LITTLE LOST THINGS

LITTLE LOST THINGS

Arms of Grace Book II

ELEANOR CHANCE

Darlington Publishing

Published by Darlington Publishing
Williamsburg, VA

eBook ISBN: 978-0-9981274-6-0
Paperback ISBN: 978-0-9981274-7-7
Hardback ISBN: 978-0-9981274-3-9
Library of Congress Control Number:2019906622

Cover Design by: Dissect Designs, London

❀ Formatted with Vellum

ALSO BY ELEANOR CHANCE

ARMS OF GRACE SERIES

Arms of Grace

Grace's Favorite Italian Dishes

OMNIBUS EDITION

The Complete Arms of Grace Series

THE MASTER'S PROTÉGÉ TRILOGY

Shades of Brilliance

Delicate Brushstrokes

The Last Masterpiece

To Mom, for believing in me from the beginning.

CHAPTER ONE

Relief washed over Grace Walker when she heard the click of Johnny's crutches in the entryway. Her son was ninety minutes late getting home from school. He'd been ignoring her calls and texts. He'd never been so late without calling, and Grace had imagined the worst, as any mother would, but she wasn't just any mother.

Her fingers froze over the keyboard of her laptop that rested on the dining room table. It was impossible to predict which Johnny would wander into the living room. Would it be her precious little man who'd always adored her or the gawky blond stranger who'd taken up residence over the summer? It was a toss-up these days. She reminded herself to relax her shoulders but braced for the storm that could erupt when she questioned him about where he'd been.

The strain on their relationship had increased so gradually in the past months that it was hard to remember when it started. It seemed only days had passed since they'd laughed over a TV show they loved or chatted about new excitements in his life while enjoying his favorite ice cream. She found herself desperately longing for those times. She missed her little man.

Her friend, Alec Emerson, had warned her that just because Johnny had cerebral palsy as the result of the traumatic brain injury he suffered as a baby, it wouldn't prevent him from experiencing typical teenage hormones. Grace should have heeded Alec's wise warning, but she'd deluded herself into believing that Johnny would be different from other teenage boys. She could have spared herself from being blindsided by his erratic behavior. She loved Johnny more than life but navigating his ever-changing moods was exhausting.

The fact that Grace was fifty-five didn't help. The parents of Johnny's friends were in their late thirties or forties, not their fifties like Grace and her husband Ryan. The physical energy she'd had when she adopted Johnny twelve years earlier had diminished in the past few years. There were days she dreaded going home after a hectic day at the doctor's office where she worked as a nurse, knowing she'd have to traverse the minefield with Johnny. She hoped this wouldn't be one of those days.

Her eyes followed Johnny as he shuffled in and dropped onto the couch. His phone was out and turned on before he uttered a word and predictions became pointless. The gawky stranger had arrived. Grace was grateful that at least he'd deigned to occupy the same space as her instead of heading straight for his bedroom. It had been a chore to get him to breathe the same air as her lately. When she asked the previous week what she'd done to upset him, he grunted that he wanted her to stop hovering and treating him like a baby. She hadn't realized she was doing that, and his words stung.

She studied him over the lid of her laptop and marveled at the young man he'd become, despite the attitude. The struggle to survive middle school with his disabilities and progress from a wheelchair to crutches two years earlier had only made him stronger. Through pain and dogged determination, he'd achieved what his doctors had declared impossible. It was a victory they'd all celebrated. She couldn't have been prouder of him and only hoped he'd continue that path of working to conquer his challenges.

She took the plunge and said, "You're late. You're supposed to answer when Dad and I text or call. I was worried. Where were you?"

Johnny lowered his phone and stared through her. "At the library. I told you I was going."

"You said you'd be back at four. You were enjoying the library so much that you lost track of time?"

Johnny shrugged.

"How'd you get home?"

His eyes moved back to the phone screen. "Ty's brother."

Grace saved her notes for the lecture she'd be giving at the hospital the following week and closed the laptop. "So, Ty, Jason and you lost track of time at the library?"

That earned her a scowl. "Ty called Jason to get us. We were studying. Midterms, remember? What's with the interrogation?"

She had forgotten about midterms, but that didn't mean she bought his story. Johnny was bright and rarely had to devote much time to studying for exams, and he'd had plenty of time to come up with an excuse for being late. She wasn't in the mood for battle, so she let it drop for the moment and switched tactics.

"You hungry? Auntie Alec dropped off some pasta and focaccia bread earlier. She was sad to miss you."

He perked up at the mention of Alec's cooking. Though their family wasn't technically related to the Emersons, they were more family than friends. Johnny had considered Alec and her husband Adam as his aunt and uncle since he was old enough to understand. It was the same for the Emerson's three children with Grace and her husband, Ryan. Grace was grateful for the bond between Johnny and Alec because Alec served as a buffer between them. It didn't hurt that Johnny still thought Alec was cool, which was no mean feat.

"Sounds good." Johnny grabbed his crutches and leveraged himself off the couch. "Cannoli, too?"

Grace stood and headed for the kitchen. "Not this time. Stay there. I'll bring it to you."

"I can get it myself, Mom."

Grace raised her hands in surrender and let him pass. *How horrible that I should dare offer to help*, she thought as she followed him to the kitchen.

JOHNNY SAVORED his aunt's mushroom ravioli while he worked up the courage to ask his mom "the question" he'd been working up the courage to ask for days. He dreaded the answer but couldn't put it off anymore. He wished he'd been more cooperative in the living room.

Just as he opened his mouth to ask, his mom said, "Speaking of your midterms, how are they going?"

Perfect opening, he thought. He put his fork down and raised his eyes to look directly at her like his dad was always bugging him to do. "They're fine. I need to ask you something. You won't like it." He felt her tense but didn't let it stop him. "We're doing a genetics assignment in biology. Everyone's talking about family traits they inherited, but I don't know anything about my family. Is there any way for me to find out? Can we go to the people where you adopted me? There has to be info about my birth parents somewhere."

His mom pressed her palms together and watched him over the tips of her fingers. He could see the wheels spinning behind her eyes and knew she was searching for a way to dodge the questions.

"As much as I wish I had those answers, there's nothing we can do. We don't know much about you before those people abandoned you at the hospital. The best we can do is get DNA testing done on you. That would give us a lot of detail about your genes."

Johnny clamped his lips shut and breathed hard through his nose. It was what he expected, but that didn't mean he liked it. He'd heard her excuses and evasions before, but his gut told him she was hiding a secret about his past. What he couldn't figure out was why or how to break through her defenses. Auntie Alec told him his mom was more stubborn than anyone she'd ever known, but he didn't need to be her flesh and blood son to be just as stubborn.

"I'll get Dad to take me, or Auntie Alec. You can't stop me."

"They won't take you, and it would be a waste of time if they did. There's nothing for anyone to tell you and your file is sealed. I'm sorry, Johnny. I can't imagine how frustrating it must be for you, but there's nothing you can do."

It drove him crazy when she made statements like that, so sure, so final, like she had an answer to everything. He'd learned it was pointless to argue, so he let it go. He'd just have to convince his dad to help him. Dad was an easier mark.

"Fine, but it's not fair. I do want a DNA test. It's better than nothing." His mom nodded and gave him that sad, pity look. "Don't do that."

She shook her head. "Do what?"

"Look at me like I'm a lost puppy. I said it's fine. I'm over it."

"Sorry, didn't know I was."

She started clearing the dishes, and Johnny gritted his teeth. As happy as he was that he'd escaped his wheelchair, there were still things he couldn't do. His friends complained all the time about chores. He'd give anything to do something as simple as loading the dishwasher.

"Don't forget about dinner tomorrow," Grace said as she rinsed his plate.

Johnny groaned. He had forgotten that his mom was having another one of her boring get-togethers. "Who's coming?"

"The Emersons, maybe Mark and Valerie if they can get away from the restaurant."

So far, the guest list didn't sound too terrible. It was always fun to see Auntie Alec and Uncle Adam, and Johnny hadn't seen his stepbrother Mark and his wife Valerie for weeks. They were so slammed with their new restaurant that getting away on a Friday night was impossible. Johnny missed their son Fisher. He was only eleven but loved video games as much as Johnny did. Sophi was nine and a girl, so Johnny never paid much attention to her, not that it mattered. She and the Emerson's twins were always in a corner giggling over some stupid thing anyway.

"Anyone else?" he asked.

"Just the Nichols."

Johnny perked up. "Is Jessie coming?" Jessie Nichol's dad worked in the same doctor's office as his mom, but Johnny didn't like Dr. Nichols much. He was always trying to diagnose him, but Jessie was cute and funny. Johnny liked her even though she went to his rival high school.

Grace turned and gave Johnny a half smile. "Would it matter if I said yes?"

"It might, but did you forget tomorrow is the homecoming game? Darnell asked a bunch of us to come over right after school and then go to the game together. I said I'd go."

She crossed her arms and leaned against the counter. *Here it comes,* he thought.

"First, I don't remember you asking if you could go right after school, and I told you about this dinner last week. Second, you have PT with Tony at three. You can go to Darnell's after we eat."

"Everyone will be leaving for the game by the time I get there. It'll be a waste." The pitch of his voice rose with each word.

"We'll eat early, and you don't have to stay until everyone leaves."

Johnny leaned on his crutches and lifted himself off the chair. "Whatever," he said just loud enough for her to hear.

His mom put her hands on her hips. "I can change my mind and not let you go."

He glanced at her before turning to the door. "Sorry. After dinner's fine."

GRACE TOSSED the extra pillows from the bed into the rocking chair and pulled back the covers. Before she could climb in, Ryan wrapped his arms around her from behind and pulled her close. He moved her hair to the side and brushed his lips on her neck.

"Hi, stranger. I feel like we haven't gone to bed together for weeks," he said.

Grace closed her eyes and smiled. Even after twelve years of marriage, he could get her revved up no matter how stressed out or tired she was. If anything, he was more attractive to her than when they'd met. His dark hair was still thick with only a slight hint of gray, and she could feel his muscles through her nightgown. She was grateful that he worked out to stay fit for his job as a state park ranger. He did it to keep up with the younger rangers, but Grace was more than willing to reap the benefits of his hard work.

"It's only been a few days, and who's fault is that?" she whispered. "You're the night-owl. You know Johnny's still awake?"

Ryan put his nose in her soft, blond hair and took a deep breath. "You smell so good. Trust me, he's not paying any attention to us. We cease to exist once he's in his room."

Talking about Johnny reminded her of their strained conversation earlier, and it killed the mood. "I wish that were true. He and I got into it this afternoon. He asked about his birth parents."

Grace felt Ryan stiffen. "Can't we talk about it in the morning?"

"I won't be able to stop thinking about it now."

Ryan gently gripped her shoulders and turned her to face him.

"Does Johnny have to intrude into every aspect of our relation-ship? We're allowed to have our own private world sometimes. "

"Sorry but it's too late for me to shut it off." Grace dropped onto the bed and patted the covers. "Let me get it out. Then, I'll willingly give you my full attention."

Ryan gave an exaggerated sigh and dropped onto the bed next to her. "That sounds promising. Make it quick."

"First, he came home late and lied about where he'd been. I'm more determined than ever to put that parental tracker on his phone."

"And I still say it's a terrible idea. It's too 'helicopter parent,' and it could backfire. He'd be furious if he found out you put the tracker on his phone without telling him. Johnny's a good kid, and we know all his friends' parents. If you're determined to do this, talk to him about it first. Explain why it's so important to you."

"He'd never agree or understand. Johnny's not a typical kid. We have his medical issues to consider, and that kidnapper Mara is still out there. Maybe she'll come and try to steal Johnny from us. She thinks he's her son. I'm installing that tracker in the morning before he wakes up."

"If Mara wanted to come for Johnny, she'd have done it by now. Forget her. You should be telling Johnny all of this, not me. Trust me, you'll regret it, and I want none of the credit."

"I'll take full responsibility."

Ryan leaned over and kissed her neck. "Good. Can we go back to where we were?"

"There's more." Ryan groaned but motioned for her to continue.

She recounted her conversation with Johnny about his birth parents. Ryan had badgered her for three years to tell Johnny about his past, but she'd refused. Johnny's life was hard enough without having to worry about old tragedies. All he knew was that he'd been abandoned at the hospital when he was six months old, and Grace had adopted him shortly before she married Ryan.

That had satisfied him until recently. She'd hoped for more time to build up the courage to tell him the truth.

"Be prepared for him to ask you to take him to see the records. You can't do it."

"If we tell him what happened, there's no reason he can't see the records. I'm sick of lying to him about this," Ryan said.

"We're not lying. We're just withholding some of the truth. I'm Johnny's mother. I'll know when the time is right."

"And I'm his father. Don't I get a say? I've raised three other children, but you seem to forget that when it fits your agenda."

Grace squeezed his hand. "I'm sorry. That wasn't fair. Of course, you have an equal say." She studied her hand resting on his arm to avoid meeting his eyes. "Maybe I'm the one who's not ready. I'm afraid telling him will turn his world upside down."

Ryan brushed a lock of her hair off her cheek and tucked it behind her ear. "It will alter his world, but we'll be there to help him set it right. You don't have to do this alone. The news will be life-altering but imagine what'll happen if he finds out from other sources. That can't happen. I won't let it."

Grace nodded, and Ryan put his arm around her. She snuggled against him and tried to force her body to relax. She forgot at times that she didn't have to face life alone. She'd had to fight the world on her own for so long before Ryan and Johnny came along.

"Be patient a little longer. I'll know when he's ready."

"Don't take too long. Time has more than run out."

PUTTING the parental tracker on Johnny's phone had gone off without a hitch. It was fortunate that he slept like the dead and hadn't stirred when she slipped his phone off the nightstand. She tested it with the app on her phone before going into the office. It showed that he was a block from the high school, which was where he should have been. She breathed a sigh of relief and went into work.

She tapped on Dr. Carter's door on the way to her office and poked her head inside.

"Morning, Grace. You're early," he said. "Come in."

"Hi, Brad. I'm not earlier than you." She walked to his desk but didn't sit down. She wasn't planning to stay long.

"Charts," he said and gestured at his monitor. "I'm finishing the report for the Campbell baby. That was a tough one. Reminded me of Johnny in some ways."

Grace nodded. Brad had been Johnny's doctor from almost the moment he was abandoned in the ER when he was six months old. Brad had taken such good care of Johnny that Grace was thrilled when he'd offered her a job seven years earlier.

"Johnny's what I'm here about," she said. "He has a half day at school, and I'd like to pick him up and do some fence mending. Things have been rocky between us lately. Would it cause too much trouble here if I left early?"

Brad leaned back in his chair and smiled. "Ah, those wonderful teenage years when our children are swapped out with Martians. It'll get better when he's twenty."

"I'd rather not wait that long," Grace said, without smiling.

"What's going on with you two?"

She crossed her arms and looked at the carpet. "Like you said, typical teenage stuff."

"By all means, take your half-day. Hope it helps. Let me know if you ever want me to talk to him and run some interference. We still have a good rapport."

"Thanks, I might take you up on that."

Grace texted Johnny as soon as she got to her office. *I'd like to pick you up after school and go for apple-cider donuts. Is that OK?*

Grace drummed her fingers on the desk while she waited for his reply, which was taking far too long.

She jumped when her phone finally dinged. *Darnell's giving Ty and me a ride home. Donuts another day?*

Grace frowned at her phone. Why was everything a battle with him? *But it's our tradition. We usually go so much earlier in the fall. You're going to Darnell's after dinner. See him then.*

After another long pause and more drumming: *Fine. SYL.*

Grace had no idea what SYL meant and wasn't sure if she'd won the skirmish or not. She'd have to wait until she saw Johnny to be sure.

THE LINE of cars in the pick-up lane stretched twice as far as usual, so Grace pulled into the closest handicapped spot. Even though it was sprinkling, it would be much quicker to park and meet Johnny at the school's front entrance. She had a few minutes until the bell rang, so she turned off the engine and sat back to decompress.

She squinted through the trails of rainwater on the windshield at the brilliant fall foliage blazing along the tree-lined street. The dreary, gray sky beyond made the colors even more striking. Autumn was Grace's favorite time of year in Richmond despite all the leaf-raking they had waiting in the front yard. She loved the bonfires in the chilly air, apple-picking, and visits to the pumpkin patch with warm apple-cider donuts.

Johnny had enjoyed all of it right along with her until that year. Having to twist his arm to go for donuts had dampened her spirits, but seeing the beautiful trees buoyed her. Maybe he'd enjoy himself once he bit into the warm, gooey pastry.

"DITCH YOUR MOM," Darnell told Johnny as they left their last class. "It's what she gets for treating you like a baby. What do you owe her anyway?"

Everything, Johnny thought. His mom constantly got on his nerves, and he wasn't excited about having to go with her, but she didn't deserve for him to bail. They'd taken their yearly trip for apple-cider donuts for as long as he could remember. He'd always looked forward to it, but it didn't seem like such a big deal that year. He was too old for that stuff. He was going to tell her it would be the last time. She had to start seeing him as fourteen instead of ten.

Darnell and his mom argued all the time, so he never had a problem ditching her. Johnny thought most of it was Darnell's fault. Johnny liked her, but Darnell was a total jerk to her some-times. As irritated as Johnny got with his mom, things weren't that bad between them. Darnell wouldn't understand why Johnny didn't want to hurt her feelings.

Not wanting to look like a chicken in front of Darnell, he said, "If I bail, she won't let me go to your house after dinner, and I wouldn't be able to stay long anyway because I have PT. My parents have to pay even if I don't show up. She'd be super pissed if I missed it. She'd probably ground me."

"You wimping out on me?"

They walked out the school's main door, and Darnell turned toward the pickup lane. Johnny was about to follow but stopped when he saw his mom coming up the front steps.

"Too late. There's my mom." For once he was glad to have her as an excuse with Darnell.

Darnell dropped his backpack and crossed his arms. "Tell her you don't want to go with her. She won't say no in front of me."

"I would if I didn't have PT. She'll make a deal out of it. I'll get to your house as fast as I can tonight."

Darnell shook his head at Johnny and picked up his pack. "Whatever."

"Hello, Darnell," his mom said and smiled when she walked up to them.

Darnell glared at her and walked away without a word. She raised her eyebrows but took Johnny's backpack without saying anything. Johnny followed her to the car, glad that she'd shown up in time to stop him from doing something stupid.

GRACE FOUND a table by the window with a clear view of the trees. She arranged their donuts, coffee, and hot apple-cider and nodded in satisfaction.

Johnny picked up a donut and said, "When is everyone coming for dinner?"

"Around six."

"Six!" Johnny groaned. "That late? Can't they come earlier?"

"Auntie Alec and Uncle Adam don't get home from work until at least five. They need time to change and get their kids ready. I'm sure you'll survive."

"Might not," he said, just loud enough for her to hear. "I'll have to wait longer to go to Darnell's." Johnny took a bite of his donut and rolled his eyes in pleasure. "I forgot how good these are."

Grace took a bite, too. "They are. I wish they sold these all year instead of just in the fall."

"You might get sick of them if they did."

"Good point," she said and wiped her hands. "Why did Darnell give me the evil eye when I picked you up?"

Johnny kept his eyes on his donuts. "You know how he is. Moody."

"Felt like more than that."

Johnny shoved half a donut in his mouth and took forever to chew it. He sipped some hot cider and put his mug down slowly.

"He's mad cause you wouldn't let me go home with him and you're making me wait until after dinner. One time he called you Hitler."

"That's harsh and more than a little unfair. Is that what you think?"

Johnny looked up from his donut. "Course not."

"This wasn't about being strict. I love our traditions and spending time with you, and we had our dinner planned long before Darnell invited you. We should honor our commitments."

"You sound like Dad. I didn't make the dinner commitment."

"Sometimes I wish you wouldn't spend so much time with Darnell. I like him, but he can be mouthy, and you're mouthier after you've been with him."

The look Johnny gave her made her wish she could suck the words back into her mouth. The last thing she wanted was to alienate him more after he'd agreed to come with her.

Johnny lowered his eyes. "He knows you don't like him. He doesn't like you, either."

"I didn't say I don't like him. I just said he can be mouthy. His mom is one of my best friends, and I don't like the way he treats her. Why don't you hang out with Kyle and Damien anymore? You've been friends since you were three."

"We still hang out at school. Can't I like Darnell and Ty, too?"

Grace rubbed her forehead. Their conversation had taken a nosedive and it was her fault. "I'm sorry, Johnny. Of course, you can. I'm just taking my frustrations out on you. Should I talk to Darnell's mom? I don't want them thinking I don't like him."

"No, don't do that. It'll only make things worse. I'll say something tonight."

"I appreciate that." Grace slowly chewed her donut to give her time to think of a way to get back on track. She patted his hand and smiled. "Thanks for coming today. I know you'd rather be with your friends. You have no idea how much spending time with you means to me. Will you forgive me?"

Johnny gave a weak smile. "It's fine, Mom. I'm not mad. I'm glad we did this. The donuts were worth missing going to Darnell's."

Grace let out her breath and leaned back. He seemed sincere, and she hoped the goodwill would last for a few more days.

CHAPTER TWO

GRACE FLINCHED when the deadbolt on the front door turned as she carried plates and silverware into the dining room to set the table. She relaxed when Alec's head peeked through the door. Grace and Ryan had caved to Alec's begging for a house key since it was safer than leaving their doors unlocked to allow Alec to barge in whenever she wanted. Alec had always refused to knock because according to her, she was "family, and family doesn't knock."

Alec breezed in and set a covered casserole dish on the sideboard with a flourish. Grace marveled at how her friend never aged. Her thick auburn hair was still dark without a strand of gray, and she didn't have a single wrinkle. Giving birth to three kids, two of them twins, hadn't altered her perfect figure a bit.

Her husband, Adam, who also had a knack for staying young and ruggedly handsome, followed Alec in carrying five-year-old Graham. Their nine-year-old twins, Rosie and Camilla, danced in behind Adam like miniatures of their mother and waved at Grace before running to find Johnny.

Grace's heart always lightened at the sight of Alec. Grace wouldn't have survived those traumatic years when Johnny was a baby without her. It was an added bonus that Ryan and Adam got on so well, too.

Adam put Graham down and said, "Where's Ryan?"

"Changing," Grace said. "I'm sure he wouldn't mind if you started the bonfire."

Adam gave Grace a peck on the cheek on his way into the backyard. Grace gathered Graham into a hug, but he squirmed free and headed for the plate of cupcakes on the sideboard.

"Not until after dinner," Alec said and turned to Grace. "It's impossible to keep up with him. He's more of a handful than the twins put together."

Graham snatched a cupcake and ran after Adam.

"Scamp," Grace said and laughed. "I only have one to worry about, not three, and Johnny's pretty self-sufficient these days. If only I could figure out what to do about his attitude." Grace shook her head and went back to setting the table.

Alec picked up the silverware and joined her. "What do you expect, that because he's disabled, he'll be perfect? I've told you before, he's a typical teenage boy. I think he does great considering."

Grace set the last plate in its place and leaned on the back of the chair. "I forget that sometimes. We've been getting into it over the smallest things. It's exhausting. He's mad at me tonight because he wanted to go to Darnell's before the game instead of staying for dinner."

It was Alec's turn to laugh. "And miss seeing me? I'm wounded. Naturally, he wants to be with his friends instead of a bunch of kids and old people. Let him go to Darnell's."

"I gave him permission to go after we eat."

Grace stared at her hands resting on the back of the chair and felt like they'd started to wrinkle overnight. Time had passed in a blur since Johnny was a baby, but the memories were as powerful as if it had been months instead of years.

"What's up with you tonight? You seem off," Alec asked.

Grace told her what had happened between her and Johnny the past few days. She lowered her voice, and said, "I put a tracker app on his phone this morning. Ryan was against it. Do you think it's too over the top?"

"Hell yes. Johnny's never anywhere by himself, so what do you think is going to happen?"

"Lots of parents use them, and their teenagers weren't kidnap victims when they were babies like Johnny. Mara is still running free out there. You never know."

Alec rested her hands on Grace's shoulders. "Let this go. It's been twelve years. Johnny's safe. Mara would have come back long before now if she wanted to get to Johnny."

Johnny came down the hallway and Alec dropped her hands.

"Hey, Auntie Alec," he said, and gave her a one-armed hug. "What were you two in such a serious convo about?"

"Grown-up stuff. What's this I hear about you wanting to bail on us?" Alec asked.

He turned and glared at Grace. "Mom, do you have to tell her everything?"

"Everything. You should know that by now," Grace said, and winked.

Johnny turned back to face Alec and smiled. "Nothing personal. I just wanted to hang out with my friends. When's dinner? I'm starving."

Ryan came out of the kitchen and said, "Just what I was wondering." He kissed Alec's cheek. "Where's Adam?"

"Outback, lighting the fire," Alec said.

Ryan rubbed his hands in excitement and headed to the backyard with Johnny close behind.

Grace said, "I'm glad Johnny has you and Steph. He hates me most of the time lately."

"He doesn't hate you. Like I said, typical teenager. But speaking of Steph, are Ryan's kids coming tonight?"

"Doubtful. Mark and Valerie are chained to that restaurant these days. They're supposed to come for dinner Monday, and we're keeping Fisher and Sophi next weekend. We haven't seen much of them since the restaurant opened. They live thirty minutes away, but it might as well be two-hundred for as much as we see them."

"I'm guessing Jen and Jason won't be here?"

"Jen's too close to her due date to travel, especially since she's carrying twins."

Alec instinctively pressed her hands to her stomach. "I remember what that was like."

"We're heading to DC in a few weeks to visit them."

"And Steph. Is she back in the country?"

"She called to tell us she got in last night. She'll stop by if she's not too jet-lagged."

Alec followed Grace into the kitchen to check the potatoes. "How's she doing after the big breakup?"

"She sounded good on the phone. Those months in Africa were what she needed to get her head straight. She got a photo spread in a nature magazine. It's a big deal apparently."

"That's perfect. Steph needs a boost after what she's been through."

"What's Steph been through?" Johnny asked as he came into the kitchen. Grace gave him a glance but didn't answer. Johnny switched to Alec. "What's wrong with Steph?"

Alec raised her eyebrows at Grace in question. Grace lowered her shoulders and gave a slight nod.

"She and Greydon broke up. The truth is, he abandoned her in some third-world backwater while she was on a shoot, that slimy snake," Alec said.

"When?" Johnny asked. "She never told me."

Grace hesitated before saying, "Three months ago."

"Three months? Why didn't *you* tell me?"

A new reason for Johnny to detest me, Grace thought. "She's been in South Africa and didn't want the entire world to know. She was heartbroken and embarrassed."

"I'm not the whole world. I'm her brother." Johnny looked at Alec. "Mom hides everything from me."

"Not true," Grace said. "Steph asked me to keep it quiet. I was respecting her wishes."

"Whatever," Johnny said. "Poor Steph, though. I always hated that Greydon."

"Don't say hate," Grace said. "Please don't mention the breakup if Steph comes over tonight. She's still sensitive."

"Steph's back? See, never tells me anything," Johnny said to Alec.

"She got in late last night, and it slipped my mind. I wasn't keeping it a secret."

Johnny turned and grunted on his way back outside.

"Take that tracker off of his phone," Alec said, but the doorbell rang, saving Grace from having to defend herself. She had no intention of removing the tracker.

She went to the door expecting to find the Nichols, but it was Stephanie. Grace gave her stepdaughter a hug before stepping back to get a look at her. She'd always been stockier than her twin sister, Jennifer, but she'd lost weight since Grace last saw her which accentuated how wiry and fit she was. Her usually short dark hair was long and fell in highlighted waves on her shoulders.

"You look amazing," Grace said. "I love your hair that way."

"You're sweet but there's no need to flatter me. I'm not fragile," Steph said and laughed.

"She's not lying," Alec said and hugged her. "You're gorgeous." Alec took her hand and dragged her inside. "Tell us everything about what happened with Greydon."

"There's time for that at dinner. Where's my Johnny?"

DINNER DIDN'T TURN out so bad, especially since Steph had come. Johnny always missed his sister when she was out of the country, but this time she'd been gone for almost a year.

He rushed to the living room as fast as he could on his crutches and hugged her. "Why didn't you tell me about Greydon?"

Steph backed away and laughed. "Hi, Johnny. Great to see you. I've missed you. How have you been?"

Johnny smiled. "Sorry. Mom just told me about Greydon. She keeps everything secret from me because she thinks I'm still a little kid."

"I heard that," his mom said. "And good job not bringing up a sensitive subject the minute Steph walks in the door."

"I asked her not to tell anyone," Steph told Johnny. "I was crushed and embarrassed. Everyone warned me about Greydon, but I didn't listen. Learn from my mistake. If everyone tells you your significant other is bad news, pay attention."

Johnny blushed and glanced at Jessie, who was looking super cute that night. "Will do."

Steph followed him to the table. "You're a speedster on those crutches now. You should enter the Paralympics."

"That would only work if video-gaming was a sport. He'd win the gold for sure," his dad said and kissed Steph's cheek. "Welcome back. Congrats on the magazine spread."

"Thanks, Dad," Steph said. "I'm on the fast track to National Geographic."

Steph kept them entertained with stories of her adventures during dinner. Johnny had planned to race through the meal so he could get to Darnell's quicker, but he was so absorbed in Steph's stories that he forgot. Her vivid descriptions of exotic locations made him wish he could go along on her next assignment, but he knew the last thing she'd want was her gimpy little stepbrother tagging along.

As soon as they finished eating, Johnny went to his room and threw some game controllers and clothes into his backpack before going to find his dad. Auntie Alec was alone in the living room flipping through a magazine when he got there.

"Where is everyone?" he asked.

"Out by the bonfire, except your mom. She kicked me out of the kitchen because I dared critique her pie crust."

"Big mistake. She's touchy about her cooking because she'll never be as good as you."

"Don't ever let her hear you say that. She'll never cook again." Alec patted the couch cushion next to her. "I have something for you." She reached down by her feet and picked up a wrapped package.

Johnny's eyes brightened. "Is this your new book?"

"It's your signed, advanced copy."

Johnny tore the paper off and ran his hand over the smooth, shiny cover. "Your illustrator did a great job with this one."

"Yes, I'm pleased with it."

Johnny beamed at her. "I'll read it tonight."

"You're taking a children's book to Darnell's?"

Johnny slid the book into his backpack. "My friends think it's cool I have a famous aunt."

"I'll sleep better at night knowing I have their approval." She winked, making Johnny laugh. "I'd hoped to do story-time with you and my kids tonight, but you got a better offer."

Adam came in from the backyard and joined them. "He's too old for children's stories, Alec. He's graduated to YA."

Alec put her arm around Johnny's shoulders and gave him a squeeze. "He's the one that pushed me to become a writer after all the hours of listening to my make-believe stories at bedtime. He'll never be too old for my books."

"I'll come over Sunday night for story-time if you'll wait," Johnny said. "What are you working on now?"

"I'm doing a new series based on these characters. The second book is in production, and I'm almost done writing the third, but

I have another project I've been working on for a long time. It's a secret. Your mom won't like it."

Johnny sat back and crossed his arms. "Mom doesn't like anything lately. Even me."

"Stop that, Johnny. You know she loves you. You know she said the same thing about you before dinner. She thinks you hate her. You two need to call a truce."

"She said that?" Johnny was shocked when Alec nodded. It bothered him that his mom thought he hated her or anything else. She made him crazy sometimes, but he still loved her. "I'll talk to her tomorrow."

"Make sure you do," Adam said. "Seeing you two butt heads is getting old. You both deserve better."

"I promise." Ryan and Steph came inside, and Johnny said, "Can I go now, Dad?"

Ryan nodded. "I'll get my keys."

Grace came out of the kitchen carrying Graham. "That'll take an hour. That man can't seem to put his keys in the same place twice."

Johnny laughed at her joke, and Grace gave him a surprised look. "We should get him one of those Binki clips Graham used to have." His mom smiled, and he felt a little less guilty for the way he'd acted earlier.

"I'll give him a ride, Dad," Steph said. "It'll give us a chance to catch up."

"Thanks," Ryan said and handed her Johnny's pack.

Johnny surprised his mom again by giving her a hug and saying "love you" on his way out.

"Love you, too. Have fun. Check in from time to time, so we know your brain hasn't melted."

"Always do," he said. "See you Sunday, Auntie Alec. Thanks for the book."

JOHNNY BUCKLED his seatbelt and took a deep breath through his nose. "Nice. New car smell."

"I splurged on myself," Steph said. "I'm still getting used to being able to afford a new car instead of old junkers. I love all the toys." She pushed the start button with a flourish.

"I can't hear the engine."

"It's electric. I'm waiting for the day when I can afford a car that drives itself."

Johnny nodded in approval. "Seems like you're over Greydon. I thought you'd be all weepy and depressed."

"I was at first, but I woke up one day and realized he wasn't worth it. I'm learning I don't need a guy to be happy. So, what's new with you? Dating anyone?"

Johnny was glad it was dark so she couldn't see him blush. He pointed at his crutches. "I'm only fourteen and not exactly a prize catch."

"What, you're like eight feet tall and have rock-star blond hair. Who wouldn't want that?"

"Only six foot, but will you come to my school and tell the girls that?" He looked out the window at the Halloween decorations on the houses they passed. He'd loved Halloween and was kind of sad that he was too old to trick-or-treat even if he'd never admit that to anyone. It was hard enough to get people to treat him like a normal person.

Thinking of being normal reminded him of his genetics assignment. He wondered if Steph would be an even easier mark than Dad and decided to test her.

"How much do you remember about me as a baby?"

"That was random. Most of it. Why?"

He told her about his assignment. "I tried to ask Mom, but she blew me off like always. You never do that. What happened to me when I was little?"

Steph was quiet for a few seconds, and he was afraid she wouldn't tell him the truth either.

"Jennifer, Mark and I came on the scene shortly before you turned two. I wasn't around much because I was away at school, but I remember when your mom took you home from the hospital. She told me about your coma and how you almost died. You had to go away for some reason before Grace adopted you. Then, you came back, and you've been with our parents since then. That's all I remember. I was too absorbed in college life to pay much attention."

"But what about my real parents? What happened to them? What happened before I ended up in the hospital?"

"Dad and Grace are your real parents, but I know what you mean. Like I said, we showed up long after that. Your mom never talked about it much. She was just so happy that you survived and that she got to adopt you. You were such a cute little smooshy-face."

Steph laughed, but Johnny didn't think it was funny. His gut told him there was more to the story, but he understood his mom not telling Steph what happened. She liked to keep secrets. Not Auntie Alec, though. She couldn't help but blab about everything. Maybe she would be his next target.

Steph pulled into Darnell's driveway and turned off the car. "Sorry I don't know more. Need help getting out?"

Johnny shook his head. "I've got it. Thanks for the ride. When will I see you again?"

"I'll come hang out on Sunday. Have fun at the game. Go Ravens!"

"We're Rams. Ravens are Jessie's school," Johnny said and laughed as he closed the door.

MARA WAS LATE GETTING BACK to the surgical unit where she was scheduled to assist the orthopedic-spine surgeon in a lengthy procedure after her break. She glanced at the TV in the surgical waiting room as she hurried past. Late or not, she skidded to a halt when she saw the image on the screen. Oblivious to the anxious family members seated behind her, she moved closer to the TV to read the closed captioning scrolling across the screen.

Her eyes hadn't deceived her. It was Alec Covington, or Alec Emerson now according to the scrolling words! *It can't be her*, Mara thought, but there Alec was, being interviewed on a cable news network. Mara grabbed the remote off an end table and turned up the sound. As she listened, her lips curled into a sneer.

Interviewer: "My children love your books. They were thrilled when I brought this latest one home." The news anchor held up a shiny children's book. "Will there be more in this series?"

Alec: "Yes, the next one is in production, and I'm writing the third. The release for that one is on hold because I've been working on a different project that has taken me several years to complete."

Interviewer: "Another children's series?"

Alec: "No, this one is a biography of my dear friend, Grace Ward Walker, and her son, Johnny. Many remember their story from twelve years ago, but I felt compelled to get the truth out to the public. Grace is a remarkable person. She's been a role model and mentor to me, and she's my biggest cheerleader."

A grainy picture of Grace from a news clipping popped up in the corner of the screen.

Alec: "You asked about my rock-climbing accident earlier. I would have given up after I broke my back from that rock-climbing fall if it hadn't been for Grace and Johnny. It's because of them that I got out of bed and learned to walk again. It's because of them that I became a writer when I couldn't be a nurse anymore. I think it's important for women, well, not just women, anyone really, to know the inner strength they have to succeed against seemingly insurmountable challenges. We don't need to be victims of our circumstances."

A recent picture of Grace and one of Johnny came on the screen. Mara moved closer to get a better look. There he was, her boy, her angel. He was so handsome and tall. She wanted to reach into the TV and stroke his silky blond hair.

Interviewer: "Sounds intriguing. What's the title and when will it hit bookshelves?"

Alec: "It's titled *Baby John Doe* and will be out in time for the holidays. It's available for pre-order at all major retailers."

Mara pressed the off button and let the remote slip from her fingers to the floor. The back popped off when it struck the tile, and every eye in the room turned toward Mara as the batteries popped out and rolled under a chair. She ignored them and stormed out of the waiting room. She ripped off her staff ID badge as she passed the information desk and tossed it into the garbage. Fighting to quell her rage, she raced out of the entrance and headed for the parking lot without looking back.

CHAPTER THREE

GRACE FOUND Ryan watching a movie in his man-cave when she got home from giving a lecture at the hospital. She checked to make sure Johnny wasn't home before tearing off her coat and climbing onto Ryan's lap.

When she came up for air after planting a passionate kiss on him, Ryan said, "Welcome home. What's gotten into you?"

"You were so seductive in your stained t-shirt and ratty sweat-pants that I couldn't resist. Want to go upstairs? Is Johnny in his room?"

Ryan leaned forward. "He wasn't here when I got home. I assumed you said he could stay out late. Where was he going tonight?"

"He didn't ask to go anywhere. He was here when I left." Grace jumped up and grabbed her phone to check the tracker app. "He's at Damien's."

"Probably just playing video games."

Grace shoved the phone in her pocket. "Still think the tracker was a bad idea?"

"Yes. We could have just called and asked."

Grace shook her head. "He knows he's not supposed to leave without telling us where he is. He's pushing boundaries."

Ryan held out his arms and motioned for her to come back to his lap. She hesitated before giving in. She wanted to be mad at Johnny but knew Ryan would coax her out of her anger. He always did.

"He should be pushing boundaries, Grace. He was a prisoner to a wheelchair for ten years. He wants his freedom. He's just a few blocks away. Call and calmly tell him it's time to come home."

Grace took some slow breaths. "Everything he does makes me so crazy. It's not like me to lose my temper. He's an expert at pushing my buttons. How will I survive four more years of this?"

Ryan chuckled. "Marie was the same way with Mark and look how well he turned out. This will get easier as Johnny gets older, but you've got to loosen your grip. He's a good kid, but he's not going to be perfect."

"I'll have to trust you on this." Grace leaned her head on Ryan's shoulder. "You call him, but put it on speaker."

Ryan tapped Johnny's name in his list of recent calls. It only rang twice before he answered.

"What's up, Dad?" he said, over the noisy background.

"Your Mom and I are wondering where you are and when you're coming home. It's getting late and I'll bet you didn't think to take your meds with you."

"I told you I was going to Damien's. Didn't you hear me?"

Ryan gave Grace a sheepish look. "I didn't. Next time make eye contact so you know I heard you."

"But you're right about my meds. Can I have thirty more minutes?"

His question was in the whiny, sing-song voice they'd never been able to resist when he was younger. Grace hadn't heard it in ages and smiled at the fond memory.

"Hi, sweetheart. It's Mom. Thirty minutes but no more. Should we come get you?"

"Nah, Jason said he'd take me home."

"Love you," Ryan said. "See you in a few." He put the phone down and grinned at Grace. "Please don't leave me."

Grace laughed and kissed him. "We both screwed up. I'll never figure out this parenting thing. I'm sorry for jumping to conclusions."

"Disaster averted, but I hope you'll reconsider removing the tracker."

Grace smiled without agreeing to reconsider. "Want to go upstairs and make out for thirty minutes?"

Ryan stood her up and took her hand. They were up the stairs in record time.

***

GRACE PULLED up to Johnny's physical therapist office the following Monday afternoon and said, "I'll get you checked in but then I have errands to run. I'll be back before you're finished." She opened her door but Johnny didn't unhook his seat belt. "You need to hurry. You know Tony doesn't like it when you're late."

Johnny didn't move. "Tony will have to deal with it. I'm sick of PT. Can't I miss just once?"

Grace set her purse down and faced him. "What's wrong? You hardly said a word on the way here. Did something happen at school?"

"No, I'm just tired, and PT hurts. Why can't I be like a normal kid who doesn't have PT three times a week for the rest of his life?"

"I know it hurts. Trust me, I know, but don't think about the rest of your life. Just focus on this session. What does Tony always say?"

"One step, one day at a time," Johnny said, mimicking Tony's gruff voice.

Grace bit her tongue to keep from laughing. "Is he right?"

He furrowed his brows. "Maybe. I don't know."

"Let's go in and see where it goes. Tell Tony you're not feeling up to much. He knows how hard you usually work. Maybe he'll go easy on you."

"Tony? Right. He's never gone easy on me."

Grace undid Johnny's seatbelt, wishing she could just take him for donuts instead of forcing him to go to PT, but as much as he hated it, it was vital that he go. "Come on, buddy. No backing out."

Johnny groaned but reached for his crutches and struggled out of the car. After Grace checked him in, she walked with Johnny to the warm-up area. Tony met them with his usual enthusiasm.

"My favorite patient," he said and held his fist up for Johnny to bump. Johnny gave a half-hearted effort and let his hand drop. "What was that? Forget your energy pills this morning?"

"Johnny's not feeling it today," Grace said.

"You sick?" Tony asked Johnny.

"Just tired," Johnny said, without raising his eyes.

"You're entitled to be tired now and then. Let's start with the tank and stretching today. We'll see what you've got in you after that."

Johnny perked up slightly. He loved getting into the warm, miniature pool that Tony called the tank. As Tony led Johnny to the pool, he turned and gave Grace a nod. She mouthed a thank you and heard him ask Johnny if he'd seen the latest episode of their favorite show. Johnny told him he had and rattled off his opinion on it. Grace breathed a sigh of relief and left them to it.

She was grateful to Tony for the magic he'd worked with Johnny over the years. He'd been vital to Johnny's success in progressing from his wheelchair to crutches. None of them would have had the strength to stick to it without him.

Grace was lost in her thoughts when someone bumped her as she walked to her car. Grace glanced up to apologize and froze when she recognized the eyes staring back at her. She'd seen those eyes only once before, on the day Johnny was abandoned in the ER, but they were indelibly etched on Grace's brain.

Before Grace recovered from the shock, the woman spun around and tore off down the street. Grace threw her purse in the car and sprinted after her. She'd never been a fast runner and was outdistanced in a hurry. By the time Grace rounded the corner, the woman had vanished. While Grace frantically searched for her, a blue sedan sped around the opposite corner with tires squealing. Grace didn't even have time to get her license plate.

She leaned against a tree to catch her breath and try to make sense of what just happened. Had it been Mara or was her mind playing tricks? Why would Mara dare come back to Richmond and risk getting caught? Had she known the time and place of Johnny's PT appointment or had their encounter been a coincidence?

Grace's hands shook so hard as she limped back to the car that it took three tries to unlock the door. Once in the driver's seat, she took out her phone to call 911 but decided to try Ryan first. He'd know what their next move should be. She dialed his number, but it went to voicemail, and she remembered he was giving a safety protocol presentation to other rangers that day. *A safety presentation of all things*, she thought. His phone would be turned off for hours. She'd have to figure it out on her own.

As she relaxed against the seat and tried to clear her thoughts, the dry-cleaning ticket on the passenger seat caught her eye. Picking up the dry cleaning and going to the bank had seemed like top priorities until she came face to face with her worst fear. Johnny was in danger. They were all in danger. Nothing else mattered.

Leaving Johnny at the PT clinic was out of the question, so Grace went inside to wait. She picked up a magazine and pretended to read, but her trembling hands made that impossible, so she laid the magazine in her lap and closed her eyes. Johnny's session was almost finished. She only had to keep it together for ten more minutes.

She sprang out of the chair when Johnny came into the waiting room and ushered him to the car in a hurry. After getting him settled, she climbed into her seat and gripped the steering wheel. Her heartbeat still pounded so loud in her ears that it was hard to hear Johnny's words.

He tapped her shoulder and she jumped. "Here," he said, and held out the dry-cleaning slip. "Where are the clothes? Didn't you go to the cleaners?"

The cleaners? Grace thought and stared at the ticket for several seconds before taking it from him and sliding it into her purse. "They were closed. The power was out for some reason."

Johnny bought her excuse and didn't interrogate her. She backed out of the parking lot and tried to stop the terrifying incident from looping in her brain. Johnny rattled on about levels and worlds from his favorite video game, but Grace only caught snatches of what he said.

"What's the matter with you? You're acting weird, and why's your hair messed up? It's not windy," he said, when they were halfway home.

Grace took a breath to center herself. She'd hoped the days of being controlled by fear were behind her, and she wasn't ready to explain Mara to Johnny. "I'm just preoccupied about a patient at work. I got a call while you were with Tony. I'm sorry. What were you saying?"

Johnny eyed her for several seconds but shrugged and went back to talking about his game.

GRACE PACED in the kitchen while she waited for Ryan to get home from work and ran into the garage the instant the door opened. She pounced on Ryan before he was out of the car.

"I saw her today, outside the PT clinic," she said in a rush.

Ryan raised his eyebrows. "Who'd you see? Was it that Midge? She can be such a pain."

Grace held up her hands to stop him. "Who's Midge? What are you talking about?"

Ryan went into the kitchen with Grace following close behind. "That one receptionist in Tony's office. She's so rude."

Grace wanted to scream as she watched Ryan sit at the kitchen table and start unlacing his boots. "There's no Midge at Tony's office. It was Mara! I saw Mara. We need to call the FBI."

Ryan's head shot up. "Mara? What are *you* talking about?" Grace dropped into a chair opposite him and told him about the incident in the parking lot. "She'd be insane to show up there, especially if there was a chance she'd run into you."

"She *is* insane, Ryan. Have you forgotten that she kidnapped Johnny from the hospital nursery two hours after he was born? Who knows what else she's capable of? We need to call Scott Michaels."

Ryan stopped pulling off his second boot and stared at her. "You mean Special Agent Scott Michaels with the FBI? He's probably retired by now, but even if he's not, what do you plan to tell him? That someone bumped into you in a parking lot?"

Grace reached down and rubbed the ache in her leg. "She ran when I chased her."

"I would have run, too, if some strange woman came chasing after me."

"I'm not some strange woman. She ran first when she recognized me. I'm sure of it."

"You saw Mara once, for less than a minute, fourteen years ago. Johnny's got you riled up with all this interrogation about the past. He's stirred up bad memories. That's all this is. You're seeing things."

Grace moved her hands from her leg to her temples. "Why won't you believe me? I'll never forget that woman's face. Never!"

"Even if it was her, why are you panicking? You keep a tight leash on Johnny, and you've got that damned tracker on his phone. What could Mara do? He's a foot taller than her, not a helpless infant."

Grace glared at him, frustrated by his denials. "Even if she's not after Johnny, she needs to pay for what she did. What if she kidnapped another child?"

Ryan put his hand on her shoulder. "Take a breath, Grace. You only saw her for a split second fourteen years ago. You have a lot on your mind. You know better than I do the kind of tricks our minds can play under stress."

Grace closed her eyes and replayed the incident in slow motion in her mind. The woman's hair was darker than Grace remembered Mara's being, but it would have been simple to dye it. A hint of wrinkles framed her mouth and eyes, which fit Mara's age, but that proved nothing. It was her eyes that struck a chord for Grace.

She switched her thoughts to the memory of Mara and her husband, Rick, racing into the ER with Johnny hanging limp and wet in their arms. The events that followed only lasted seconds, but Grace and Mara had locked eyes as Rick tore Mara from Johnny and dragged her out into the storm. Grace would never forget the anguish and loss in Mara's eyes. It was the pain of a mother losing her child. Grace understood that kind of pain.

The anguish was missing from her eyes in the parking lot earlier, but the loss remained. Mara had only been Johnny's mother for months after she kidnapped him, and it occurred to Grace that Mara could have remarried and had children of her own. The thought disgusted her, but could Mara still suffer the pain of losing him after so many years? It seemed unlikely, and Grace wondered if she had conjured Mara up out of her own fears.

She opened her eyes and said, "I'll admit there's a minuscule chance I'm wrong, but whether or not that was Mara today, she's managed to evade the FBI all these years. Who knows if they're even looking for her? We can't afford to get complacent. Not ever."

"I'm not saying we should. We'll continue to keep close tabs on Johnny and contact the FBI immediately if she shows up again, but we can't go seeing trouble around every corner. Whoever she was, hopefully you scared her off." He finished removing his boot and glanced at Grace. "Did you tell Johnny what happened?"

Grace shook her head and got up to put a plate in the sink to avoid facing him. "I made up a story for why I was shaken up."

"More lies? Isn't hiding the truth about Mara more dangerous than telling him? If Mara is back in the picture, Johnny needs to be on his guard more than anyone."

"I couldn't talk to him about it. I was too freaked out. And if Mara *is* back, telling Johnny is the least of our worries."

Ryan stood and kissed the top of her head. "I'm going to change. Don't mention this to Alec when she gets here. She'll blow it out of proportion, and half of Richmond will know by morning."

Grace groaned. She'd forgotten Alec was coming over to plan their Thanksgiving menu. All she wanted to do was climb into bed and hide under the covers. "I'll do my best, but she always knows when I'm keeping a secret."

Ryan looked her in the eye. "So does Johnny."

———

ALEC READ from the list she'd typed into her tablet two hours later. "Along with the turkey, wild rice stuffing, and red garlic potatoes, I'm planning to make my famous pumpkin Agnolotti. We just need to come up with a light vegetable. Is Ryan still insisting on broccoli cheese casserole?" When Grace didn't respond, she said, "Are you listening? Where are you tonight?"

Grace's gaze shifted from the carpet under the dining room table to Alec. Despite Ryan's warning, she'd been battling with herself about whether or not to tell Alec about Mara. Hoping for a more understanding response that she'd gotten from Ryan, she gave in and spilled the whole story.

"I haven't stopped shaking since I saw her. I wanted to call Agent Scott Michaels at the FBI, but Ryan thinks I'm paranoid."

"Look at me," Alec said, and put her hand on Grace's shoulder. "It happened so fast, and you've had Mara on the brain lately. That lunatic wouldn't dare show her face in Richmond and risk getting caught. She's most likely rotting in prison for some other crime."

Grace rubbed her forehead. What Alec said made sense, but she was having a hard time convincing herself. "I'm losing my mind."

"No, you're not. It's just all the stress with Johnny."

"You sound like Ryan."

"Just get the big reveal with Johnny over with. You've been agonizing over it for weeks."

"I was happy to let it go. You and Ryan are the ones pressuring me, but you can relax. We're telling Johnny Thanksgiving weekend." Alec picked up her phone and started tapping. "What are you doing?"

"Putting it in my calendar so you can't conveniently forget."

"Don't bother. Ryan will be holding my feet to the fire."

"Good man." She squeezed Grace's hand. "I know you, better than anyone but Ryan. Maybe better than Ryan. You'll obsess about Mara until you drive yourself and the rest of us crazy. Johnny has all of us to protect him. Forget Mara and focus on reality, not ghosts. By Christmas, you'll be wondering why you kept Johnny's past from him for so long and this Mara thing will be a faint memory. On another topic, have you considered that Johnny will want to meet Craig once he knows the truth?"

"I've tried not to think of it, but we won't stand in his way if he does. He has a right to know his biological father."

"Speaking of, have you heard from that jerk lately?"

Grace shook her head. "Not since his daughter was born three years ago. I've heard from Craig exactly five times since the day he relinquished his parental rights to Johnny. First, when Kristen left him, then when he married Melanie, and when Samuel, Charlie, and Laurel were born."

Alec crossed her arms and huffed. "What do you notice about those events? All about him. He never calls to find out how Johnny's doing?"

"Never, but he's doing me a favor. The less I have to think about Craig Stuart, the better, especially now."

"Then let's shift gears, be grateful for our amazing lives, and plan our Thanksgiving dinner." When Grace smiled, Alec said, "See what I did there?"

"I get it. Funny. Now, tell me again what you're fixing. I didn't hear a word you said."

CHAPTER FOUR

GRACE WALKED into Johnny's room after clearing up the Thanksgiving dinner and frowned at the mess on his floor. Jeans, sweatshirts and even underwear were strewn in every direction, and she could guess from the wrappers and dishes the contents of every meal that he'd eaten for the past week.

"How can you even maneuver in here on your crutches? It's a miracle you haven't broken your neck."

Johnny was lying on his bed in a stained t-shirt watching something on his tablet. "I'll clean it tomorrow before I leave," he said, without taking his eyes off the screen.

"You said that two days ago. Do you need help?"

"I'll manage."

Grace knew that meant he had no intention of cleaning his room. Ryan had convinced her to stop doing it for him, but it made her teeth itch to let it go. The room smelled like the inside of a garbage can in a locker room and made her eyes water. She didn't know how he could stand it. She motioned for him to scoot over and sat next to him on the bed.

"I wanted to thank you for staying tonight after dinner and

not leaving to hang out with your friends. It meant a lot to me and everyone else."

"It's cool. I had fun, and I'm kind of tired. I kind of have a headache." Grace reached over to feel his forehead, but it was cool. Johnny moved his head to the side. "Don't freak out, Mom. I'm not sick. It's just a tiny headache."

The smallest symptom could turn into a major ordeal with Johnny, so Grace was always on her guard. Aside from the cerebral palsy from his head injury as a baby, he suffered lung and heart damage from going without oxygen when he almost drowned after being thrown out of a capsized boat in the James River. The slightest cold could send him to the hospital.

"Probably too many video games." Johnny lowered his tablet and rolled his eyes at her. "Besides cleaning your room, what are your plans for tomorrow?"

Johnny sat up and looked her in the eye. "Can we do my DNA test in the morning? You said I could have one."

Grace had been so relieved when he'd let the matter drop that his question caught her off guard. A DNA test would be pointless once they had their talk with Johnny on Sunday night.

"I completely forgot, but tomorrow is Black Friday. I'm not leaving this house."

"You always have an excuse." He crossed his arms and looked at the wall.

"It may be an excuse, but it's a legitimate one. We won't be able to do anything about it until Monday. I know a geneticist I trust. I'll call her and find out the best way to go about this."

"You'll conveniently forget by then."

Grace pulled a sheet of paper from a notepad on his desk and wrote a promise to call her friend on Monday. She added her signature with a flourish and taped the note to his mirror. "Satisfied?"

"That's a binding legal contract." He smiled and swung his feet to the floor. "I'll hold you to it." He picked up his crutches and stood, towering over her. She wondered if he'd keep growing until she wouldn't be able to see his face anymore. "What are you smiling at?" he asked.

She tipped her head to get a good look at him. "Remember how much you loved *Jack and the Beanstalk* when you were little? You used to ask us to read it over and over. I always thought of you as Jack, not the giant in the story."

"I'll let you know if I start craving man-flesh."

"Good to know," Grace said and laughed. It was the most pleasant moment they'd shared in as long as Grace could remember. He seemed like the old Johnny. Not wanting to spoil it, she chose not to pester him about the state of his room. The mess would be there tomorrow. "So, what are your plans?"

"The movies, remember? I did ask."

"That's right. You're brave to venture out. The theater will be packed."

"We have tickets with assigned seats. It's all good." He leaned on one crutch and bent down to pick up some trash, which he tossed in the overflowing trash can. "Three points," he said and did a fist pump.

She was glad to see him making an effort. "Do you and your friends need a ride? There won't be anywhere to park."

"Jason's taking us. We're going an hour early. Could you drive me to Ty's?"

" I just need to be back before four. We're having friends over for a game night."

"I want to leave at one, so that'll work."

"Good." She stood on a stack of his textbooks and kissed his cheek. "It was a nice day. I have much to be thankful for."

JOHNNY WAITED until his mom was down the hallway before grabbing his backpack. He ignored his growing guilt for lying to her while he dug out clean clothes from one of the piles on his floor and shoved them in his bag before dropping onto the bed to think about what he was about to do. Johnny recognized that his mom was making an effort to get along with him. It felt good to laugh with her instead of arguing and reminiscing about *Jack and the Beanstalk* had struck a chord, but he and his friends had made their plans weeks earlier. He refused to back out so close to launch. He'd be home before his parents knew he'd left Richmond.

He dumped the meds he needed for the weekend, and a few extras just in case, into a baggie and added them into the pack. His game controllers went in last. He'd grab his toothbrush and toiletries after he showered in the morning. When he was done, he laid down to finish his video and do his best to shove thoughts of his mom out of his throbbing head.

GRACE WAS glad Alec and Adam stayed behind when the other guests left after their game night, but she hoped they wouldn't stay too long. Grace was relaxed and looking forward to some alone time with Ryan. Johnny had called earlier to ask if he could spend the night at Ty's, and she hadn't hesitated before saying yes. Grace and Ryan needed time to rekindle their relationship without Johnny distracting them.

When the Emersons started making moves to leave, Alec took a wrapped package out of her tote bag and handed it to Grace. "An early Christmas gift. You may not speak to me again after you read it, but I was driven to write it. My agent and publisher went crazy for the idea. It's an advanced copy, but the book comes out next week."

Grace studied the package. It was much too heavy to be a children's book. Alec hadn't mentioned that she was working on anything else. Grace slowly tore the paper away to see a picture of herself staring back at her. It was one Alec had taken at a park years earlier. Off to the side, there was a blurred-out image of a baby. The title read "Baby John Doe."

Grace's hands started to shake. "What is this, Alec?" Before Alec could answer, Grace caught Adam and Ryan giving each other a conspiring look. She glared at Ryan. "Did you know about this?"

Alec stepped between them. "I made him promise not to tell you. Adam urged me to tell you, but I knew you'd try to talk me out if it."

Grace gritted her teeth. "What is this?" she hissed.

"A biography of Johnny and you that I've been working on for years. I hadn't planned to publish it, but I mentioned it to my agent one day when I was behind on my deadline for another book, and she told me to write up a proposal for the publisher. They ate it up. I've been so worried that you'd find out. The publisher has been putting out advanced publicity, and I've already mentioned it in a few interviews."

Grace lowered herself into a chair and tried to fight her rising terror. She had secrets that only Alec and Ryan shared. She knew the truth about her disastrous affair with Jay Morgan. Worse, she knew about the attempted suicide. Had she laid her deepest secrets bare for the entire world to see?

"How could you do this to me? You're the last person I thought could betray my trust." She let the book fall to the floor. "You were right, I don't ever want to speak to you again. Get out of my house and leave your key."

Adam kneeled in front of her and put his hand on her arm. "Read it before you throw away a fifteen-year friendship. It's brilliant, and most of the facts are already public. Alec just added more depth and detail. There's nothing intimate or too personal that only we would know. She did include the truth about Jay Morgan and what happened to him, but not your relationship with him."

Grace brushed Adam's hand away. "Don't defend her. You all knew what this would do to me, and you've backed me into a corner, making me tell Johnny about his past on your timetable."

"You told me three weeks ago that you're telling him this weekend. I put it in my phone, remember?"

"But you're forcing my hand. What would you have done if I wasn't ready? Or would that matter to you? We're just the little people in the way of Alec Emerson's quest for fame and fortune."

Alec leaned over with her face inches from Grace's. "How dare you say that after all I've done for you? I wrote it because I want the world to know the incredible person I've treasured like a sister all these years. I want women to see how you succeed against insurmountable odds and believe it's possible for them to do the same. What you did was remarkable. No, more than that, it was miraculous."

"You should have told me. You could have waited until Johnny knew the truth. You're forcing me into telling him because that's what you've wanted all along."

"It's what I want, too," Ryan said. "The rest of the world knows the story. It's a miracle Johnny hasn't found out yet."

"You all seem to know what's best for my son and me."

"Our son," Ryan said.

"We'll tell Johnny as planned on Sunday." She pointed to the book on the floor, "But I'm not reading that."

GRACE STROKED the cold sheets on Ryan's side of the bed when she woke the next morning. She'd made Ryan sleep in his man-cave, which made her angrier at everyone. Not only had Alec betrayed her, but she'd ruined her first night alone with Ryan in longer than Grace could remember. They'd had a rare argument. Ryan said now she knew how it felt to have secrets kept from her like she was doing to Johnny. She'd thrown a pillow at him and sent him to the basement. What made her angriest was knowing that he was right.

She tossed in bed for hours before getting up to apologize for overreacting. They'd never gone to bed mad. Alec should have told her about the book, but it was true that the story was already out there. She had no right to take it out on Ryan. He was up getting the boxes of Christmas decorations out when she found him.

"It's the Saturday after Thanksgiving," Ryan said. "Time to decorate for Christmas."

"You still want to do that with me after the way I treated you?" She took the box he held and set it on the couch before pulling him into her arms. "Forgive me for last night. I felt betrayed, but you weren't the cause. That said, I don't like that you kept secrets from me. As much as I've kept from Johnny, I have nothing to hide from you. You're not hiding anything else, are you?"

"How can you ask that? You know how I feel about secrets. It's been killing me to hide it from you."

She gave him a tender kiss. "I *am* sorry. Is it too late to make up for lost time? The decorations can wait."

Ryan led her to the sofa and pulled her onto his lap. "I've always wanted to make love to you in my man-cave but never dared with Johnny and his friends always coming and going. Would you mind?"

In answer, she laced her fingers in his hair and gave him a deep, lingering kiss. "Does that answer your question?"

CHAPTER FIVE

GRACE AND RYAN showered and took a nap after making love. She woke more rested than she'd felt in days. They ate a leisurely lunch of Thanksgiving leftovers, then went back to the Christmas decorations.

They'd used an artificial tree for the past few years, but Grace had pressed Ryan to get a live one. He agreed but wanted to get it at a lot in town. Grace insisted on going to a tree farm in the country where they could cut one down. They drove to a farm just west of Richmond and found the perfect tree. Ryan wasn't thrilled at all the work it took to get it home and into the house, but once it was set up, he agreed it was worth it. He strung the lights, but Grace said she wanted to wait for Johnny to decorate it.

Grace's phone rang as she was getting the leftovers out of the fridge for a second round. It was Darnell's mom, Jayda.

"Happy Thanksgiving," Grace said. "How was your holiday? We missed you at our game night."

"As much as I wish I could make my own Thanksgiving, it's worth it to go to Jordan's mom's, so we don't have to go for

Christmas. It wasn't too terrible. Better than usual. I bet yours was amazing with Alec cooking."

"Indescribable. I had to put on my stretchy pants. What are you and Jordan doing tonight? Did you know we're supposed to get snow?"

"They were just calling for a dusting. Whenever the weatherman says that we get two feet. We're just staying in and getting out the decorations. I was calling to tell Darnell we're going to pick him up before the roads get too bad. He's not answering his phone. Would you mind asking him to call?"

"Darnell's not here. I think he's at Ty's with Johnny."

The line went quiet. "The boys aren't at Ty's. I was just talking to Ashley. They haven't been there. She said the kids were at your house, and Darnell told me he was spending the night with you."

Grace's gut twisted into a knot. "Hang on," she said and muted the phone. "Have you talked to Johnny today?" she asked Ryan.

He shook his head. "What's wrong?"

She unmuted the phone without answering him. "I'll hunt them down and call you right back. Don't worry. They're probably at Damien's."

She hung up and told Ryan what was going on. She opened the app and waited for the results to appear. It showed him in Charlottesville.

"What's he doing there?" Ryan asked.

"Call him," she said.

Ryan tried but Johnny didn't answer. "Maybe they're at Sonya's."

Grace hadn't thought of that. Darnell's older sister went to the University of Virginia. She hoped the boys had driven up there to spend the day with her.

"I need to call Jayda, but how do I explain that I know where Johnny is without telling her about the tracker? She'll think I'm nuts."

"Tell her the truth. We need to know what's going on and quick. If we have five inches of snow here, there must be twice that in Charlottesville."

Grace dialed Jayda. She explained about the tracker, and said, "Is Sonya still home for the break or did she go back today?"

When Jayda didn't respond, Grace had her answer.

"She's still here. She's going back in the morning if the roads are clear." Grace heard Sonya and Jordan in the background, asking what was happening. After Jayda explained, she said, "Sonya didn't know anything about the boys going to Charlottesville. She thought Darnell was at your house. Jordan wants to know if he can ride up there with Ryan in your 4X4."

Grace had put the phone on speaker, so Ryan said, "Tell him I'll be there in five minutes."

"Thanks so much. Don't worry, Grace. I'm sure they're fine. They probably went to the game and got stuck. They'll be home safe in a few hours. I'll let Ashley know."

Grace thanked her and sank into a chair after hanging up. Just when she thought things were back to normal with Johnny, he pulled this stunt. "Keep me posted," she said as Ryan rushed past on his way to the garage. She covered up with an afghan and settled in for the long night ahead

---

GRACE CHECKED her watch while she paced the living room. Only two minutes since the last time she checked. Alec had offered to sit with her, but Grace told her to stay home. She didn't need to be worrying about Alec out in the storm along with everyone else. Ryan had called two hours earlier to say they were on their way back. The trip normally took less than an hour, and Grace had imagined all kinds of terrible scenarios.

Grace had tried to watch a favorite Christmas movie and read a book she'd bought the week before, but she couldn't focus. Only pacing helped. Just when she thought she'd go out of her mind, the garage door opened. She ran to the kitchen to greet her men, not sure if she wanted to hug Johnny or shake him.

They went into the living room to talk after Johnny dumped his belongings in the bedroom. Grace had tried to plan what she would say, but all she knew was that she had to control her temper. Advice from the child-psychology books she'd read over the years flooded into her mind but none of it seemed to apply to her situation. In her opinion, the books would be most effective for thumping him over the head.

She was about to lecture him when he said, "I'm so sorry, Mom. What I did was stupid and selfish. I put myself and other people in danger, including Dad. I deserve whatever punishment you give me."

She was shocked into silence until she realized that Ryan had probably practiced that speech with him on the way home. Rather than question it, she said, "I appreciate the apology, but sometimes a simple sorry isn't enough. Help me understand why you did it? Why *were* you there?"

Johnny stared at the carpet and said, "Jason has a friend at UVA. He had extra tickets to the game, and I've always wanted to see them play. Jason drove us up last night, and we stayed in his friend's dorm. It was an early game, so we were going to watch it and be back before our parents knew we were gone. We didn't know it was going to snow."

"Whose brilliant idea was this?" Ryan asked.

"Let me guess," Grace said. "Darnell."

Johnny squirmed. "Why do you blame everything on him. Maybe it was my idea?"

"Was it?" Grace asked. Johnny shook his head. "It doesn't matter whose idea it was. Why didn't you just ask if you could go? Dad and I would have driven you and your friends this morning. You didn't have to lie."

Grace caught Ryan raising his eyebrows. She ignored him but the irony wasn't lost on her.

"We wanted to see what college was like with no parents. That's all. We didn't do anything bad. We could've drank, but we didn't."

"Am I supposed to congratulate you on that? I'm glad you made that choice, but in your case, you would have ended up in a coma if you drank," Ryan said.

Johnny nodded. "I know." No one spoke for several seconds. "So, what's my punishment?" He cringed while he waited for their answer.

"Dad and I need to talk about that, but I have one more question. Are you sorry because you got caught or because you feel bad about it?"

Johnny raised his chin and looked her in the eye. "Both. I do wish I hadn't got caught, but I swear I was going to tell you when I got home. I felt sick about doing it, especially after our talk last night, but I didn't want to look like a momma's boy. I'm sure you don't believe I was going to tell you, but it's the truth."

"Thanks for your honesty. Go in the other room and give us ten minutes to decide your fate," Ryan said.

Johnny started for the hallway but stopped after a few steps. "How'd you know where I was? We didn't tell anyone."

Ryan looked at Grace, waiting for her to answer. She'd dreaded that question, but since he'd been honest with her, he deserved the same.

"I put a parental tracker on your phone several weeks ago, so I'll always know where you are. I didn't do it because I don't trust you. I did it because it's a dangerous world, and I want you to be safe. And because of your medical issues."

Ryan's mouth dropped open, and Johnny's face reddened. "What do you mean a tracker? Like you can read my texts and stuff and see what I do on my phone?"

"No, it's only a GPS tracker so I can see where you are."

Johnny breathing quickened, and his face got redder. He glanced at Ryan, who held up his hands. "Don't blame your dad. He tried to stop me, but I bet he's glad now that I did it. You'd still be stranded in Charlottesville."

"You put a tracker on me like I'm a dog? How could you do that? You always talk about trust. Where's your trust now?"

Grace stood and glared up at him. "You're questioning my trust after what you just did? This night could have ended much worse. You should be thanking me."

"Thanking you?' He spat the words. "I hate you." He turned and stormed down the hallway as fast as his crutches would carry him.

"Johnny! Come back here!" Ryan said, but Johnny ignored him and slammed his door.

It was Grace's turn to stare openmouthed. Her precious little man, her Johnny, hated her.

She started to go after him, but Ryan grabbed her around the waist. "You'll only make it worse. Give him time."

Grace struggled to get free, but she was no match for Ryan. She slumped against him, and a sob escaped her lips. "You heard what he said? He hates me."

Ryan turned Grace to face him and pulled her to his chest. "He doesn't mean it. You know he loves you. He's just mad. You remember how it was to be that age. Teenagers always hate their parents. If not, you're doing it wrong. That's what Mom used to say."

"My parents were long gone before I was Johnny's age. My grandparents were overwhelmed by having my brothers and me thrust on them when Mama died. I did my best to be the perfect little girl to ease their burden. After they died, and I was sent to my aunt and uncle, I thought it was my chance to be a normal teenager, but I was just in their way. They were glad to see me go when I was forced to marry Danny at sixteen." Grace pulled away and looked into Ryan's eyes. "We've sheltered Johnny from the brutalities of the real world. That's mostly my doing. He has no idea how good he has it."

Ryan tenderly brushed a lock of hair from her forehead. "Sometimes I forget what your life was like before we met. Let me deal with Johnny. I'll get him to see some sense. You two can hold a peace summit tomorrow when you're calmer." Grace nodded and leaned back into his arms. "Are you willing to remove the tracker? You were right about it this time, but it might be a good gesture for initiating the peace process."

Grace gave a weak smile. "You missed your calling. You should work at the UN. I'm sure I'll regret it, but I'll get rid of the tracker. I should have talked to Johnny before I put it on his phone. He's never given us a reason not to trust him until tonight."

"I know it's not easy to be the bigger person after what he did."

"It's not, but I'm the adult. Maybe we'll revisit the issue once things are back to normal, if they ever are."

"They will be, and sooner than you think. Johnny doesn't hold grudges."

Grace pulled away and gazed down the hall. "We should postpone the big talk about Johnny's past for a week or two until our relationship is on a stronger footing. If I tell him the truth now, he will hate me forever."

"As anxious as I am to get it over with, I agree with you. No more than a week or two, though, please."

Grace reached her hand out to Ryan. "I'm ready to get it behind us, too. I'm tired of carrying this weight. I just want to be a typical family doing everyday things."

"Not sure what a typical family is, but we'll get there."

"I'm going to bed and pretend to sleep. Good luck in there," Grace said, gesturing toward Johnny's room.

Ryan smiled and kissed her. "This will be forgotten by tomorrow night."

Grace watched him go, doubting his prediction but wishing more than anything for him to be right.

***

JOHNNY DROPPED onto his bed and started pulling stuff out of his backpack and tossing it to the floor. He didn't care if his mom wanted him to keep his room clean or not. Darnell was right, what did he owe her? He was still shocked that she'd had the nerve to put that tracker on his phone. She'd violated his personal space and proved she thought he was a baby who couldn't take care of himself.

He stared at his phone lying beside him on the bed. The sight of it disgusted him. He wanted to text Darnell and tell him what his mom had done, but he wasn't convinced that she couldn't read his messages. He wondered what other ways she'd devised to spy on him. He considered searching his room for hidden cameras but didn't get the chance before his dad walked in and motioned for him to move over and make room on the bed.

Johnny scooted back and leaned on the headboard. "What do you want?"

His dad's look warned him to lose the attitude. "Your mom and I aren't the ones at fault. We'll get to the tracker in a minute, but first we need to talk about whether or not your apology was sincere."

"Everything I said was true. I *was* going to tell you. I did feel guilty. That's the first time I've done anything like that. Mom should know that since she's been spying on me like I'm some drug dealer."

His dad studied him for several seconds. "I'm choosing to believe you. Did you mean what you said to Mom? Do you hate her?"

Johnny raised his chin and was about to say yes, but it wasn't true. He was furious and felt betrayed, but he didn't hate her. He let out his breath and lowered his shoulders.

"Of course not, but what she did was wrong, and it made me mad. I love Mom, but don't ask me to forgive her. She broke my trust."

"Fair enough, and she happens to agree with you on that. I tried to stop her, but you know how she is when she's determined."

Johnny rolled his eyes. "More than anyone. Why did she do it? Was it really because she's worried about my safety? Seems like a cop-out."

"She did do it for safety reasons. She could have handled it better, but she did it for the right reasons. She worries about you. Being your mother hasn't been easy for her, but she loves you more than her own life."

Johnny sat forward. "Why is she so worried? I know I've been sick a lot. That tracker doesn't change that."

"She has her reasons. Leave it at that. She's agreed to remove the tracker, but you have to offer up a compromise, too. What you said destroyed your mother. Her actions didn't deserve that. No one deserves that, and you're going to fix it. I'm tired of you being at each other's throats."

Johnny crossed his arms and leaned back. "I'm pretty pissed."

His dad got up and kissed the top of his head before he could duck away. "Think about how she feels."

Johnny watched him go, not wanting to think about his mom's feelings. She'd always been a great mom, even if she did baby him too much, but what she did went too far.

Since he was off the hook until morning, he let it go and finished unpacking his clothes. The receipt from the food he bought at the game fluttered to the floor when he pulled out the last handful. Seeing it reminded Johnny that his dad hadn't handed down his punishment. Maybe apologizing to his mom would get him a lighter sentence. He flopped back on the bed, willing to give it some thought.

STEPH'S RINGTONE blared in Johnny's ear the following morning. He glanced at his phone. It was only nine. On a Sunday morning. What was Steph thinking? When he shook his head to clear it and sat up, memories of the previous night flooded his brain. He was tempted to chuck his phone at the wall, but it wasn't Steph's fault, and if he broke his phone, his parents would make him pay for a new one.

He groaned and tapped the answer button to get it before it went to voicemail. "What do you want, Sis?"

Steph laughed. "I was calling to see if you're still alive. I was afraid either the storm or your mom did you in."

Johnny gritted his teeth. Did the whole family always have to know his every move? "How'd you find out so fast?"

"Are you kidding? You had us all scared to death. Dad called after you went to bed to let me know you were okay. Why'd you take off like that? I'd have driven you and your friends to Charlottesville."

Johnny felt guilty all over again. He hadn't thought about anyone else when he'd left with his friends. "I had a ride. I didn't want to bother you, but I should have told Mom and Dad. Did Dad tell you about the tracker?"

"He did. I tried to get your mom to talk to you first. She wishes she had, but maybe she did the right thing after the stunt you pulled."

"I've learned my lesson."

"Hope so. Good luck today. You're going to need it."

Johnny could hear Steph laughing as she hung up. He didn't see anything funny about it. He rolled onto his back and was about to cover his head when his text alert buzzed. He picked the phone up and saw that it was his other stepsister, Jen.

Call when you wake up.

He called instead of replying. "Hey, Jen, what's up?"

"You're already awake? Or did I wake you?"

"Steph just called," Johnny said and smiled. He'd never admit it to anyone, but he liked that his sisters worried about him. "How are you feeling?" he asked to avoid the reason she was calling. "Thanksgiving wasn't the same without you and Jason."

"I'm as big as a house. I don't know if I'll survive the four weeks until these babies arrive. I don't know how my mom did this."

"Focus on how great it'll be. I'm excited to be an uncle again, especially since it's boys. I love Mark and Valerie's kids, and the Emersons are great, but there are too many girls."

"You have Fisher and Graham, but Jason agrees with you. So why did you run off and scare all of us to death?"

Johnny gave Jen the same excuses he gave Steph and told her he was sorry. "I'll see you when we come up to DC before Christmas. Hang in there. It'll go by fast."

"Doubt it, but thanks. Behave yourself and apologize to Grace. You broke her heart."

"I will. I promise."

"Love you," Jen said and hung up.

Johnny smiled at his phone, waiting for Mark or Valerie to call until he realized they'd be at the restaurant in the middle of brunch service. He decided to get up and face the inevitable.

"Did you sleep?" Ryan asked Grace as he came into the dining room. "Every time I woke, you were staring at the ceiling.

Grace pushed her notepad aside and gave him a weak smile. "You must have only done that twice, because I slept most of the night, surprisingly. I guess I've finally trained myself to sleep through a crisis."

"I'd hardly call this a crisis. It's just typical family turmoil. What were you writing?" he asked and glanced at her notes.

"Just putting a few thoughts down to keep them straight for our peace summit. It helps keep my emotions in check."

"I'll get Johnny so we can get his over with and enjoy the rest of our day. It's back to the real world tomorrow. Hopefully, he's awake, so we can avoid that battle."

"I heard him on the phone a few minutes ago. He sounded in a good mood, so there's a glimmer of hope."

Grace gave her notes one last check but closed her notebook. Maybe she was making too much of what Johnny had done. Though Ryan didn't excuse their son's behavior, he didn't seem too worked up about it either. Grace decided to take a cue from Ryan and not make it a big deal. Parents of teenagers dealt with these situations all the time. She and Ryan were fortunate that Johnny rarely gave them trouble.

She turned her focus to the highlights from the past few days. Thanksgiving weekend had gone by fast and hadn't exactly been the break she'd hoped for. Thanksgiving Day had been pleasant, though. She'd been glad that Mark, Valerie, and their kids had joined them for the feast. They saw too little of them because of the demands of their restaurant. Even though Jen and Jason hadn't been able to come to dinner because Jen was too close to her due date, Grace was thrilled that two new members would be added to their clan when the twins were born. She couldn't imagine managing twins, but she couldn't wait to meet her grandsons.

She was smiling at the thought when Ryan came into the room with Johnny following close behind.

"That wasn't the look I expected," Johnny said.

"I was thinking about Jen and the babies. I can't wait for them to arrive," Grace said.

"I was just talking to her. She feels the same way, but for different reasons. She said she's as big as a house."

Ryan took out his phone and pulled up his latest text from Jen with a picture. "More like a toothpick with an olive on it. I don't know how she keeps from tipping over." Grace and Johnny laughed when Ryan showed them the picture. He slipped his phone back into his pocket and said, "Let's sit in the living room. It's more comfortable."

Once they were seated, Grace said, "Let me see your phone. I'll take the tracker off with you watching."

Johnny smirked as he handed it to her. "Guess you know the unlock PIN."

Grace ignored his comment. She uninstalled the tracker and gave him back his phone. "I should have talked to you before installing that app. I hope you'll believe that it wasn't because I don't trust you. It's a dangerous world. I worry about you after all we've been through. I'm sorry."

Johnny stared at his phone for several seconds. Without looking at her, he said softly, "Don't apologize to me, Mom. You should have talked to me, but what I said to you last night was so bad. I didn't mean it. I promise not to say that to you ever again. You know I love you. You're a great mom. You do so much for me, and I never thank you. I'm so sorry. I hope you'll forgive me, and that this won't ruin things between us. Oh, and I shouldn't have run off without telling you."

Grace ignored the tears rolling down her cheeks. His words were genuine and far more than she'd hoped to hear. She went to him and put her arm around his shoulders.

"Thank you. You're forgiven. I've dealt with some tough things in my life, but one thing I couldn't bear was the idea of you not loving me. Our relationship has been rocky lately, but I promise I'll try harder if you will."

Johnny wiped a tear off the end of his nose before he nodded. As much as he tried to be grown up, he was still her little man.

"Shortest peace summit in history, but we're not finished," Ryan said. "There's still your punishment to deal out." Johnny groaned but looked Ryan in the eye. "Your mom and I agreed last night that you can't have or go to any sleepovers until after Christmas break. As sorry as I know you are, what you did was dangerous, and you need time to think about it. You can still have friends over and go to their houses, but no sleepovers, and we expect you to be honest about where you are at all times."

"Fair enough. I deserve that."

"And we'd like you to spend a little more time with us," Ryan said. "I know we're your boring parents, but you're only fourteen and family is important. It's no more than I expected from my kids when they were your age. You can ask them."

Johnny grimaced. "How much more time?"

Grace chuckled and said, "Is the idea that painful? Just a few hours a week. We'd like to start today. Decorate the Christmas tree with us."

Johnny's eyes brightened. Decorating the tree had always been one of his favorite holiday activities. Grace had fond memories of his eyes lighting up as they took each ornament from the box and reminisced about where it had come from on their travels or what it represented.

"Can we start now?" Johnny asked.

Ryan rubbed his hands together and jumped up to get the boxes of ornaments from the basement, leaving the two of them in awkward silence. Even though this skirmish was resolved, getting back to normal would take time. Grace watched Johnny pick at a thread on his hoodie and wondered again how time had passed so quickly without her noticing.

"We good?" she asked softly.

He jerked his head up and stared at her. "Yeah, Mom. Can we just forget all this drama?"

"Please," Grace said and smiled. "I'm too old for drama."

CHAPTER SIX

You guys want to come over and finish our game marathon? Johnny asked his friends in a group text when he got home from school the following day. *Already did my homework and parents won't be home for hours.*

Darnell texted back a minute later. *Thought you were grounded.*

Only from sleepovers.

Ty chimed in next. *You got off easy. I'm grounded from life until Christmas. I'm lucky they let me keep my phone.*

Johnny was surprised. Ty's parents were usually pretty lax, and it had been his brother that drove them to Charlottesville.

That sucks, Johnny typed. *Anyone else?*

When no one responded after several minutes, he gave up and went to get a snack. He was relieved to see there were still a few leftovers from Thanksgiving. He didn't know what his mom was fixing for dinner, but he knew it wouldn't be near as good as anything Auntie Alec made.

He heaped the food on a plate and maneuvered to the table, wishing he could take the food to his room and eat while he played video games. He reminded himself to talk to his dad about coming up with a way to carry things to his room that couldn't go in his backpack.

After he wolfed down his food, he carried his game console to the basement to play on his dad's big-screen TV instead of the small one in his room. It took five grueling trips up and down the stairs, but once he got it set up, the graphics and sound system made the hard work worth it.

He played for half an hour before a message popped up saying his controller batteries were dying. He tossed the controller on the couch and bent down to get his crutches so he could look for batteries in the storage room. He noticed a book sticking out from under the sofa, but all he could see was a picture of a baby in the corner of the cover. He picked up the book, wondering why his dad had a book about a baby in his man-cave.

He studied the cover. A photo of his mom when she was younger stared back at him. The title read, *Baby John Doe*. his gut tightened, and his heart started to pound. At the bottom of the cover was a blurb that read, "The true story of one woman's harrowing battle to save a life." The author, Alexandra Emerson.

Dread crept up Johnny's spine. Logic told him to shove the book under the sofa, but the temptation to open the book drown out his logic. His hands trembled as he flipped through the pages to the first chapter. The chapter heading said, "Grace Ward – The Beginning." Johnny skipped past that part to where his story began.

What he read for the following two hours tore what he thought was the truth about his life to shreds. He was kidnapped the day he was born. The kidnappers were never caught. His mother died giving birth to him. His father was alive, living in New Mexico and knew about him. He'd lived with his father for a few months before his father rejected him and gave him up to Grace and Ryan. Worse yet, Ryan and Grace, Alec and Adam, all of them, they'd known the truth all along.

Johnny slammed the book shut and stared at the cover. Alec's name jumped out at him. How could she keep those dark truths from him? She was always spouting off about the importance of honesty. Nothing about their relationship was honest. And there was Steph, Jen, Mark. These people were nothing to him. They'd pretended to care, to want to be a part of his life, but they'd kept the biggest secret about who he was from him.

His parents must have forced them to lie. No, not his parents. Ryan and Grace Walker, the imposters he'd loved and trusted. They were strangers to him now. They were liars. Grace most of all. Waves of nausea washed over Johnny when the magnitude of her betrayal sank in. He collapsed into the cushions, too numb to cry or scream or flee.

GRACE WALKED into the kitchen through the garage and set her purse on the table. The house was silent and dark. The back of her neck prickled. Johnny usually flipped on every light and had at least two TVs blaring by the time she got home from work.

Grace went through to the hallway and nearly tripped over Johnny's backpack. She was about to pick it up to take to his room, but she left it where it was. He'd never learn to put his things where they belonged if she always did it for him. She wanted to call him to come get it, but their truce was fragile, and she didn't want to jeopardize it. There would be time to train him later. Instead, she pasted on a smile and went to ask how his day had gone.

He wasn't in his room, but it only took seconds to figure out where he was. Perfect outlines of dust rested on the empty shelf where his game console usually sat. Since Ryan had remodeled the basement to create his man-cave, Johnny had spent almost as much time there as his dad. She tossed the wet towel he'd left on the floor after his shower that morning into his clothes hamper and headed for the basement.

While she descended the stairs, she rehearsed how she'd deflect him if he asked about the DNA testing. The promise she'd scribbled down to talk to her colleague had been sitting on the end of Johnny's bed. She pushed the basement door open and found Johnny hunched over on the sofa with his head resting in his hands. The familiar knot of dread tightened in her gut.

As she rushed to his side, her eye caught Alec's book lying at Johnny's feet. She froze as the dread of a different sort washed over her. She dropped to her knees and picked up the book. "Johnny," she whispered, "We were going to tell you. Please, let me explain."

He looked at her with his face twisted in a pain she'd never seen there before, not even on his worst days. Without speaking, he grabbed his crutches and raised himself off of the sofa. His legs shook, but he managed to hold himself upright.

"Stay away from me! I don't want any more of your lies. You knew! You knew my mother was dead. You know who my father is and where he lives. You knew I'd been kidnapped. Kidnapped! And the kidnappers weren't caught." He lowered his face close to hers and between gasps for air said, "That's why you were tracking me. That's why you always kept me on a short leash. You're afraid they'll come back for me, and you didn't even warn me."

"Johnny, calm down. You shouldn't get so agitated. It could bring on a seizure. I'll tell you the whole story but sit down and get control of yourself."

She put her hand on his arm, but he jerked it away. "Don't touch me," he hissed.

"You two down there?" Ryan called from the top of the stairs. "What's all the shouting?"

"We're here," Grace said, just loud enough for Ryan to hear.

He stopped and the smile slid from his face when he saw

Grace and Johnny facing each other with Alec's book on the floor between them. "No," he whispered.

"Why did you bring that down here? I told you I wanted it locked up in our room. Look at what you've done," Grace said.

"I thought is was hidden under the couch, but don't hang this on me. I've been the one begging you to tell him the truth. This is all on you." He stepped closer to Johnny. "Take a few breaths and sit down. Let's talk this out."

"Shut up!" Johnny screamed. "One of your stupid talks won't fix this. Nothing will fix this. You're liars, and you're not my parents. You're nothing to me. Stay away from me." He locked his eyes on Grace. "I hate you. I mean it this time. I never want to see you again, ever!"

He turned on his crutches and started for the stairs.

"Don't leave like this, please," Ryan pleaded. "Where will you go?"

Johnny ignored him, and Grace started to follow but Ryan stopped her. She fought like a mad woman to break free, but Ryan held her tighter.

"Let him go, Grace. He needs time to process what's he's just learned. Nothing we say now will reach him. Just let him go."

When Grace stopped struggling, Ryan loosened his grip, and Grace dropped to the floor, too stunned to move. Johnny's crutches thumped on the floor above their heads until the front door slammed. Then all was quiet, and Grace knew it would be the last she'd ever see of her precious little man.

MARA CLIMBED out of the shrubs where she'd been crouching near the corner of Grace's house listening to the argument taking place on the other side of the wall. She grinned as she rubbed the stiffness out of her thighs and walked her dog to the front of the house on his short leash. She waited in the shadows for Johnny to come through the front door. Her patience was rewarded less than a minute later.

"Can you and Jason come get me, Ty?" she heard him say. "I don't want to talk about why, but it's pretty bad. I'll need to stay at your house for a while." Mara watched Johnny and listened for a few seconds. "None of that matters," he finally said. "Just come get me now."

The emotion in his voice was clear. He was losing it. *Pay dirt*, she thought. The long hours of crouching in the cold, waiting for her ideal moment had paid off. She scanned the street to make sure it was empty before casually stepping onto the sidewalk and heading away from Johnny. She had the urge to run but forced herself to walk like any dog-owner out for a leisurely stroll. Johnny was too distraught to notice a woman walking her dog.

She picked up her pace once she rounded the corner. Her car waited halfway down the block. She got in and tossed the dog into the backseat. She estimated that she had less than a minute to get to Johnny before his friends showed up. She had to time it right or her perfect chance would be wasted.

***

JOHNNY FACED the direction Ty's brother would come from, wondering what was taking so long. For a second, he worried that Ty's mom wouldn't let them get Johnny since Ty was still grounded. He was also afraid his mom had called to warn them. The thought made him freeze. Grace wasn't his mom. He didn't have a mom. His mom was dead.

His legs went weaker than usual, so he transferred his weight on his arms before lowering himself to the top step of the stoop. His body shook uncontrollably. He was afraid he'd pass out before Ty got there to rescue him. He couldn't let that happen. He steadied his breathing, taking slow even breaths the way Tony had taught him. That helped a little, but he was going to need something much stronger to survive the nightmare he was facing.

He turned to look for Ty just as a blue car slowed and came to a stop near the driveway. A woman Johnny didn't recognize was driving. She smiled and rolled down the passenger window.

"Johnny?" she asked. When he nodded, she said, "I'm Ty's aunt, Mara. He said you need a ride."

Johnny was up and had his backpack over his shoulders before she could escape. He crossed the lawn to her car in record time.

Once they were moving, he said, "Thanks for picking me up. I didn't know Ty had an aunt around here."

"I was happy to help. I don't live in Richmond. I came into town for Thanksgiving. Are you all right? Ty said you sounded upset on the phone."

There was no way Johnny could explain to this stranger, so he mumbled something about getting in a fight with his parents and looked out the window. He was relieved that she didn't press him for more.

They rode in silence for a few more blocks, but when Mara passed the turn to Ty's house, he said, "It's that way. You missed the street."

"We're going to our cousin's house in the country. They invited us to dinner. Ty said you wouldn't mind."

Johnny wondered why Ty hadn't told him about the cousin on the phone, but he liked the idea of getting as far away from his parents as possible. Thinking of home made him feel sick. He was afraid he'd puke all over the car.

Mara glanced at him out of the corner of his eye. "You sure you're okay?" He wasn't okay, far from it, but he didn't answer. Mara took out bottled water from the pocket in her door and held it out to Johnny.

"Drink this. It'll help. I'm a nurse."

Johnny took the water and downed it in five gulps. Mara was right. It did help for a minute until his head got a strange heavy feeling. His vision blurred, and the last sight he remembered before everything went black was Mara staring at him with an eerie grin.

MARA WAS RELIEVED that Johnny went out so quickly. He was such a big boy, her boy, that she hadn't been sure of the correct dose to put in his water. She worried it would be too much and he'd overdose or not enough so it wouldn't do the job. His health problems meant she had to be extra cautious.

She alternated between watching Johnny sleep and watching the road. Her plan had worked so smoothly that she wanted to shout for joy. It was just like the first time she'd taken him as her son when he was born. If it hadn't been for that damned hurricane all those years earlier, she would have been the one to raise Johnny. He never would have gotten hurt, and she wouldn't have had to give him up to that perfect little Grace Walker.

All of that was behind her. Her next task was convincing Johnny that he belonged to her. Since he'd seen Alec's book and knew the truth, she'd had to concoct an ironclad story. It had taken time, but she was ready to answer his questions when he woke up and discovered he wasn't at Ty's cousin's house.

Johnny's text alert buzzed three or four times. It must have been Ty wondering where Johnny had disappeared to, or Grace begging her baby to come home. A minute later, the phone rang. Johnny stirred but didn't open his eyes. Mara gingerly took the phone from his hand and looked at the caller ID. It was Ty. She wasn't worried about him. Even if he told Grace that Johnny had asked for a ride but wasn't there when he showed up, they'd just assume he'd gone with another friend. By the time they realized he was gone, Mara would have him safely settled in his real home.

She lowered the window and threw Johnny's phone into the snow pile on the far side of the road. By the time anyone got around to tracing it, the battery would be wet and ruined. She congratulated herself for being clever enough to think of every detail. She had a new phone waiting for him that no one could trace.

She did a U-turn at the next intersection and headed for the city. She was glad she wouldn't have to plot and plan and stalk anymore. After more than fourteen years of agonized waiting, she was ready to begin the life she deserved as Johnny's mother.

CHAPTER SEVEN

GRACE DREW a deep breath through the paper bag and held it for a moment before exhaling. She'd resisted when Ryan first thrust the bag at her but breathing into it helped. She took another breath and scanned the room with her eyes. The architecture and furnishings felt foreign even though this had been her home and safe haven for years. The house had become nothing more than an empty shell without Johnny.

She lowered the bag and said, "This has turned out worse than my nightmares."

Ryan stopped his pacing. "Breathe," he said and motioned for her to put the bag back to her lips.

Grace threw the bag on the floor and stood to face him with her hands on her hips. "Why did you take that infernal book downstairs? Why couldn't you have left it alone? You ruined all our plans. You and Alec. Why'd she write that damned thing in the first place?"

"Drop the melodrama, Grace. I'm not in the mood, and I told you I didn't bring that book down here."

"Then how did it get here?"

He exhaled and shook his head. "How should I know? Maybe

Johnny found it upstairs and brought it down here. Who cares? This isn't my fault or Alec's. If you'd told him the truth years ago, we could have avoided this. I've hated lying to him. So have Alec, Adam and my kids. You forced us all into this horrible situation, but what matters now is that we've got to pull together and do damage control. Call Tony in the morning to see if he'll help. Johnny respects him, and Tony doesn't know anything about Johnny's past. He's the only person who hasn't been lying to him."

Grace dropped her hands to her sides and looked toward the window as if she expected to see Johnny in the darkness beyond. "Don't keep saying we lied. It wasn't lying. It was protecting him. We just didn't tell him the whole story."

"Rationalize all you want, but telling half-truths is lying. You as much as looked him in the eye and told him his birth parents were dead."

She slumped onto the sofa and covered her face with her hands. As much as she hated to admit it, Ryan was right. They were all at fault, her most of all. She had used the excuse of trying to protect Johnny by not telling him his history, but she was only protecting herself. He'd deserved to know. Now, it was too late. She'd never get the chance to convince him they'd been on the verge of telling him before he saw the book.

"Where do you think he is?" she asked softly. "How long has he been gone?"

"Three hours. I'm sure he's at Ty's or Darnell's."

"I wonder why their parents haven't called. They must be dying to know what happened. Should we call them?"

Ryan sat next to her and shook his head. "Let's give him his space. It'll take time to recover from this emotional earthquake. Call Jayda and Ashley tomorrow if we haven't heard from Johnny by then."

Grace's phone buzzed in her pocket and made her jump. She tore it out as fast as she could get her hands to work. She looked at the screen and frowned when she saw it was Alec. She let it go to voicemail and tossed her phone on the ottoman.

Ryan peeked at the screen before it went dark. "Why'd you do that?"

"I have nothing to say to Alec. How could she write that book knowing what it would do to me, how it would affect me? Do my feelings mean nothing to her after all these years?"

"She'll just keep calling until you answer. Her reasons for writing the book are the opposite of what you said. She wrote it because of how much she admires and respects you. The book is good. I hope once we're through this crisis, you'll read it. I think it will surprise you."

Her phone rang again, but she ignored it. She couldn't believe what Ryan was saying. Did he truly understand her so little after all their years together? She'd spent her adult life burying the horrors of her past. Now, all he and Alec wanted to do was dig them up and expose them to the world. Once again, her past was threatening to destroy the life she'd worked so hard to build. How could they not understand?

"Did you forget that I'm intimately acquainted with that story? I know it better than Alec. Why in God's name would I read it? How would you feel if someone wrote a book about the months Marie suffered through her cancer before she died and then asked you to read it?" The pained look in Ryan's eyes was her answer. "Now, you understand."

"This situation is completely different, but I wouldn't mind if the story could lighten even one person's burden." Ryan rubbed his face. "I'm too exhausted to talk about this now. I'm going to bed. You coming?"

Ryan stood and held his hand out to her, but she didn't take it. "I won't be sleeping tonight. I already texted Brad and told him what happened and that I wouldn't be in tomorrow. Maybe I'll scrub the kitchen floor."

"That's ridiculous. Staying awake for days won't bring Johnny home or turn back the clock. Come to bed, take a sleeping pill and watch a movie with me until you fall asleep."

Grace scowled at him. "You know I can't stand taking those things. Scrubbing the floor works better than any sleeping pill and without the side effects."

Ryan knelt in front of her and cupped her chin in his hand. "Look at me." When Grace raised her eyes, he said, "I'm not your enemy. If we're going to reunite this family, we need to support each other. I'd give anything to undo this, but I can't. Neither can you. I love you. Don't push me away."

She looked into his eyes and remembered all he had done for her. He'd stood by her and Johnny through their worst trials and greatest triumphs. More than that, she owed him her life.

She kissed him tenderly and wrapped her arms around his neck. "I'll never understand why you stay with me. Forgive me for acting like the old Grace. I feel like I'm in a scene from a TV movie." She held his hand and let him help her up. "I'll come to bed and even let you pick what to watch."

"I stay because there's nowhere I'd rather be. Stop worrying, Grace. I'm not going anywhere."

———

GRACE WOKE IN A FOG. *Damned sleeping pills*. She pushed herself to a sitting position and squinted at the clock. Nine-thirty! Ryan's side of the bed was empty and the house was quiet. He probably thought he'd done her a favor by letting her sleep, but she'd wanted to get up early and find Johnny before he left for school. She grabbed her phone, but there were no messages or texts. At least the hospital hadn't called. Too much stress could cause Johnny to have seizures. What he'd gone through the day before was the worst shock he'd ever had.

She climbed out of bed and headed for the bathroom, but she

stopped when her phone rang. She went back to the bed and checked the caller ID. It was Johnny's school.

When she answered, the attendance secretary said, "I'm calling to find out why Johnny's absent since you didn't notify us that he wouldn't be here. Is he ill, or did he have an appointment this morning?"

"He's not there? You're sure?" Grace asked, trying to steady the tremor in her voice.

"His homeroom teacher marked him absent. I can check with her, but he's kind of hard to miss."

Grace didn't want to get into their problems with the school secretary, so she said, "I just checked my phone and remembered that Johnny did have an appointment this morning. His father took him. He should be back after lunch. I'll call if his appointment runs long."

"No need. Just let us know if he'll be absent tomorrow. Thank you," she said and hung up.

Grace didn't know who to call first. Ryan would have told her if he'd talked to Johnny, so she dialed Jayda. She hated to bother her at work, but it was an emergency.

When she picked up, Grace said, "Did Johnny stay at your house last night? The school just called, and he's not there. Do you know where he is?"

Grace heard Jayda's hesitation. "You don't know where Johnny was last night?"

"He found out about the kidnapping and Craig. He knows everything. It's a long story. Was he at your house?"

"No, Grace. I'm sorry. I haven't seen Johnny since before Thanksgiving. Do you want me to help you find him?"

"No, you're the first person I called, and you're at work. I'm sure he spent the night with Ty. I'll try Ashley."

"Please text me as soon as you find him. Good luck."

"Thanks, I will."

Grace hung up and called Ashley as fast as she could. Once she explained what was happening, Ashley said, "I haven't seen Johnny, but the boys were playing video games in the basement pretty late last night. Maybe they sneaked Johnny in." Ashley paused and Grace heard her walk downstairs. "He's not here. Let me check Ty's room. Johnny shouldn't have been here last night. Besides the fact that it was a school night, Ty's still grounded from that stunt they pulled over the weekend. If Johnny was here, Ty's going to get it."

Grace gave a fake laugh. She couldn't have cared less about Ty's punishment. She just needed to find her son.

"He's not here. I'll text Ty to see if he knows what's going on, but his phone is supposed to be turned off when he's in class. He may not get back to me until lunch. Please, let me know if you find him before then."

"I will and call as soon as you hear from Ty," Grace said.

She ran her hand through her hair and started pacing the room. She called Ryan next. He needed to know Johnny was missing. She ran through the places he could be while she waited for Ryan to answer. If Ty and Darnell hadn't seen him, it was worse than she thought. Her last hope was that he really was with Ryan and he hadn't wanted to call and wake her.

"You're up," Ryan said and chuckled. "You were dead to the world when I left. I thought you'd sleep..."

"Johnny's missing," Grace said. She told him what was going on in a rush. "Is he with you? Have you heard from him?"

"No, Grace. Oh my God! Where do you think he is? I'm coming home now."

"Call your kids and see if he contacted them. I'm going to try Alec and Adam. I know that's a long shot since he's probably mad at them, too. I'll call Kyle and Damien's parents after that."

"Call the instant you know anything."

"You do the same."

She was calmer after talking to Ryan and working with him to find Johnny made her feel less alone.

She dialed Alec next, and she picked up after the first ring.

"It's about time," Alec said. "I knew you wouldn't hide from me forever. Does this mean you've forgiven me for writing the book?"

"That's not why I'm calling. Johnny's missing. Did he call you last night?"

"What do you mean Johnny's missing?"

Grace told her about the blow up the night before and her role in it, but she didn't care about blame. If Alec was in the dark, it meant she hadn't heard from Johnny.

"I'm sick about this, Grace. Johnny hasn't contacted us. I'm coming over, and we're going to find him. You shouldn't be out looking alone."

"Don't come over. Ryan's on his way home. We have more people to call. Maybe he's at Steph's. If we don't find him soon, I'm calling the police."

She hung up before Alec could protest, and dialed Kyle's mom, but got the same response, and with Damien's mom, too. The last person she could think of was Tony. She felt like she was going to burst out of her skin waiting for the PT receptionist.

When she asked for Tony, the receptionist said, "I'm sorry, but Tony's out with the flu. We don't expect him back until Thursday."

Johnny had Tony's cell number, but Grace didn't, and she knew the receptionist would never give it to her. "I know Tony's sick, but it's extremely urgent that I talk to him. Could you please call him and ask him to call me as soon as he can?"

The receptionist hesitated. "Can one of the other physical therapists help? I hate to bother him."

"No, I need to speak to Tony. I'll take full responsibility for bothering him."

"Fine, Mrs. Walker. I'll give him your message."

"Thank you. I wouldn't ask if it weren't an emergency."

She hung up and took the phone into the bathroom so she'd

hear it while she showered and dressed. Half an hour passed with no calls or texts.

She called Ryan as soon as she toweled off and threw on some clothes. "Where are you? Please, tell me you found him."

"I guess that means you haven't had any luck either. None of my kids know where he is. Steph is freaking out. She's on her way to the house. I'll be right behind her"

"My last hope is that Tony will call and tell me he knows where he is. He's out sick with the flu so Johnny could be with him."

"He would have let us know. If Johnny is missing, Tony would know the anguish we're going through."

Call waiting beeped. "There's Tony. I'll put it on conference call."

She told their story one more time, desperate to hear good news.

"I'm sorry to say I have no idea where Johnny is. Call the police immediately. And please keep me posted. I'm sure he's fine. Probably hiding out somewhere you haven't thought of yet. Check and see if he's been on social media."

"We will, Tony. Get better."

After Tony hung up, Ryan said, "I know I probably don't need to ask but have you called Johnny's phone?"

"Ten times. It rang the first few times, but now it's going straight to voicemail."

"It's time to call 911."

"I'm calling Agent Michaels. He knows Johnny's history, and I don't want to waste time with the local police."

"He wasn't kidnapped. He ran away. Local cops will know where to look for a runaway."

"I'm calling Scott Michaels."

"Do you think he's still at the Richmond office after twelve years?"

"Why are you arguing with me? If I'm wrong, they'll point me to the police."

"Do what you think is best. See you in twenty."

GRACE DUG through the pile of business cards she kept in her bedside table until she found Agent Michael's number. He'd been the agent to handle the search for Johnny's biological parents when he was a baby, and he knew about the kidnapping. Even if he'd left the Richmond office, she hoped whoever answered could tell her how to find Johnny.

"Michaels," Scott said when he answered. "Who is this? How did you get this number?"

Grace recognized his voice without him identifying himself. "It's Grace Walker. Do you remember me? You might know me as Grace Ward."

"Of course, Grace. How are you? Scratch that. I'm guessing this isn't a social call to catch up."

"Johnny's missing. We haven't seen him since about six-thirty last night. We thought he spent a night with a friend. When the school called to say he didn't show up today, Ryan and I started calling everyone we could think of. No one has seen him."

"Hang on," Agent Michaels said and put her on hold.

Grace was irritated that he cut her off so abruptly. What could be more important than a missing, disabled teenager? She took a breath and told herself to trust that he had a good reason. He'd come through for them when Johnny was a baby when they were desperate to find out where he'd come from. Agent Michaels would know what to do.

He kept Grace waiting for almost five minutes before he came back on the line. "Sorry for keeping you waiting so long," he said. "It took a minute to pull Johnny's file. While I scroll through it, give me the details of why you think Johnny's missing? Has there been any family trouble?"

Grace dreaded having to divulge what she'd done to one more person. She felt guiltier and angrier with herself after each retelling, but Johnny's disappearance wasn't about her. She'd suffer whatever it took to find him. Grace gave Agent Michaels all the details and held her breath while she waited for him to respond.

He whistled and said, "That's rough. Why didn't you tell him about his past? You hadn't done anything wrong. In fact, you saved his life."

"Long story. I had my reasons. Does that matter now?"

"No, you're right. You can sort that out once he's home. You've done the right thing to contact me. Most likely he's holed up at a friend's house licking his wounds, but given his health issues and history, we need to treat this as a missing person's case. I just gave instructions for one of my agents to enter him into the missing person database," he said. "I'll need some updated information. We'll need recent photos too. Give them to Agent Shepherd when she gets there."

"You don't want us to come to your office?" Grace asked. That's what they'd done when they worked with him in the past.

"No, stay where you are. It's better to set up a base of operations in your home. Agent Shepherd will take the lead on the case and coordinate with local law enforcement agencies. We won't stop working until Johnny is safe at home."

"You're not coming?" Grace asked, disappointed that they'd have to work with a stranger.

"No, I'm the Special Agent in Charge of this field office now. I'll be involved in the case, but Agent Shepherd will head operations. Hopefully, Johnny will be home before she has time to set up. Now, how tall is Johnny? What color is his hair? Oh, and he's not in a wheelchair?"

"No, he walks with crutches. He's six foot, has broad shoulders, but he's kind of gawky. His hair is still blond."

Agent Michaels whistled again. "Six foot? Big boy. And on crutches. Shouldn't be hard to locate. How's his health? Does he have his meds?"

Grace broke down at the question. He'd taken his backpack but hadn't gone to his room before he stormed out. She was sickened that she had no idea if he had his meds. Grace wiped her cheeks with her sleeve and cleared her throat. "I don't know."

"That's fine," he said and continued to ask her a series of questions. Grace was grateful that she could answer them. "The majority of runaways in a similar situation show up after a day or two. I'm sure Johnny's a smart kid with you as his mother. He knows where his bread is buttered. Agent Shepherd knows her stuff, and she's a mom, too. Trust her as you would me. I'll stick my head in when I can. Don't hesitate to call at this number any time."

The doorbell rang as she was about to thank him. "Someone's at the door. Maybe it's Johnny," she said and disconnected the call.

JOHNNY'S EYELIDS felt like lead weights. It took three tries and fierce concentration to force them open. He looked around the unfamiliar room and snapped them shut again. His heart started to pound, and his breath quickened. He had no memory of how he'd gotten into this room. The last thing he remembered was calling Ty to come rescue him, but he'd ended up on a narrow, creaky bed in a small shabby bedroom he'd never seen.

He swung his feet to the floor and raised himself into a sitting position. The room spun for a few seconds, but he focused on a paper tacked to the wall across from him to make it stop. When the dizziness faded, he was relieved to see his crutches leaning against a table next to the bed. He wasn't steady enough to stand yet, but he was glad he'd have his crutches when he was ready to make his getaway.

He was wearing sweatpants and a t-shirt that didn't belong to him and wondered who'd changed his clothes. He pulled the waistband of the sweatpants down to check his underwear. At least those were his, so whoever changed him hadn't seen him naked.

There was a terrible taste in his mouth, and his head pounded as hard as his heart. *Did I have a seizure?* he wondered. He didn't feel like he usually did after a seizure. This feeling was something new.

When his head cleared, he realized he needed to pee. As nervous as he was about standing, he was more afraid of wetting his pants. He reached for his crutches and pushed himself onto his legs. He took a few seconds to make sure he was stable before moving when it occurred to him that he didn't know where the bathroom was.

He decided to risk finding out who had brought him to that strange place. "Hello," he said. The word came out like a croak. He cleared his throat and tried again. "Is anyone there?"

Seconds later, footsteps thumped on what sounded like wooden stairs. His heart raced faster, but he didn't back down. He had to know what was happening to him. He braced the backs of his legs against the bed in case he had to use his crutches as a weapon.

The woman who entered the room looked familiar, but Johnny couldn't remember why. She wore a nurses' uniform, and her black hair was pulled up with a clip. He wondered if she worked with Grace or in one of his doctors' offices. She was a little taller than Grace, but not by much, and she had a slight build. Johnny was sure he could take her if she attacked him.

He shifted his weight to his left leg and pointed his right crutch at her. "Stay there. Who are you? Why'd you bring me here?"

"I guess you figured out that I'm not Ty's aunt," she said, with a smile.

Memories from the night before flooded his brain. That was how he knew her. "How did you know about Ty? Where are we?"

"Calm down, Johnny. You have nothing to fear from me. I'd never hurt you. Sit down. Let me explain."

She took a step toward him, and Johnny leaned away with his crutch still pointed at her. "I said, stay there."

She stopped and held up her hands in surrender. "I'll stay here but sit down before you fall. I can see your legs shaking."

Johnny stared at her for a few seconds before slowly lowering himself onto the bed. She was right. His legs were about to give out. He wouldn't be able to defend himself very well if he was flat on his back.

"That's better." She gestured to a chair in the corner. "Do you mind if I sit, too? I can't reach you from there."

She continued grinning at him, probably trying to put him at ease, but Johnny thought it was creepy. He nodded anyway. He'd rather have her sitting.

Making himself look as threatening as he could, he said, "What's your name? Where are we? Did you kidnap me? Why does everyone keep kidnapping me?"

"My name is Mara Brennen. We're at my home in Richmond. You'll see The James if you look out the window. And I didn't kidnap you, Johnny. I brought you home. You see, I'm your mother."

Johnny would have jumped up if he could. Instead, he stared at her in shock. "No, you can't be my mother," he stammered. "My mother's dead. She died having me." He lowered his voice and looked at the floor. "That's the first time I've said that. I just found out yesterday."

"What you found out are more lies. Whatever you read in Alec's book, whatever Grace and Ryan told you, all lies. If you're willing to listen, I'll tell you the story of who you truly are."

GRACE RAN for the door expecting to see her Johnny. Instead, she swung the door wide to find an attractive thirty-something woman of about five-five with her brown hair tied neatly into a ponytail. She wore a tailored black pant-suit with a fitted white blouse. Grace was surprised she wasn't wearing dark sunglasses. She peeked around her, looking for the black SUV, but it was only a late-model silver sedan.

The woman showed Grace her credentials. "I'm Special Agent Nichol Shepherd. Are you Grace Walker?"

Grace nodded and moved aside to let the agent inside. "How'd you get here so fast?"

"Didn't have far to go, and we're always prepared to move quickly when a missing minor is involved."

Before Grace could close the door, two more sedans pulled up to the house. Four people got out and retrieved various cases from the backseats and trunks. They came to the door and stared at Grace. She stepped aside to let them in as well.

While Agent Shepherd made introductions, Steph burst in through the kitchen and wrapped Grace in a suffocating hug.

"She's not one of mine," Agent Shepherd said.

Grace unwrapped herself. "My stepdaughter, Stephanie Walker," Grace told Agent Shepherd and turned to Steph. "What are you doing here? There's nothing you can do."

Steph took Grace's hand and pulled her along as they followed Agent Shepherd into the living room. "You're kidding, right? My baby brother is missing. Did you think I wouldn't come?"

The rest of the FBI entourage followed them into the living room. They formed a half-circle behind Agent Shepherd and stared at Grace.

"Where should we set up, boss?" a young man in a t-shirt, hoodie and ball cap asked. He looked young enough to be the older brother to one of Johnny's friends. Grace suddenly felt old and tired. She dropped onto the couch and rubbed her temples. Agent Shepherd raised an eyebrow in question.

"I don't care," Grace said. "Set up wherever you want."

Steph sat next to Grace and took her hand. "In here is fine," she told Agent Shepherd.

Agent Shepherd cocked her head at the rest of them and they jumped into motion. Within minutes, they had their equipment spread over the top of the dining room table. Agent Shepherd carried one of the dining room chairs over to the living room and sat facing Grace.

"I'll collect the photos Special Agent Michaels asked for before I interview you. We need to get the fliers made. Do you have those ready?"

Grace shook her head. "I didn't have time, but it will only take a minute."

As Grace got up to gather the photos of Johnny, Ryan rushed into the living room from the kitchen as Steph had done. He threw his arms around Grace and whispered into her ear. "I'm here, and Johnny's going to be fine. He's just furious with us and hiding at a friend's house. That's all this is."

Grace fought her tears and nodded without a word. Ryan stepped back and hugged Steph before acknowledging the other people in the room. With his arm around Grace's shoulder, he extended his right hand to Agent Shepherd. "Ryan Walker, Johnny's dad."

Agent Shepherd introduced herself. "Your wife was about to get some photos of your son for me. Would you mind answering questions while she does?"

"I'd be happy to," Ryan said and sat on the couch where Grace had been.

Grace was halfway to the kitchen to grab the pictures of Johnny when the doorbell rang. *What now?* she thought and went to answer it. Before she could turn the knob, two agents flanked her at the door.

"From now on, use the peephole before opening the door," the agent Shepherd had introduced as Crawford said. "Just in case."

Just in case what? Grace wondered. She stood on her tiptoes and saw two police officers on the stoop. She stepped back and gestured for Agent Crawford to open the door. "Be my guest. He probably wants to talk to you," she said.

Agent Crawford introduced himself and Grace to the officers and ushered them to Agent Shepherd. Grace didn't go after them. She peeked at the cars lining the curb just as a car marked Sheriff pulled in behind the police car. She waited for the sheriff and what must have been a deputy at the door. After more introductions, she pointed them to the rest of the group and escaped to the kitchen.

She leaned on the table and tried to ignore her pounding heart. Scott Michaels hadn't been kidding when he'd said they'd pull out all the stops to find Johnny. Grace was more than grateful and would do anything to help find her son, but the mushrooming crowd in her living room was suffocating her.

Less than twenty-four hours earlier, she'd been going about an ordinary day. Now, her world had been thrown off its axis. Alec had once told her that she'd had enough trauma in her life for ten people. That number had bumped up to fifteen.

She didn't have time to stand there pitying herself, so she shook her head to clear it and grabbed a stack of random photos from the drawer where she kept them. She didn't dare look at them as she turned to rejoin the others. Before she made it to the living room, the kitchen door swung open and Alec burst through it. She pulled Grace into a hug and held her for a long minute before moving away. She laid her hand on Grace's shoulders and studied her face

"How can this be happening? Where is our boy? What do you need from me?"

Grace shrugged free of Alec's hands and turned her back. "I told you not to come. The living room is full to bursting as it is. There's nothing you can do, and having you here only adds to my stress."

"Stop it, Grace. I'm not leaving your side until Johnny is under this roof. I'm not just here for you. Johnny is family. I've known him as long as you have, and I love him almost as much as you do. Now, sit down and tell me what they're saying. What's the plan?"

Grace sank onto a chair and reached for Alec's hand as she took the chair facing her. "I'm still mad at you. I'm trying not to blame you even though it's your fault."

"Don't act like you're squeaky clean in this, but there will be time to assign blame later."

"Don't interrupt," Grace snapped. "Having said that, I'm glad you ignored me and came. I hate to admit that I can't function without my Alec."

Alec covered Grace's hand with hers. Images of times they'd huddled together during their multitude of traumas flooded Grace's mind. Instead of weakening her already fragile mental state, they gave her strength. They'd conquered those obstacles. They'd survive this together.

"Thank you, friend, for understanding me better than anyone in the world."

"That's better. Now, let's get to work."

Grace stood and scooped the pictures from the table. She grasped Alec's hand and led her to the base of operations, which only minutes before had been an ordinary room and an ordinary house. The chaos reminded Grace that being ordinary had been an illusion, but with Alec and Ryan at her side, she could face what the world threw at her.

"I'VE RECORDED Ryan's account of what happened. Now I'd like yours," Agent Shepherd said.

Every eye turned on Grace. She hadn't expected to perform for an audience, and her courage wavered, but Ryan and Alec each squeezed a hand, and she felt their strength flow into her.

"Things have been rocky between Johnny and me lately, but we had called a truce on Sunday. Everything was fine. Then, he came home from school yesterday and found Alec's book."

Agent Shepherd held up their copy and Grace cringed.

"Your husband told me Johnny's history. I've read his original file."

"You understand why he was so upset?"

Agent Shepherd nodded.

"He learned the devastating secrets we kept from him with no one there to explain. We had a terrible argument and he stormed out. I wanted to go after him, but Ryan said to let him go blow off steam. I should have gone with my gut and stopped him. How could I let my baby go?"

"Stop blaming yourself," Agent Shepherd said. "That's just a useless waste of the energy you'll need to get you through this. Tell me what happened next."

"We went to bed and watched a movie. I thought Johnny would come home after a few hours, or at least by morning to get ready for school, but he didn't. Ryan let me sleep late. I got up around nine-thirty, which is rare for me, especially after what happened the night before. If I hadn't slept so long, I would have figured out that Johnny was missing much sooner.

"The school called shortly after I woke up to find out why he was absent. We're supposed to call if he's going to be absent. After that, we started calling his friends and family." She mentioned Johnny calling Ty and not being there when Ty's brother showed up to get him.

"This gives us a solid timeframe. I've asked Ryan to make a list of anyone he's contacted. I'd like you to do the same. We also need a list of anyone you can think of that Johnny has frequent contact with. While you're doing that, I'm going to interview Mrs. Emerson and Ms. Walker. When I'm finished, we're going to get the word out on all social media platforms, get posters made and posted, and start canvassing your neighborhood. If you think of anything else that will aid in the search, please tell one of us immediately."

When Grace gave Ryan a worried glance, Agent Shepherd said, "I feel confident that Johnny is hiding out somewhere you wouldn't think to look. We'll do our best to have him home for dinner."

Grace wasn't so sure. She was afraid that Johnny got impatient waiting for Ty to come, decided to walk instead, and had a seizure. He could be lying passed out in some freezing-cold ditch.

When Grace told Agent Shepherd that, Sheriff Granderson said, "My deputy is searching the streets in the immediate area," the sheriff said. "If he were on the street, he would have been spotted by now."

That comforted Grace some, but not enough to convince her she was wrong.

"I'm glad you brought up Johnny's health concerns," Agent Shepherd said. "We'll need a list of all his doctors, therapists, medications, and medical conditions. Does Johnny have any regularly scheduled appointments?"

"Just physical therapy. We've spoken with Johnny's long-time physical therapist. He hasn't heard from him," Grace said.

"He wants to help in the search," Ryan added.

Agent Shepherd turned to face Alec. "Mrs. Emerson, has your book been released to the public? If not, when does it come out?"

"Next Tuesday, but why does that matter? And please, call me Alec."

"Has there been pre-release publicity?"

"Yes, the usual."

"In the unlikely event that this case continues into next week, the tie with your book might heighten national awareness. This is one of those rare times where sensationalism can have a positive outcome."

"The book is available for pre-order. I'll talk to my publicist. Maybe we can step things up a few days early."

"Give me her name. I'll contact her directly," Agent Shepherd said.

"You're going to use your book to help find Johnny?" Grace asked. "That's what caused this."

"We might as well use my evil book for good, then," Alec said. "You never know if someone might see his picture and recognize him."

"My thoughts also," Agent Shepherd said. She faced the agents and officers waiting for her signal to get started. "I have everything I need. You know your assignments. Let's get rolling. I don't want to lose any more time."

The group sprang into action as one. When Agent Shepherd's phone buzzed, she answered it and crossed to the opposite side of the room to speak privately.

Ryan put his hand on Grace's shoulder. "As much as you don't like it, using Alec's book release is a good idea. We need to exploit every resource available. I've been involved in missing person searches at the park. The slightest scrap of information can make a difference."

"If Johnny finds out, it might make him dig in deeper. We need to draw him out, not chase him off."

"Forget about Alec's book," Steph said. "Johnny will be home before dark. Trust me, he can't survive for long without his game controllers."

CHAPTER EIGHT

JOHNNY DID his best to make himself fierce and stare Mara down. "Why should I believe you any more than Grace? My whole life is a lie. How do I know you'll tell me the truth?"

"I'll be right back," Mara said and rushed out of the room before he could ask any more questions.

He stared after her in shock. *What a lunatic,* he thought. *I've got to get out of here.* He was trying to get up to search for his phone when Mara came in and held out a bag of takeout food to Johnny. "Eat while I explain. You need your meds, too." She held up her hand and the baggie of meds Johnny had packed for the weekend dangled from her fingers. "Is this everything you need, or did you leave some of your medications at home?"

It was the second time she'd shocked him. Johnny didn't like how unpredictable she was. It threw him off kilter. He grabbed the bag from her. "Where'd you get these? Did you go through my pack? You had no right."

Mara sat down and smiled. "Relax. I wasn't trying to violate your privacy, but I know you're on various medications and had to see what you had on hand. Why are you so worked up? I didn't find anything *interesting* in your backpack."

His head pounded harder when the memory of his departure from Grace's house flashed in his mind. All he had was what he'd needed for school. He wasn't planning on leaving forever. He must have forgotten to take the bag of meds out of his pack when he got home Sunday night, but Mara was right. He needed to take his meds. He had no idea how long it had been since his last dose.

"That's all I have with me. It's only four days' worth."

She scrunched up her face. "Four days? That's it?"

"I wasn't packing for a kidnapping," he snapped.

He had to eat before he could take his medicine, so he opened the bag of food. It was his usual order from his favorite burrito place. She'd even gotten the salsa he liked. The thought that Mara knew that gave him goosebumps. And how had she known he's on medications?

I have a stalker, he thought and smiled as he took the items out of the bag and placed them on the nightstand. He wasn't sure why that struck him as funny. He should have been terrified but was only a little creeped out, but when Mara watched him with laser focus as he ate, the goosebumps returned.

"Not kidnapping," she said. "You're my son. You belong to me. I'll have to figure out your prescription situation, though," she said, just loud enough for him to hear.

"Take me to my house when Ryan and Grace are at work." He took a huge bite of burrito. "That way I won't have to talk to those people," he said through his mouthful of food.

She jumped up and ran at him, stopping inches from his feet. "No!"

He backed away and instinctively threw his arm across his face. "Chill out. What's your problem?"

Mara took a few breaths and visibly relaxed. "I'm sorry. You upset me with the idea of going to that house. Your life there is gone. We're starting a new one together. We've got to find another way to stretch your meds. Maybe we can cut your doses in half."

Johnny's hands shook as he set his burrito on the wrapper. "I can't do that. I'll get sick, and are you saying I can't even go get my stuff? I can't see my friends? I want to call and let them know I'm okay. Where's my phone?"

"I destroyed it so they can't track you."

"You did what?" Johnny wanted to punch her. His phone was his lifeline. Mara had cut him off from everyone and everything he'd ever known. "I'm not doing anything you say unless you tell me what's going on, or I'm out of here. I may be slower than you, but I'm stronger."

Mara went back to her chair without a word.

"You say you're my mother. How is that possible? Alec's book said that the DNA tests done when I was a baby showed this Craig Stuart is my biological father. He was in New Mexico. Is he your husband? Where is he? Are you taking me to him? The book said his wife died when I was born."

The questions that had been swimming in his brain spilled out of him. He'd been trying to make sense of what he'd read in Alec's book for the past twenty-four hours. Then, this Mara showed up and threw him into a completely different world. He was desperate for a thread of truth to grab onto and pull himself to safety.

Mara gripped the armrests on her chair as she watched him. Johnny could tell she was high strung, and for all his bravado, he was afraid to set her off. If she was capable of kidnapping, what else might she do? Even if she was his mother, he wasn't sure he wanted to stay with her. He thought of Adam's friend, Paul, who was a lawyer. He didn't know his number, but he could Google it.

"I said I'm going to tell you the truth of who you are and I will," Mara said, interrupting his thoughts, "but first, we need a few ground rules. You're not allowed to contact anyone for the next few days. Your friends might be worried about you, but if you call them, you could be traced. We can't have that."

"How can I contact anyone? You destroyed my phone."

Mara held up her hand to stop him. "Don't interrupt. Don't leave this house or spend too much time near the windows. You can move freely inside otherwise. I'm a nurse, and I have a job, but I took a few days off to get you settled. When I go back to work, you're going to have to keep yourself entertained until I have enough money to take you to Portland, Oregon. That's where we'll live. I only came to Richmond to get you."

"Portland? I don't want to go to Portland. Why can't I stay here and go to my school with my friends? What about school? I'll get behind in my classes."

"I have a copy of your class schedule. I've got the textbooks that aren't online downstairs. You'll have to study on your own, but I'll help as much as I can. I told you to forget your old life. It no longer exists for you. The sooner you let it go, the better."

Johnny got his crutches and pushed himself off the bed. He went to Mara and glared down at her. "And what if I don't?"

Mara laughed. "Is that supposed to scare me? When you hear my story, you'll want to stay. Sit down and listen."

Johnny had expected to frighten her and was disappointed that it didn't work. He sighed in defeat and obeyed to keep her talking. He hated to admit that he was dying to hear what this strange woman had to say.

MARA WAS RELIEVED when Johnny went back to sit on the bed. Even if he was on crutches, he was a big boy and could probably hurt her if he'd tried. She had to establish her dominance over him from the beginning, or her plan would fail. It wouldn't be easy to manipulate him into leaving the only life he'd ever known.

He picked up his burrito and took a bite. Through his mouthful of food, he said, "I'm waiting. What's this great story you have to tell me?"

She gave him the comforting, motherly smile she'd practiced.

"I can't believe you're sitting here with me after all these years. I've dreamed of this day since you were six months old. We're going to have a wonderful life together, Johnny. By the way, your real name is Kyle. Can I call you that?"

"No. It's too late for that. I've been Johnny my whole life."

Mara frowned. "Not your whole life. For six months, you were Kyle."

"Call me Kyle if you want, but I'm not changing my name."

She shrugged. "Fair enough. Here's how it happened. I was with a man named Rick. He wasn't a good guy. He couldn't keep a job. He ran up lots of debt."

"Why did you stay with him?"

"I was young and ignorant. I thought I loved him. One day, I came to my senses and left him, but some of the debts followed me, and I was desperate for money. I had a job as a nurse but was only getting two shifts a week. It wasn't enough to get out of the hole Rick dug for me. I found out by a fluke that a friend of mine knew a couple who was looking for a surrogate mother. Do you know what that is?"

Johnny slowly shook his head. "I've never heard of that. I'm sure I'll regret this, but what is it?"

"A surrogate mother is a person who has an embryo implanted in her from another couple who can't have a child on their own. She carries and delivers the baby for the couple. They were offering $50,000 plus expenses and other fees. It was more than I needed to pay off my debts and still have money in the bank. I wouldn't even have to stop working until just before the baby was due. I passed the application process, and the implantation worked. You were born healthy and perfect."

She stopped and glanced at Johnny. She laughed at the disgusted look on his face but could tell he was buying her story. She knew from following him the previous few weeks that even though he cared most about video games and hanging out with his friends, he was intelligent and a good student. She was satisfied that he had a typical teenage life despite his disabilities. As much as she loathed Grace, she was grateful that she'd raised her boy well.

"Does that mean Craig Stuart and his wife are my biological parents?" Johnny asked, breaking into her thoughts.

"Yes, but I felt like your real mother. I carried you and went through the pain to give birth to you. When the time came to turn you over, I couldn't do it. I offered to find a way to return their money, but they only wanted you. I'd signed a paper promising not to keep you, but I couldn't let you go. You were my son."

"That sounds horrible. Why would you do something so crazy in the first place?"

"I told you. I was desperate, and you wouldn't exist if I hadn't done it."

"I guess it's better than you dealing drugs or whoring."

"Watch your mouth," she snapped and smiled at his reaction. Scolding him made her feel like a real mother.

"How did you end up with me?"

"I contacted Rick. He'd had run-ins with the law, so I figured he wouldn't have a problem helping me. He agreed if I promised to get back together with him. I'd have done anything to keep you, so I said yes.

"We formulated a plan to get you out of the hospital. It worked like a breeze. We brought you to Richmond and started a new life with you as our son. Rick found a job and agreed to behave himself. I stayed home and took care of you. We had six months of bliss until that damned hurricane came."

Mara was pleased to see Johnny watching her as she wiped her tears.

"Grace told me about the hurricane, but she didn't know how I got hurt. What happened?"

"We were evacuating in Rick's fishing boat because our street was flooded. The boat capsized, and you hit your head when you went into the water. We rushed you to the hospital, but Rick wouldn't let me stay with you because he was too afraid we'd get caught. He forced me to leave you. It was the worst day of my life. I've never gotten over it."

Johnny stared at her in shock, and she didn't have to fake her anguish. Even though she'd fabricated the story to that point, leaving Johnny at the hospital had been the worst thing she'd ever had to do.

After watching her for several seconds, he said, "Grace told me what happened after that, at least I think she did, except for the part about Craig Stuart trying to get me back. Why did he lie and tell people my mother died when I was born?"

"He was ashamed to admit that they'd used a surrogate."

"But didn't the FBI know? After reading about my kidnapping in the book, I Googled news stories on my phone. What really happened to my biological mother?"

"Maybe Craig paid the FBI off. He's rich. I don't care. She got sick and died not long after you were born. Leukemia, I think. Maybe the stress of losing you was too much for her. What matters is that you're here now, where you've belonged all along."

Johnny had finished his food. He wadded up the wrappers and held them out to Mara. "Thanks for the food. That's a wild story. Seems too farfetched to believe."

"It is wild, but how could I make up a story like that? I swear to you that you're my son."

Johnny digested that for a second before saying, "I have two more questions. Why did you take so long to come for me, and how did you know I called Ty for a ride last night?"

"I'll answer the rest of your questions later. I won't lie to you the way that Grace has your entire life. Take your medicine and rest. You've been through a shock, and we don't want to bring on a seizure."

Johnny nodded and rolled onto his back. "I am pretty freaked out and tired, but I won't let this go. If you want me to trust you and go with you to Portland, you need to always tell me the truth. If I find out that you've told me one lie, I'm gone."

"You have my word."

She covered him up and kissed his forehead. She was relieved that he was out before she made it to the door. She could have conjured up some quick answers to his questions, but she needed to have all the threads in place. If her story unraveled, she wouldn't get another chance to persuade Johnny.

BY THE TIME Johnny had been gone for twenty-four hours, Grace and Ryan had compiled lists of friends and others Johnny had frequent contact with. Investigators on Agent Shepherd's task force had already questioned them. They'd gone to the school to interview teachers and administrators to see if they recalled friends no one else had mentioned. Their search had been a dead end.

Even before the sheriff did a press conference on the evening news, all of Richmond knew Johnny was missing. Every friend or neighbor had called, texted or stopped by to offer sympathy and support, and news of Johnny's disappearance had gone viral on social media. Even Johnny's doctors and teachers had come by to offer help. Their house had become Grand Central Station. So many different people came and went that Grace lost track. She'd escaped to her room a few times, but hiding didn't drown out the sounds of controlled chaos taking place just beyond the walls.

Grace was touched by their generosity, but the only person she wanted to see come through the front door was Johnny. Rehashing the story to every well-wisher who showed up got old for Grace in a hurry. Alec and Steph clued into her fatigue and started running interference. Ryan was running on pure adren- aline, but Grace was exhausted. She was a reluctant expert in dealing with trauma and understood the importance of pacing herself in a crisis, but she'd passed her saturation point. Losing Johnny was her worst nightmare and she was staring it in the face.

Jayda showed up at dinnertime with her arms full of bags of food from their favorite restaurant. Darnell followed her inside carrying more. They'd brought enough for the family and entire task force. Grace had lost her appetite, but the smell of Italian food wafting from the bags made her stomach growl. When Ryan took out his wallet to pay Jayda, she refused.

"We gathered a fund from the neighbors to pay, and we're setting up a schedule online for the days to come, just in case. Don't give your meals another thought."

Ryan's eyes glistened as he returned his wallet to his pocket. Grace hugged Jayda without a word, overwhelmed by her kindness.

"We can only imagine what you're going through, but I know you'd do the same for us if we were in your position. You know how much we all love Johnny."

"I do," Grace whispered and squeezed her hand.

Ryan took the bags from Jayda, and he and Darnell set the food on the dining room table. When he was done, Darnell turned toward Grace. "I'm sorry I was a jerk to you. Johnny talks about what a good mom you are all the time. That's not how he says it, but it's what he means. He felt bad for lying to you about Charlottesville."

Grace's voice broke as she said thank you. She turned away to hide her tears.

Ty came in with Ashley and gave Darnell a fist bump. "Hey, man. Any news?"

"Not yet," Darnell said.

"I'm sorry about Johnny, Mrs. Walker," Ty said. "I feel like it's my fault. If Jason and I had turned off our game and gotten here faster, he wouldn't be gone."

"It's not your fault," Grace said. "I'll tell him that as soon as he's home."

Ashley hugged Grace and kissed her cheek. "I've been telling him the same thing, but it's better coming from you."

"Do you mind if we hang out in Johnny's room for a while?" Darnell asked.

"Please do," Grace said. "Maybe it won't seem so empty."

Ryan announced that the food was ready and when members of the task force lined up to load their plates, Agent Shepherd said, "Grace and Ryan first."

The group parted for the two of them. Ryan handed Grace a plate and motioned for her to serve herself. She dished the small amount she thought she could stomach and took her plate to the kitchen, hoping for some peace and quiet. Ryan and Alec were close behind, followed by Steph. The rest of the group gave them their privacy.

No one spoke while they ate. What was there left to say?

Ryan's phone buzzed on the table. He picked it up and read the screen. "It's Mark. He'll be here as soon as they finish the last service at the restaurant. Valerie will come after she drops the kids at school tomorrow." He smiled and set the phone on the table. "He says they'll bring food for everyone after they close each night, so we don't have to worry about meals. At least we'll have plenty to eat."

"More food? Did you tell him about Jayda's dinner fund?" Grace asked.

"I did, but he insists. He said it makes him feel like he's doing his part to contribute."

"Thank him for me."

Ryan picked up his phone and texted Mark. "Done."

"Johnny would love this," Steph said. "We'll have to keep it going to celebrate once he's home."

Steph's words broke Grace's defenses. She covered her face with her hands and gave in to her tears. Ryan pulled her against his chest, wiping his own eyes.

When Grace's crying slowed, Steph said, "I don't feel like

crying. I'm too pissed. Wish I knew where to direct my anger. At Johnny for taking off without telling us? At the person hiding him from us? She pointed at the window. "At that random guy out walking his dog?"

"None of this makes sense," Ryan said. "Did Johnny call an Uber or get on a bus to somewhere? Where would he go?"

"If I find out he's being stupid and hiding from us, he's going to get it from me for putting us through this," Steph said.

"You'll have to wait in line," Alec said.

All Grace could imagine was her little man shivering in the cold and dark. He may have been a fourteen-year-old giant, but he knew so little of the world and she was to blame for that.

Ryan stood and stretched. "Agent Shepherd said they're organizing a search party for the morning with as many people from the community as they can get. It'll be an early start, so we should get to bed and pretend to sleep."

"No way I'm even pretending to sleep with my baby out there alone," Grace said.

Adam came in with a plate of food in one hand and a box from Juliana's Bakery in the other.

"Hey, babe," Alec said when he leaned down to kiss her.

He put the box on the table and said, "What good is a Walker family crisis without cannoli from Juliana's?"

Alec flipped the lid open and handed Grace two cannoli. She put them on her plate and stared, not even capable of choking down a bite of her favorite food.

Adam took a medicine bottle from his jacket pocket and handed it to Grace. It was a prescription for a strong sedative with her name on the label. "Take one of those right now while I'm watching."

He sat next to Alec and scooted Grace's water bottle closer to her. She grudgingly fished out one of the pills and popped it in her mouth before washing it down with a gulp of water. "Satisfied?" she said.

"The last thing we need is you suffering a collapse from sleep deprivation." He reached into his pocket and took out another bottle. "Ryan, you take one, too."

Ryan shook his head. "I'll be able to sleep. I can hardly keep my eyes open now."

"Don't hesitate to take one if you need to," Adam said. "After I eat, I'll shoo all unnecessary bodies out and make up the couch bed in the man-cave. Steph, you take the guest room. There's an overnight bag for you in the car, Alec."

"You don't have to sleep here. Go home, or you'll all be sleep deprived, too," Grace said. "By the way, where are your children?"

"I called the nanny. She's agreed to stay as long as we need her," Alec said. "I told you I was staying until Johnny's home and I meant it."

GRACE PULLED her coat tighter the following morning as she gazed over the crowd that huddled in the church parking lot and spilled into the street at the end of their block. The task force had sent out a call for volunteers to help in the search for Johnny. At least a hundred people waited for instructions from the sheriff. Grace didn't recognize most of them, and she was touched by their willingness to sacrifice their time and comfort to come to the aid of a stranger.

Further up the street was the line of news vans and reporters standing behind yellow police tape. The sight reminded Grace of the days when she was trying to garner support for keeping Johnny on life support when he was a baby. The news media had been both a hindrance and help back then. She hoped they'd be cooperative in keeping awareness of Johnny's disappearance alive. News cycles changed the instant public interest waned. With Johnny's history, their story might stick a little longer.

Grace joined Alec, Adam, and Ryan at the front of the crowd.

Ryan had tried to talk her into staying back in case Johnny came home, but officers were posted at the house to notify them if he did. There was no way she was going to sit on her comfy couch wondering while everyone else was sacrificing to search for her son in the thirty-degree weather.

She inched close to Ryan and reached for his hand. He gave her a weak smile and squeezed her shoulder. He was pale, and his eyes were puffy and red-rimmed. For all his professing he'd have no trouble sleeping, Grace heard him tossing and getting up and down all night. Even with the sedative, she'd only slept three and a half hours.

Sheriff Granderson stepped in front of the group, and everyone quieted. "We want to thank all of you for answering the call to help in this search. Johnathan James Walker has been missing for approximately thirty-six hours. His family was unaware he was missing for the first eighteen hours, and though we began looking for him as soon as we became aware of his disappearance, we didn't want groups out searching last night in the dark. We've lost valuable time, so we need to get moving as quickly as possible."

He turned to one of his deputies, who handed him a stack of papers. "Is there anyone here under age eighteen?" No hands went up, so he said, "Good. We're providing each group with a map, fliers with Johnny's pictures, and instructions for how to properly and safely conduct this search. Please read and follow them carefully. The most important points to remember are not to touch any evidence, but to take pictures of anything you believe will help the investigation. If you find anything, mark it with the flags we'll hand out and contact one of us immediately. Take care for your own safety and don't take unnecessary risks. Go slowly, scanning your surroundings carefully, and be respectful of the property of your neighbors. Stay within arm's length of the others in your group and don't get separated. We don't want to lose anyone else. We'll break you into groups of ten. Assign one person to carry the map of your grid. Please, stay within your grid, so we don't have overlaps or holes. Let's get going and bring this boy home alive and well."

The sheriff's words should have encouraged her, but a sick foreboding crept over Grace while he talked. Images of Johnny's dead, frozen body hidden under a bush flashed in her mind. She'd seen enough crime shows to know that the longer someone was missing, the less chance they'd be found alive. As angry as Johnny had been, he was too much of a homebody to have stayed away so long, and there's no way he would have gone so long without texting Darnell or Ty.

Alec gave her a soft tap on the shoulder, and she jumped. "I know that look. What's twisting in that brain of yours?"

"He's dead, isn't he, Alec? We're wasting our time. I can't do this."

She started toward home, but Alec grabbed her arm to stop her. "I won't let you quit this early in the game. Look at all these people who still believe Johnny's alive. Even in the minuscule chance he's not, God forbid, we need to find him. We're going to find him alive, and Johnny needs you."

"He never wants to see me again. Ever. Those were his last words to me. Mine is not the face he wants to see."

"He's had time to cool off, and he's waiting for you to rescue him like you always have. Remember that day in the PICU? You told me Johnny's spirit cried out to you. He's calling you now. He's alive, Grace. I feel it. Search your heart. You'll believe it, too."

Alec's words were like a punch in the gut. Johnny was her reason for existing, and Alec was right, he needed her. She'd lost sight of that in the chaos. No one else was quitting. How could she?

She gave Alec a quick hug. "I told you I can't do this without you. Point me in the right direction."

Alec led her to where Adam and Ryan waited with the map and the rest of their group. Steph chose to team up with a group closer to her age, thinking they could cover the more difficult areas. Adam described their search zone and lined them up to begin. Grace pushed her dark thoughts aside and focused on finding her boy.

THE TEMPERATURE HAD REACHED sixty-five by four o'clock. The sky was overcast, but the searchers had ditched their coats and gloves to work in shirt sleeves. *Crazy Richmond weather*, Grace thought as her group searched the last corner of their third grid, but the warmth was preferable to the chill. If Johnny were exposed to the elements, there'd be no risk of hypothermia.

Grace rubbed her neck and extended her arm to make sure Ryan was still within reach. He reached back for her when she tapped his forearm. The feel of his skin under her fingers was comforting. *Not alone*, she thought.

"How are you holding up?" he asked.

"I'm exhausted. I need to take a break when we go for our next grid assignment," she said. "How about you?"

"Tired but fine. I have a few more hours in me. I keep telling you to exercise more."

"Not the time for a lecture, but you may be right."

They were searching a small stand of trees a few blocks from their street. Grace pushed some undergrowth aside with a stick she'd found. Johnny was far too big to fit under that bush, but the action made her feel she was doing something productive. She heard a rustle in the bushes to her left and swung around to check it out, but Adam beat her to the bush in the direction of the sound.

"It's a fawn trapped in some dead blackberry canes," he said.

He freed the fawn, and it leaped away at top speed. *Where is your mother?* Grace thought. *Is she out searching these woods for you? Or did she give up and go back to her comfy hollow?*

"I think we can call this one," Ryan said. "Let's head back to the command center."

Grace was hyper-vigilant while they walked back to the church. She scanned every inch of the area around her, desperately looking for the slightest clue that might point to Johnny. But it was just road and dirt and houses and trees. Her hope started to waver, but she reminded herself of what Alec had said that morning and gathered her strength. She was committed for the long haul.

She and Ryan each got a text just as they reached the church. It was from Agent Shepherd. *Calling off the search. Johnny's phone recovered twenty-five miles west on Route 60.*

"What the?" Ryan said and ran for the command trailer with Grace close behind.

SHERIFF GRANDERSON WAS THANKING the volunteers for their time and hard work, and sending them home when Grace and Ryan reached the parking lot. They found Agent Shepherd on her phone inside the trailer. She waved for them to wait and hung up. They both bombarded her with questions.

"We've been pinging Johnny's phone since we found out he was missing and got nothing. Then, an hour ago, we got a response. The sheriff in Powhatan County dispatched some units to find it. They just got back to me. They're on the way here with the phone for you to identify, but they're pretty convinced it's his. The deputy I spoke with said the phone had obviously been there for a day or so. All I can think of is that it got wet and dried out in the warmer weather."

"How did his phone end up in Powhatan?" Ryan asked.

"How bad is this? Don't lie to me, Agent Shepherd," Grace said.

"I'd never lie to you," Agent Shepherd said. "And please, call me Nichol. I need more information before I can answer your question. Does Johnny have any family or friends in Powhatan that you forgot to put on the list? Is there any connection to that area?"

Grace and Ryan shook their heads. "I have some colleagues that live out there, and I work in that area occasionally, but other than that, I can't think of anyone," Ryan said.

"Neither can I," Grace said. "And that's outside Johnny's school district. I don't know how he'd know anyone in that area unless a friend moved there that we don't know about. So, how bad is it?"

"Well, it's not good, and honestly, it's confusing. It's possible Johnny threw his phone out a car window or lost it, and someone else took it and dropped it in Powhatan, but it's time to switch the investigation from likely runaway to abduction. We'll ratchet the search up a notch. Go back to your house. I'll meet you there."

Grace was too distraught to speak on their walk to the house. When she got there, one of the officers told her they'd allowed Johnny's friends in to play video games in the basement.

"You allowed them in yesterday, so I didn't think you'd mind. I can ask them to leave if you'd like," he said.

She wasn't thrilled to have the house full of Johnny's friends, but it occurred to her they might know something about Johnny's phone. "It's fine," she told the officer. "I'll take care of it."

She went to the basement but stopped on the bottom stair. She hadn't been there since the argument with Johnny, and her gut tightened into a knot. She switched her gaze to the boys sprawled around the room and took a breath. Seeing their familiar faces calmed her. She took the last step and told them about Johnny's phone.

"Does he know anyone in Powhatan?" she asked.

"My cousin lives there, and Johnny went to his house with me one time a long time ago," Damien said. "I don't know if he'd even remember. If he did, I doubt he'd know how to get there."

"Go tell Agent Shepherd please, and give her his phone number and address," Grace said. She looked at the other boys, but they shook their heads. "Did you hear anything at school?"

"No, and it's all anyone talked about," Darnell said. "We're keeping the word out there for Johnny. Someone has to have seen him. He's hard to miss."

Grace thanked them and went upstairs just as Ryan was telling Steph, Alec, and Adam about Johnny's phone.

Agent Shepherd came in as he finished. "We want to request Johnny's phone records. I need your permission since he's on your account. Otherwise, we have to get a warrant."

"Of course," Grace said.

"Having access to the records will tell us when his signal went dead. He or someone else may have erased his activity, although most people don't know how to wipe phones correctly. Do you know how to unlock his phone?"

The tracker, Grace thought as the memory of sneaking it onto his phone flashed into her mind. She rushed at Ryan and grabbed the front of his shirt.

"What are you doing, Grace?" he asked, trying to break free of her grip.

"You made me take the tracker off his phone. If you hadn't, we would have known where he was from the minute he left here. It's your fault, and you" She pointed at Alec. "You were all so worried about Johnny's privacy and feelings. All I cared about was his safety. Still glad you made me get rid of it? I don't know why I listened to you."

She let go of his shirt but didn't move. Alec reached out to calm her down, but she slapped her hand away. "You think you know everything, but I'm his mother. I know what's best for him. I've always known. From now on, you have no say. He's my son!"

She went to her room and slammed the door expecting Ryan

to follow but was relieved when he didn't. One of his soothing lectures was the last thing she needed.

As much as Ryan and Alec were at fault, Grace blamed herself for listening to them. Hadn't all the years, all the challenges she'd faced taught her to trust her instincts? She'd gotten lax. She'd never make that mistake again.

She paced the room trying to quiet her shaking limbs, not from fear or shock, but from rage. She hadn't been so angry in years. She stopped pacing at the realization that she was moving through the stages of grief. She'd hit them all in the past twenty-four hours, except for acceptance. She'd never reach that stage.

There was a tap on the door. "Go away," she yelled.

"Grace, it's Scott Michaels."

She climbed off the bed and unlocked the door for him. "Sorry," she said and rubbed her face. "I thought you were Ryan."

She sat on the end of the bed and motioned for Scott to take the rocking chair in the corner.

"Ryan explained about the tracker," Scott said. "In his defense, that app probably wouldn't have helped much. Johnny's phone had been lying on the side of the road for hours by the time you realized he was gone."

Grace didn't want to hear Scott defend Ryan. She was pissed and needed a scapegoat, but she said, "Makes sense."

"Speaking of Johnny's phone." He leaned forward and handed it to her. "Would you mind unlocking it?"

She tapped the fingerprint sensor, and the home screen lit up. "What can his phone tell you?"

"I'll scroll through his texts, his web search, and call history. We'll also examine the SIM card. There might be evidence that will lead us directly to him." While Scott searched through Johnny's phone, he said, "The Bureau has activated the closest Child Abduction Rapid Deployment, or CARD, team. They're an elite unit that has specialized training in recovering abducted children. They have a high success rate. I regret not activating them sooner, but I truly believed Johnny was hiding out with a friend. That's still possible, but I hope the delay won't prove too costly."

"I'm not sure it would have made a difference," Grace said. "We've been searching for him since we knew he was gone. What more could they have done?"

Scott left her question unanswered. "It wouldn't have been easy for someone to force Johnny into their car unnoticed. He's so conspicuous. He may have called someone we haven't thought of for a ride and then ditched his phone to throw us off the trail. He's an angry teenage boy after all."

"I pray you're right. What else can we do now?"

"The CARD team will arrive in the next hour. In the meantime, we'll pull together evidence we've gathered and figure out where we're going to find your boy."

CHAPTER NINE

JOHNNY TOSSED the handheld video game Mara had given him onto the bed and got up to look out the window. It was eleven at night, but he'd slept so much during the day that he was wide awake. The stream of events from the past two days played nonstop in his brain. He'd been cut off from all the people and places familiar to him. He had moments where he wondered if that life had existed or if it had just been a bizarre dream.

It felt like the time they had stayed at a lake house with the Emersons one summer. There was a powerful thunderstorm one night and the dock broke loose. It had floated to the middle of the lake by morning. Johnny felt like he was on that dock, torn from his moorings and floating free in unknown waters. He was a kid who'd had three mothers, but he had no home.

He heard the TV downstairs, so he got his crutches and went to see what Mara was watching. She'd left him alone most of the day and hadn't said much. He was still waiting for her to answer his questions. He'd let it go because she was so on edge most of the time, and he was afraid to set her off.

She'd told him after dinner that she was going out the next day to try to get his prescriptions refilled. It would be a relief to have the house to himself, even if it was only an hour. He needed time to figure out if he was going to stay with Mara or try to escape. If he was going to leave, he needed a plan.

He went downstairs and found Mara was asleep on the couch. He tapped her arm with his crutch to wake her. She flew off the couch and spun to face him, crouched and ready to strike.

"Easy *John Wick*, it's just me," he said.

Mara rubbed her eyes and stretched. "You startled me. I'm not used to having anyone else in the house. What time is it?"

"Eleven. I'm hungry. Do we have anything good?" He went to the kitchen and started rummaging through the cupboards. He found pretty meager pickings, so he tried the fridge.

Mara dropped onto the couch with a moan. "You're hungry again? I'll have to get used to feeding a growing teenage boy. There are frozen meals and desserts in the freezer." Johnny found a pizza and maneuvered it to the microwave. "Need help?" she asked.

"I got it. Don't baby me like Grace always does. Tony says I need to learn to fend for myself if I ever want to live on my own, which I do."

She shrugged and covered up with a quilt. "Less work for me. Knock yourself out."

Johnny cooked his pizza and managed to carry it to the recliner after a few near disasters. After a few bites, he said, "When are you going to answer my questions?"

Mara ignored him and grabbed the TV remote. "I'm too tired to get into it now. We'll talk in the morning."

"This morning you said we'd talk tonight. It's tonight."

"Fine, if it'll get you to quit pestering me." She turned off the TV and sat forward facing Johnny. "I didn't come for you sooner because after we left you at the hospital, Rick made us go into hiding in Montana. He was paranoid and thought someone would link us to your disappearance. We stayed in Bozeman for two years until I couldn't take living with Rick anymore. I'd never forgiven him for making me abandon you, and he was unstable."

He was unstable, Johnny thought, but he didn't interrupt her.

"I had my own near misses with the law, but I settled in Portland after being on the run for three years. I got a new identity and started a new life. I've been biding my time until I had all the pieces in place to bring you home. I saw Alec Emerson on TV going on about that damned book of hers. That lit the fire under me to come and rescue you from these people."

Her story made sense, so Johnny didn't question it. He felt the same way about Alec's book and wished he'd never seen it. Even if it was a false reality, he could have been sleeping in his comfortable bed in a home with people who had always cared for him. Maybe ignorance was better than his new reality.

"What about the other question? How did you know about my call to Ty?"

"I've kept a close watch on you since I got to Richmond. I was outside the Walkers' house when you had your argument with them. I heard the whole thing. I ran for my car and got to you before Ty's brother. That's it. No big mystery."

"So you have been stalking me? Creepy."

"How else could I know when it was safe to take you?"

"Why didn't you just tell me who you were and ask me to go with you? You didn't have to drug and kidnap me."

"I couldn't take the risk. Would you have believed me before you knew the truth?"

She didn't wait for him to respond but picked up the remote and flipped through the channels. She stopped when a picture of Johnny flashed on the screen. He sat forward and stared. It was from Thanksgiving a few days earlier. He was in the kitchen leaning on his crutches holding pumpkin pie with Alec laughing in the background. The sight disgusted him and overwhelmed him with longing.

"Turn it off," he said.

"I need to hear this." She turned up the volume.

Johnny wanted to cover his ears and run but couldn't tear his eyes from the screen. The news anchor described a national-wide manhunt underway to find Johnny. The FBI suspected kidnapping. They showed pictures of the Walkers and Emersons huddled together comforting each other. Johnny felt guilt, sadness, and a good mix of satisfaction. The Walkers were good people who had gone through tough times raising him, but they'd lied to him. Part of him was glad that they were getting what they deserved.

Footage of a search party of hundreds of people came up, and he felt bad for his friends and other people that mattered to him. They hadn't done anything to hurt him and didn't deserve to worry. He was shocked that so many total strangers were nice enough to take the time to look for him. He'd wait for the right time to ask Mara if he could text his friends that he was alive and safe.

When the news switched to another story, he glanced at Mara. She was beaming.

"What are you so happy about? There's a manhunt out for us."

"No, they're looking for you. They don't know anything about me, and we're going to keep it that way. I'm going to dye and cut your hair tomorrow and pierce your ears."

Johnny frowned at her. "What if I won't let you? I'll be a bigger freak than I already am."

"You'll let me," she said, staring him down. "We have to change your appearance as much as possible. Too bad I can't do anything about your height or crutches. You're too conspicuous."

Johnny pointed a crutch at her and sneered. "Sorry to inconvenience you."

"Don't be a smart ass. I'm your mother. You can't talk to me that way."

"Whatever. I'm going to my room."

He left his half-eaten pizza on the chair and worked his way upstairs. He'd thought being with Mara would mean freedom from Grace's hovering. He was beginning to wonder if being with this wacko would be worse, but he was willing to give Mara a chance. Life with her would at least be unpredictable.

RYAN AND ALEC jumped up when Grace followed Scott into the living room

Ryan said, "I'm so sorry, babe. Can we talk about this?"

"Scott says it probably wouldn't have made a difference, and I trust him. Let's drop it for now," Grace said.

"What about me?" Alec asked.

"Your crimes are piling up," Grace said. "You'll owe me. All I want to do now is figure out where Johnny is."

"I've run dry of ideas. I'm going to take one of Adam's magic pills and sleep," Ryan said. He kissed Grace's cheek before she could duck out of the way and waved to the rest as he went down the hallway.

"Since the CARD team is on their way, I sent Nichol home for a good night's sleep. I'll stay tonight. I'll be in the corner with Johnny's phone until they get here."

Grace nodded and dropped onto the couch next to Alec.

Alec squeezed Grace's hand. Without looking at her, she said, "Since you're already mad at me, there's something I want to bring up."

"You have the worst timing of anyone I've ever known. Can't this wait?"

"No, it might actually help with the search for Johnny. I think you should call Craig."

Grace sat forward and frowned at Alec. "He must know about Johnny by now. The FBI has Johnny's old file. I'm sure they sent an investigator to Craig's house."

"It should come from you. He may not be Johnny's father on

paper, but he is Johnny's biological father. He deserves to know what's happening."

"Craig gave up the right to know about Johnny's life when he signed away his parental rights. I've given him multiple chances to be a part of Johnny's world, but he's always refused. I don't owe him anything." Grace fell back and rubbed her temples. "The last thing I want is for our first call in five years to be the news that I lied to Johnny and drove him away. Craig will blame me. He wouldn't be wrong, but I don't want to hear it from him."

"He'd hear from me if he tried to blame you. This is no one's fault but the person who has Johnny."

"Then why should I call Craig?"

"Maybe he knows something. Maybe he decided he wants Johnny after all. Who knows? It wouldn't hurt to find out."

"The FBI can question him all they want." Grace shook her hand free of Alec's and covered her face. "I failed Johnny. I had one job, to keep him safe, and I failed. I should have pushed Craig to take him when he was a baby. It was where Johnny belonged."

"Drop the self-pity. Since the day Mara dumped Johnny in the ER, he hasn't belonged anywhere but with you. There isn't a person on earth who could have loved him as you have. A bad guy is responsible for Johnny's disappearance. I won't stand for you blaming yourself."

"Do you think a bad guy has Johnny?"

The doorbell rang before Alec could answer. An officer guarding the door looked through the peephole before opening the door and admitting the six-person C.A.R.D team. They introduced themselves.

While Scott brought them up to speed, Grace studied the one who had introduced himself as Special Agent Reid, the team commander. He was roughly six-three with light brown hair and a closely shaved beard. Enough muscles bulged in his arms that it looked like he'd be able to lift a car, but he had a kind face and the concern was clear in his eyes when he gazed at Grace. Something in his look told her she could trust him.

"We studied the records on the way here," he said. "We'll work from here tonight, but since it appears unlikely that Johnny's in the immediate area, we'll move to the Richmond field office in the morning. We'll have access to better resources there. I alerted Agent Shepherd, and I promise to keep you in the loop, Mrs. Walker. We'll be calling on you for additional information as evidence comes to light. We have a ninety-percent success rate. I won't stop until I find your boy."

She noticed that he didn't say he'd bring him home alive, but she understood that wasn't a promise he could make.

"Thank you, Agent Reid. We're placing Johnny and ourselves in your hands," Grace said.

Alec shook his hand and introduced herself. "We're thrilled you're here, but Grace needs to rest, and my husband's been asleep downstairs for two hours. I'm going to join him." She kissed Grace's cheek. "See you in the morning. Don't forget what I said."

Grace watched her go before reluctantly going to face her demons for another night.

JOHNNY ADMIRED himself in the full-length mirror. He'd resisted letting Mara give him a makeover, but he had to admit he liked his new look. It had taken months of pestering to get Grace to let him grow his hair longer, and he'd been reluctant to see Mara chop off his hard work and dye it black, but she'd done a decent job. She spiked it with gel and dyed his eyebrows black, too. Without his crutches, even his friends might not have recognized him.

Piercing his ears had been a different story. He'd tried to talk Mara into using clip-ons, but she insisted on poking holes in his ears. She used ice to numb his lobes, but it still hurt like hell when she stuck the needle through. His ears had been throbbing ever since. Mara assured the pain would be gone by morning. She showed him how to take care of them to avoid infection. At least she was a nurse and had disinfected his earlobes before starting.

When she came at him with the nostril ring, he fought her off, refusing to let her stick a needle through his nose. She laughed and told him to relax. He was relieved to find out it was a fake that clipped to his nostril. When she finished, she handed him a black hoodie and a pair of ripped jeans. He changed and nodded in satisfaction.

He joined Mara downstairs and said, "I look like a gimpy badass."

She laughed and gave him a fist bump. She was wearing her nurse's uniform and said she had to go to the hospital.

"I thought you weren't working until tomorrow," Johnny said.

"I have to get your prescriptions filled. You only have enough left for a day and a half. Since your mom, I mean Grace, never got them filled where I work, I shouldn't have a problem. Remember what I said, don't contact anyone and stay away from the windows. Your textbooks and my laptop are on the table. Get started on your homework while I'm gone."

"Can't I have one more day? Who's going to know?"

"I don't want you to get behind, so you'll be up with your classes when we get to Portland. Don't get on your school website. Just do your best to figure out what you should be studying."

He rolled his eyes but didn't argue. Mara went sort of nuts whenever he disagreed with her. He had no intention of doing schoolwork, but he'd be able to fake it easily enough.

She left through the front door and locked the double-sided deadbolt from the outside. He'd never seen a lock like that. He checked the door that led to the backyard, but it had the same kind of lock. The few windows on the first floor had bars on the windows, but it wouldn't have mattered if they didn't. There was no way he could climb out with his bum legs. So much for his plan to just walk out the front door and call a friend to rescue him. He'd have to come up with a better strategy.

He bristled at the realization that he was Mara's prisoner. He felt like the victim in one of those real-life crime dramas about kidnapped teenagers he'd seen. As unpredictable as Mara was, Johnny was grateful that she wasn't as terrifying as the kidnappers in those stories. When the search for him calmed down, he'd talk to her about giving him a key and gauge her reaction. Maybe she was locking him in for his own protection?

Ignoring Mara's orders to stay away from the windows, he looked out the one by the front door to see what the neighborhood was like. Mara's house was on the corner. The houses on the adjacent corners were rundown and in need of paint jobs, but the yards were in decent shape. One house down the block had a beat-up car parked on the grass and a sagging porch, but the rest Johnny could see looked fine.

He left the front and went to check out the backyard. The door had a small window, but he had a view of the whole block. It was a good size yard with a six-foot cedar fence like the Walker's had. It needed a good power-wash, but it looked sturdy. Three bare old oak trees stood in the middle of the lawn, which was mostly dead weeds and leaves, but it was a nice space. Ryan would have had it looking great in an afternoon. A whitewashed shed stood in the far corner. Johnny could see junk piled high through the windows and wondered why Mara had a shed full of rusty metal.

He went to his room next to get a wider view of the area. Most of the yards and houses were like Mara's, but the yards were in better shape. A narrow ally ran behind her house to the end of the block. That would be a good way to escape without being seen if he could get a key to the back door and find a way to open the lock on the gate. He'd had more time to search for a key when she went to work the next day.

He gave up his reconnaissance and went to the kitchen to cook another pizza. It was easier to carry his food to the recliner than it had been the night before. He settled into the recliner and turned on the TV. He flipped through the channels making sure to avoid the news networks. The last thing he wanted was to see the dopey picture of him holding the Thanksgiving pie staring back at him from the screen.

MARA CLIPPED her hospital badge to her uniform pocket and took the elevator to the Internal Medicine floor. She hoped for a busy day so no one would notice her moving around the floor, but all was quiet.

Deciding she had no choice but to risk it, she went to a computer at the far end of the nurses' station and logged into the system. She was hoping to find patients on medications similar to Johnny's. She wished she'd been able to get there earlier when doctors were doing rounds so she'd be less conspicuous. The next best choice was to go at lunchtime when most patients would get their midday meds. She'd checked the patient boards and computers until she found what she needed.

She scanned the barcode on her badge at the door to the med room. The door popped open, and she looked both ways before entering. Her hands shook as she logged into the med dispenser. She wished she'd practiced getting the drugs out while she was on duty. She didn't know how the system would respond if she didn't have patients assigned to her that day, but the finger pad lit up. She pressed her index finger onto the sensor, and the patient drug list showed on the screen. She blew out her breath and looked at the patient names and room numbers she'd written on the palm of her hand.

She was about to press the screen to dispense the drugs she needed when the charge nurse walked by and glanced at Mara through the glass door. She would know that Mara wasn't on duty since she was in charge of scheduling, so Mara casually signed out of the system and walked to the closest patient room. Fortunately, that room was empty. Mara held the door open a crack to spy on the charge nurse. She sat down at the nurses' station and stared at the computer. Mara would be in her line of sight if she tried to get to the med room.

She waited thirty more minutes, but the charge nurse didn't move. When she finally turned away to speak to another nurse, Mara exited the room and started in the opposite direction, but the charge-nurse saw her and called her name. Mara pasted on a smile when the charge nurse waved her over and walked to the nurses' station as casually as she could.

"Hi, Candice. What do you need?"

Candice crossed her arms and leaned back in her chair. "What are you doing here, Mara? You're not scheduled until tomorrow."

Mara chuckled. "I know that now. I got my days confused. Since I was here, I decided to stop in and say hello to a few of my patients. Do you need me to stay and help out for the rest of the shift?"

Candice shook her head. "What were you doing in the med room when I came back from break?"

"Med room?" She tapped her chin in fake confusion and pretended to consider for a moment before grinning. "I left my sweater in there during my last shift." She hooked her thumbs in the pockets to show Candice for emphasis.

"Then why were you at the dispenser terminal?"

"I was checking to see if Dr. Barrett uped Mr. Patterson's BP meds. We were having trouble keeping his BP stable last week. How's he doing, by the way?"

"He was discharged yesterday," Candice said and eyed Mara with suspicion.

"That's great. Explains why I couldn't find him in the computer. See you tomorrow," she said and waved as she turned to leave.

"Wait," Candice said. Mara held her breath. "Check with me the next time you come in when you're off duty and stay out of the med room unless you're getting prescriptions for a patient."

"Sure, Candice," Mara said and grinned at her.

She left as quickly as she could without arousing suspicion and headed for the exit to the stairwell. She went down two flights before stopping to kick a metal trashcan. It tumbled to the ground floor, making a deafening racket all the way to the bottom. Mara cursed and held her breath again as she waited for someone to check out the cause of the noise.

When no one came after half a minute, she sank onto the stairs to get a grip and figure out her next move. She had no chance of getting Johnny's drugs from the hospital thanks to Candice. She'd considered trying the following day when she was on duty, but Candice would be watching her. Her only other option was to get refills at Grace's usual pharmacy. That move carried a risk of alerting the authorities, but after years on the run, Mara was expert at avoiding detection.

She was furious as she drove home for not taking Johnny's need for prescriptions into account when planning her strategy to get him out of Richmond. She'd been careful to consider every factor, except the one most likely to derail her plan.

THE HOUSE WAS TOO QUIET. After two days of chaos, the FBI had pulled up stakes and returned to their field office but left two uniformed police officers behind to guard the house. Grace was left wondering how to occupy herself.

Alec had gone to the school after they called to tell her Rosie had been pushed off the slide and may have broken her wrist.

Grace would have gone with her, but she didn't dare leave the house again in case Johnny miraculously came home. Ryan had suffered another sleepless night despite Adam's magic pills, so he was in the room with his noise-canceling headphones trying to take a nap.

Grace took her laptop to the dining room table and opened her notes for a lecture she'd been scheduled to teach before Johnny's disappearance. The university had supplied a long-term substitute for her just in case the situation dragged on longer than they hoped. She'd need her notes for the next time she taught, so she had to keep them updated. She only typed three words before stopping to stare at the screen for long minutes before remembering what she was doing. "This is hopeless," she announced to the empty room.

She closed the document and opened a video app to look for a movie to watch. She found a classic Jerry Lewis comedy and carried her laptop to the couch. Her phone rang two minutes later. She let it ring for ten seconds before getting up the courage to answer. Every call in the past two days had been nothing but terrible news. She peeked to see who it was and frowned at the name on the screen.

"Hello, Craig. I've been expecting your call," she said and closed her eyes. *Here it comes*, she thought.

"Why didn't you call me? I saw the news about Johnny on CNN last night and got a call from the FBI five minutes later. I told them I hadn't seen or heard from Johnny, but they came and interrogated me and searched the house anyway. The investigator just left. Melanie and the kids are terrified, except for Sam, who thought it was cool. What the hell is going on, Grace?"

"The FBI didn't tell you?"

"No, all they did was ask questions and refuse to answer our questions. They treated me like a criminal. I would have appreciated some warning."

"It didn't occur to me to call you," she said and crossed her fingers for lying. "You're nothing to Johnny. He doesn't even know you exist, which is what you requested."

"My son, who was kidnapped on the day he was born, goes missing. I need to know that, even if just as a courtesy."

Grace rubbed her temples and toyed with the idea of hanging up on him. He had no right to question her actions, and she wasn't obligated to listen to him rant, but she explained the story in full detail despite her reluctance. He'd hear it eventually. It was better coming from her.

"Why did you lie to him? What would the truth have hurt? You used to say you'd tell him about me when he was old enough. What were you waiting for? His college graduation?"

"If you wanted Johnny to know you were his father, you should have been a father to him all these years. This was your choice. We honored your wishes." She hovered her thumb over the button to hang up but didn't have the heart to do it. She knew that deep down, Craig loved Johnny.

"Clearly, I made the wrong choice," he continued. "What kind of mother have you been? You've lied to him, and worse, allowed him to be taken right out from under your nose."

"You mean like you did the day he was born."

Grace cringed as soon as the words spilled out of her mouth. What she'd said was inexcusable. Craig had been at his dying wife's side when Mara and Rick took Johnny. No one was to blame but them. *That Mara,* Grace thought. *She's the cause of all this anguish not Craig. No one but her.*

Grace jumped up as the memory of chasing Mara across the parking lot flashed into her mind like a giant, orange neon sign.

"I'm sorry, Craig. I've got to go." She hung up, ignoring the protests she heard before the line went dead.

Grace ran to her bedroom and clicked on the light.

Ryan sat up and pulled off his headphones. "What the hell, Grace? Did they find Johnny?" She put her hands on his shoulders. "No, but I know where he is. Mara has him."

Ryan rubbed his eyes and tried to focus on her face. "Did you say Mara?"

"Get dressed. We're going to the FBI." Ryan started pulling on his jeans without questioning her. "I told you it was Mara I saw in that parking lot. You and Alec convinced me I was just paranoid. I forgot about the incident until I was just talking to Craig..."

Ryan froze with his leg halfway into his pants. "Craig? You called Craig? Are you insane?"

"I didn't. He called me. He had to make sure I understand what a terrible mother I am, but our conversation reminded me of Mara. She has our son. We have to find her."

Ryan nodded as he zipped his pants and slipped on his shoes. "I'm ready."

As he held out his hand to Grace, she felt the first glimmer of hope since Johnny vanished.

GRACE HAD CALLED Scott Michaels on the way to the FBI field office. By the time they reached the lobby, Agent Shepherd was waiting for them. After checking them through security, she escorted them to a small conference room adjacent to Scott's office. He came in two minutes later with Agent Reid from the CARD team and a man he introduced as Anderson Nettles, their forensic sketch artist.

"Please, give Mr. Nettles a description of Mara before we do anything else. Then, explain to me why you think she has Johnny. She's eluded us for years. I'm skeptical she would come back and risk capture," Scott said, "so, convince me."

"I agree," Agent Reid said, "but we don't have any concrete leads at this point, so I'll take whatever I can get. We've been getting hundreds of calls on the tip line, but none of them look promising yet."

Mr. Nettles took out a spiral bound book with pages of headshots and asked Grace to point out ones that had facial aspects like Mara's. Once he had the base elements to go on, he began to sketch on an artist's pad. He finished the initial sketch quickly and asked Grace if the drawing was close. She suggested some minor changes. After Mr. Nettles made the corrections and Grace approved them, he uploaded the information into facial composite software. Grace was shocked at how much the full-color finished product resembled Mara.

"That's her," Grace said. "The likeness is remarkable."

"Odds are she's changed her appearance since you ran into her, but if the facial structure is accurate, someone might recognize her," Agent Shepherd said.

Scott asked Agent Shepherd to get the sketch to media outlets immediately. When she left the room, he turned to Grace. "Tell me what happened when you thought you saw Mara."

"I don't just think I saw her. I did see her. I remembered her from when I saw her at the hospital when she abandoned Johnny. I'll never forget her eyes. She was older, and her hair color was different, but it was her."

"I believe you. Please continue," Agent Reid said.

Grace glanced at him and nodded, relieved he didn't discount her statement. "I dropped Johnny off for his appointment with the physical therapist. Mara bumped me as I was walking to my car. Our eyes only locked for an instant, but it felt like slow motion. When she saw me staring at her, she took off running, but she was too fast, and I lost her. She had a car waiting around the corner. She sped off a minute later, but I couldn't get her license plate."

"Why didn't you report it at the time?" Scott asked. "Having a heads up that she was back in town might have prevented this."

Grace glanced at Ryan and started to answer, but he stopped her. "That was my fault. I thought she had imagined seeing Mara, and I discouraged her from coming to you."

"Alec did, too," Grace said. "She and Ryan convinced me I was just paranoid, but it was real. It happened several weeks ago. I'd forgotten the incident until today."

"If it was Mara, Johnny's disappearance makes a whole lot more sense. We've been hunting Mara for twelve years and zilch. Your description is the only lead we have," Scott said.

Grace stood and faced Scott. "Mara has Johnny. She considers him to be her son, so I don't think she'll hurt him. She'll slip up eventually, or Johnny will find a way to alert us. He's smart. We're going to find him."

"I'm convinced," Scott said. "Talk to Alec. If you two remember anything else about Mara, no matter how insignificant, call immediately."

"I'll make sure she does," Ryan said. "If that psycho does anything to hurt my boy, I'll never forgive myself."

"I'M SICK ABOUT THIS," Ryan said on the ride home. "I got our son kidnapped."

A portion of Grace agreed with him, but she said, "We'll talk about it when we get home. Alec should be there. I don't have the energy to go through it twice."

"I noticed that you didn't disagree with me," Ryan said and was silent for the rest of the drive. Grace resisted the urge to comfort him. She was at fault for listening to him, but the lion's share of the blame was his. She wanted him to feel it. Maybe then he'd learn to listen to her more closely in the future.

ALEC AND ADAM were in the living room with their kids when Grace and Ryan got home. Poor Rosie had a neon pink cast on her arm, but she was happy to see Grace. They all were. Grace hugged each one and asked Rosie about her arm.

"That stupid Thomas Landon pushed me off the slide," she said and cradled her cast against her stomach.

"Don't say stupid," Alec said.

"But he is," Rosie whined.

"I'll take the kids home," Adam said. "You and Alec have things to discuss and don't need us underfoot."

"I want to stay with Aunt Grace," Graham said and wrapped his arms around her calf. "Where's Johnny?"

Adam pulled Graham off Grace and lifted him onto his shoulders. "You'll see Johnny later. How about we get pizza on the way home?"

"Yes," Graham said and pumped his fist.

Once Adam shuffled the kids out the door, Alec said, "Let me have it."

"What's the point?" Grace sat on the couch with her elbows resting on her knees. "Will it bring Johnny home sooner?"

"No, but it's not healthy to bottle up your feelings. Scream at me, slam the door in my face, kick me out."

"She's right," Ryan said. "Because of us, our son is with that madwoman. If you'd reported seeing Mara, they would have been on the lookout for her. We would have protected Johnny better, like keeping the tracker on his phone. We could have prevented this."

"What do you want me to say? That I'm furious with both of you? I am furious, but this isn't about the three of us. Our total focus needs to be on finding Johnny. Nothing else matters. I'll save the screaming for when he's home."

"Fine, but for what that's worth, I *am* deeply sorry," Alec said. "What do you need from me now?"

"Scott wants us to rehash that phone call from Mara twelve years ago. We might remember some clue that will lead the CARD team to her. There has to be something."

"It was so long ago, but I'll try," Alec said and sat on the loveseat facing Grace.

"What can I do?" Ryan asked.

"Heat up some dinner. I haven't eaten since breakfast, and I have an appetite for the first time in days."

"What do you want?"

"I don't care. Between Mark and the neighbors, there's enough food for an army. Just throw something on a plate."

"I'll pack up some of it and put it in the freezer. It'll give me something productive to do."

"He's a good man," Alec said after Ryan went to the kitchen. "He loves you, and he's devoted the last twelve years of his life to you and Johnny. More importantly, you owe him your life. He may have been wrong about this, but don't let that get in the way of what you've built with him. You need a united front more than you ever have."

"Why do you always have to be right? It's infuriating," Grace said. "Give me my two minutes to be pissed at both of you. I'll be the martyr and bigger person after that. I just need my two minutes."

"Deal. Let's talk about Mara."

CHAPTER TEN

JOHNNY IGNORED the news at first, but his curiosity got the better of his reluctance. The fact that the whole country was watching news reports about him was too tantalizing. He flipped to a cable news channel, but the story was about a sleazy politician. *What's the news in that?* Johnny thought and smiled. It was five minutes to the hour, so he decided to wait for the headlines to start.

His patience paid off, but instead of a picture of him, a color sketch of Mara appeared on the screen with her first name in the caption. He was shocked that they'd found out about her so fast. He watched the report for fifteen more minutes and felt another pang of guilt when the newscaster begged the public for any information on him or Mara.

She'd been gone a long time, and Johnny started to worry she'd been caught. That meant the FBI could be coming for him. He wasn't sure how he felt about her getting arrested for kidnapping. Mara had taken him from the hospital as a baby, but she'd done that out of love. She kind of was his mother. He'd also gotten into the car willingly on Monday night, so had she committed a crime this time?

His emotions flitted between wanting to punish the Walkers and wanting to get away from Mara. He wondered if Tony would take him in until he figured out who his real family was? He wondered the same about Craig Stuart. He was the only person in the whole mess related to Johnny by blood.

He went to Mara's laptop and searched for Craig's name. The results turned up his name, address, architectural firm, and Facebook account. *This guy should safeguard his info better*. He was about to click the link to Craig's Facebook when he heard Mara's key in the lock. He closed the browser and went back to the couch.

Mara came in with her arms full of grocery bags. "What were you doing? You look guilty." She dumped the bags on the counter and glared at Johnny.

His face twisted into a sneer. "Nothing, just reading my homework. What's your problem?"

"Lose the attitude. It won't work with me, and I'm in no mood."

"What's for dinner?" He got up and started rummaging through the bags, hoping she would let it go. "Did you get my prescriptions?"

"I got some salad and chicken. You can't just live on pizza."

"You sound like Grace." He fished a plastic salad container out and took it to the table. "I happen to like salad and chicken though."

She put a rotisserie chicken on the table in front of him. "There you go. I couldn't get your meds. Do you know which pharmacy Grace uses? Do you think you could log into the pharmacy app to order refills?"

"Sure, I do it all the time. I'm not sure if I remember the password, and since you got rid of my phone, we might have to recover it."

"Which pharmacy?" He told her, and he made a note of the PIN she used to unlock her phone before she downloaded the app. "I'm too stressed to deal with it tonight, and you have enough doses to last until the day after tomorrow. Try to remember the password."

He repeated her PIN in his head while he ate. He went upstairs as soon as he finished. Mara hardly noticed him leave. If becoming the sudden mother of a disabled teenager was getting to her after two days, there was no hope of her being able to handle it forever.

———

JOHNNY HUNG OUT in his room and forced himself to stay awake until Mara turned off her bedroom light. She'd gone to bed earlier than the night before, but he gave it an extra half hour to be safe before sneaking into her room. His crutches clicked on the wood floor, so he had to sneak along at a snail's pace.

He held his breath as he opened her door an inch at a time, terrified that it would squeak in such an old house, but it didn't make a sound. He was relieved when he got inside that the faint glow from the streetlamp outside her window made it, so he didn't need his phone flashlight. The outline of her cellphone was easy to spot on the nightstand. He stretched his arm forward without budging another muscle and curled his fingers around the phone. He slid it a millimeter at a time to the edge. Once he had a good grip, he picked it up and slid it into his pocket. Mara hadn't even stirred.

He risked getting out of there faster than he came in and made sure to close the door securely. He stopped in the bathroom doorway between their rooms to catch his breath. Once he stopped shaking, he went downstairs without clicking on the hall light. He sat at the table and opened Mara's laptop to pull up the page with Craig's information. It was two hours earlier in Albuquerque where Craig lived, so it wouldn't be too late to call, but Johnny had another call to make first.

THE FULL MOON reflected off the glass patio table in the backyard. As Grace stared through the back door, ghosts of backyard family cookouts on long summer days shimmered across the lawn. It was a time when she'd learned to allow herself to accept happiness. She imagined Ryan lifting Johnny into a swing while Alec's twins toddled in the grass. So many pleasant memories. Would there ever be more?

Ryan came up behind her. "I know you're furious with me," he said softly, "but can I sleep in our bed tonight?"

"Not furious. Frustrated," she whispered. "I love you with my whole soul. I'm just angry and feeling betrayed. My emotions have taken on a mind of their own in the past two days. You may sleep with me if we can call it sleep."

Ryan wrapped his arms around her waist, and she leaned into his warmth. "You were very far away just now."

Grace closed her eyes. "Not far away, but long ago, remembering Johnny as a little boy. Such carefree times."

"Carefree isn't the word I would use to describe Johnny's childhood. There was always a crisis around the next corner."

"As hard as those times were, Johnny's medical problems were expected. We knew how to face them. I would take all those times over this nightmare. I feel paralyzed."

Ryan turned Grace to face him and cupped her chin in his hand. "This isn't all on you. There's a mass of experts around the country doing what they can to recover Johnny and capture Mara. Like you said, she'll slip up. We'll have them both."

"My confidence is slipping. I was so hopeful after I remembered seeing her, but we have zero leads. Alec and I racked our brains for anything Mara may have said on that phone call twelve years ago that will lead us to her. We came up empty."

"It's after eleven. Let's go to bed. Maybe the answers will come in your sleep."

Grace's phone buzzed and she jumped. Her hands shook as she took it from her robe pocket. The number was blocked, but she answered in case it was news of Johnny.

"Hello," she said, trying to keep her voice steady. "Who is this?"

"It's Johnny," the voice on the other end said.

"Johnny?" she gasped.

"Speaker," Ryan said and waved to the two police officers guarding the front door.

As Grace clicked it to speaker, Johnny said, "Yes, remember me? Your pretend son?"

Grace's legs gave out, she nearly dropped the phone. Ryan helped her to a dining room chair.

"Where are you? Are you safe? Are you hurt? We'll come to you now."

Officer Layton walked to the kitchen and made a call while Officer Perez motioned for Grace to hand him the phone. He opened the app the FBI had installed to record her calls before handing it back to her.

"I'm with my *real* mother, and I'm not going anywhere with you," Johnny said, almost spitting the words. "Mara's taking good care of me. She told me how she gave birth to me in New Mexico, but my biological father was going to take me away from her. She escaped with me to Richmond, but Rick made her leave me at the hospital after I got hurt during the hurricane. You had my whole life to tell me the truth. Too late."

"That's a lie. We can prove it. Don't listen to Mara," Ryan said. "Tell us where you are. We'll rescue you and explain everything. Are you still in Richmond?"

"Shut up, Ryan. Like I told Grace, it's too late. I'll never trust anything you say. I'm going to live with Mara. She's my new family. My real family. Call off the FBI. I don't need them to find me."

"I'll never stop looking for you until the day I die," Grace sobbed. "Mara's an insane and dangerous criminal. Don't trust her. She's not your mother. She kidnapped you."

The line went quiet for five seconds. Grace prayed that she was getting through to him, but he said, "I have to go. This is the last time you'll ever hear from me. Forget me and call off the feds. I'm staying where I am."

The officer signaled for Grace to keep him talking.

"Johnny, this is us. We love you more than life itself. Haven't we taken good care of you and loved you? We've given you a happy life with everything you wanted. I saved your life when you were a baby. Mara's the one who kidnapped and abandoned you. She doesn't care about you."

"You're the liar. I hope you get what you deserve."

The line went dead. "Johnny," Grace whispered. Nothing but silence answered. "Johnny," she cried. "Don't go!" Officer Perez tenderly took the phone from her hand. She stared at him uncomprehending before doubling over as waves of nausea washed over her. "Call back. Get Johnny back," she told Officer Perez between gasps.

"Working on it," he said and tapped the screen. The call went to a message saying the voicemail hadn't been set up. He tried again and got the same answer.

"Can you trace the call?" Ryan asked.

"Possibly. My partner notified Special Agent Reid. He's on his way and will be able to answer your questions."

Grace groaned and dropped to her knees. Ryan squatted next to her and rubbed her back. "Johnny's alive. He's alive and safe."

"Safe with Mara? That lunatic? Who knows what she's capable of?"

"Did you hear how strong he sounded? He had the strength to get mad at us. He said Mara's taking good care of him. This is great news, Grace. Johnny's alive!"

The basement door opened, and Alec came in rubbing her eyes. "Did they find Johnny?"

"No, he called," Officer Perez said, and played the recording for her.

"Oh my God, he's alive. Our boy is alive. When are we going after him?" she asked as Agent Reid came in with Scott Michaels.

"Thank you for getting here so fast," Ryan said.

"We were still at the office," Scott said. "Get us up to speed."

Officer Perez played the recording one more time.

"Copy that and get it sent to the techs to be analyzed," Agent Reid said.

"Was the call long enough to trace?" Alec asked.

"Calls don't need to be a certain length to trace. That's a myth. All we need is to learn where the call originated," Scott said. "I have a standing warrant to request phone records from your carrier. Agent Shepherd is contacting them now. It shouldn't take long to find out where the call was initiated. Pinpointing the general location will take longer. It'll be much quicker if the origination was local, but we doubt that's the case. I wager Mara's halfway across the country with Johnny by now if they're still in the States."

Grace stood and faced him. "They're close. Mara would be foolish to take Johnny too far from his doctors and pharmacy, at least at first. She'll need his medical and prescription records. That might help you catch her."

"That might be true, but she's had a long time to plan this," Ryan said. "Can't she just falsify the records when they get where they're going?

"It's possible, but she'd make things harder on herself," Scott said. "Let's hope you're right, Grace, but keep in mind, she's not rational. We might be able to use that to our advantage."

The agents and officers went into the kitchen, leaving the three of them alone. Alec hugged Grace. "Things will move fast now," she said. "Johnny will be home by morning."

"From your mouth to God's ear," Grace said. "Should we wake Steph?"

"Let her sleep. If you're right, Alec, Johnny may be here to greet her in the morning," Ryan said.

"I'll text Adam in case he's awake worrying, but I won't call. He's got his hands full with Rosie and her broken arm."

Grace went to the living room and sank onto the couch. After the shock of Johnny's call, her stomach was reeling, and every muscle ached. Johnny had to be home by morning. She wouldn't survive the trauma for another day.

JOHNNY SHOVED Mara's phone in the pocket of his sweatpants when he heard her bedroom door creak. She stomped down the stairs and stopped inches from where he sat.

"Who were you talking to? Answer me. No games." When he hesitated, she grabbed the collar of his t-shirt and pulled his face closer to hers. "Tell me," she hissed.

"I called Grace," he said.

She gripped him tighter. "How?"

His body started to shake. He hated to show weakness and did his best to hide it from Mara, but she was too close not to notice. It wounded his pride to be afraid of this little woman. If he had the use of his legs, she wouldn't have dared threaten him. He pulled her phone out and handed it to her.

"You snuck into my room and stole my phone?"

"Borrowed." The word came out as a squeak, so he cleared his throat. "I was going to put it back after I called Grace and Ryan to rub their face in it. You should have heard them begging me to tell them where we are, but I didn't."

Mara loosened her grip in slow motion, but Johnny sensed her rage building. He reached for his crutches, but she kicked them out of reach.

"You idiot. I told you they can track our phones."

Johnny smiled nervously. "I made sure to keep the call short."

"How long you were on doesn't matter. They could trace it the instant the call connected. You don't know anything. This isn't a game."

She ripped the back off her phone and took out the sim card. Johnny watched in shock as she tossed the card into the sink and turned on the garbage disposal. She let it run for a full minute. She took the rest of the phone to the garage without a word, and Johnny heard hammering a few seconds later. When the pounding stopped, Mara came in carrying the shattered bits of her phone in a zippered baggie.

"We have to leave. Go pack your things," she ordered and ran up the stairs.

Johnny lowered himself to the floor and dragged his body the five feet to his crutches. It took all his strength to get to his feet, and even longer to climb the stairs. Mara was ready to go by the time he made it to his room. He picked up his backpack, but she yanked it from his hands.

"Let me do it, or we'll be here for a week."

She tossed his shoes at him and started stuffing his few belongings into the backpack. Johnny kept his eyes lowered while he put on his shoes and tied the laces. He hated to admit it, but she was right to be mad at him. He'd made thoughtless mistakes and screwed up her plans. Because of him, Mara was being forced to abandon her home.

"Where are we going?" he asked as he followed her down the stairs.

"I haven't had time to figure that out thanks to you. How could you be so stupid? Haven't you ever played a video game or watched a crime show?"

"I'm sorry, Mara. I was angry and wanted to get back at Grace. I didn't think."

"No kidding. I'm warning you, no more stunts like that." They reached the front door and she motioned for him to stop. "Wait here while I make sure no one will see you getting into the car."

She left the front door open while she carried their bags to the car. After checking the street, she waved for him to join her. It was the first time Johnny had been out of the house in more than two days. The chilly night air felt good on his skin. He wished he had time to enjoy it but climbed into the car as quickly as he could. It wasn't fast enough for Mara who barked at him to hurry until his seatbelt was hooked.

Johnny watched the house fade in the side mirror as Mara sped down the street. Even though he'd been a prisoner there, he'd just started getting used to the old house and was sad to leave. Who knew where his crazy new mom would take him next?

AGENT REID INSTRUCTED the driver of the SWAT unit to park a block from the address they'd gleaned from the phone records. Their initial drive-by assessment had yielded little information. The house was dark and there was no sign of activity. Reid asked to see the live drone footage on the laptop in Agent Cameron's hands. She shook her head as she handed it to him. Nothing there either. After commanding twenty similar raids, Reid's gut told him they were too late. He radioed instructions to his team waiting in their assault gear.

"We don't know what awaits us inside the house. Mara may be armed, but my hope is she's fast asleep, blissfully unaware we're coming. Elliott, take your group and set up along the north street. Prince, your team covers the back. Enter through the gate off the alley. The rest of us will take the front. Cameron will monitor the drone feed to make sure no one goes out a window or other egress. Pull up in front of the house," he said to the driver before going back on his radio. "Let's get our target and bring Johnny home, alive and well."

The driver pulled up to the curb in front of the narrow two-story corner house. Reid's team silently spilled out of the van and was in place within seconds. When Reid gave the signal, his team rushed the front door. It was unlocked and ajar. They moved in just as Prince came in from the back with his team. They swarmed the house and found no one. What they did find was evidence that Johnny had been there.

"Damn it. Missed them but not by much. The house is warm even though the front door was cracked. Get forensics in here," Reid said before calling SAC Michaels to give him the news. "We're on her heels, sir. It's just a matter of time."

"Get back here while we wait for the forensics report. We'll see what other leads we can dig up," Michaels said.

"Yes, sir," Reid said and hung up. "Elliott and Prince wait here to work with forensics. I'll send a driver for you later."

The agents nodded, and Reid rounded up the rest of his team. He was determined it would be the last time Mara slipped through his grasp.

JOHNNY WOKE up wanting his life back.

After leaving Mara's house the night before, they'd driven around greater Richmond for two hours before ending up at the drab motel on the rundown edge of the city. Johnny had tried to stay awake to memorize the routes Mara took, but riding in the dark car at three in the morning had lulled him to sleep. Next thing he knew, Mara was shaking him awake after she checked in. Once inside the room, he'd fallen onto the hard, squeaky bed without even bothering to take off his shoes. He was out in two minutes.

It was still dark when he woke, but he wasn't sure if that was from the blackout curtains or the hour. He instinctively reached for his phone and swore when he realized it was gone. He looked across the small room to see if Mara had heard him, but her bed was empty. A sliver of light glowed under the bathroom door.

Johnny wondered if Mara had slept at all. He felt like he'd only been out for an hour or so, not that it mattered. He could nap all day if he wanted. He had nothing else to do.

He rolled back onto his pillow and imagined what he'd be doing if he were home. First, he had to figure out what day it was. He was more disoriented and adrift than he'd been at Mara's. He'd lost track of time. If he'd had his phone, he could tell not only the time and day but where he was with the GPS, too.

He depended on his phone for so much. He wanted it back, just like he wanted his clothes, his friends, and the comfy bed that was long enough, that his feet didn't hang off the end. He felt a rush of emotions but couldn't decide which was more powerful, his anger or his homesickness. If he could make himself dig deep enough to forgive Grace, he would escape from Mara and go home, but he didn't even have the strength to think about it that morning.

He picked up the remote, turned on the TV, crossing his fingers for cable. When the channel guide popped on, he sighed in relief. He doubted the motel had any kind of decent internet, so at least with cable he wouldn't be completely isolated from the world.

The display on the TV read 7:15, Thursday morning. Only a week had passed since Thanksgiving. It was almost impossible to wrap his mind around after all he'd been through in the past seven days. He recalled talking with Grace in his room after Thanksgiving dinner. Part of him wished he could turn back time and return to being Blissfully Ignorant Johnny.

He flipped to a news channel to find out if the world was still talking about him. Sure enough, there was his horrible school picture from a few months earlier. Why had his mom picked that picture and the one with the pumpkin pie to give to the FBI? His mom's phone was full of better ones where he didn't look like a grinning idiot.

The image switched from his photo to the sketch of Mara. He

was about to click it off when she came out of the bathroom and told him to wait. She moved inches from the screen and stared.

"Turn it up," she ordered. Johnny pressed the volume button a few times. "More." He did it again until she nodded.

"There is a $25,000 reward for information that leads to the capture of this woman, known only as Mara, and the recovery of Johnathan James Walker," the news anchor said.

Mara whipped around and glared at him. "Did you tell someone what I look like?" When Johnny shook his head, she leaned closer to him. "How did they find out about me? How do they know what I look like? It had to be you."

"How could I have told anyone? I never left your house until last night."

"You called Grace. Who else did you call? The police?"

Johnny scooted closer to the headboard. "Why would I do that? I stayed with you by choice, remember? Grace was the only person I called. You would have seen that if you'd checked your phone before smashing it to death. I only had your phone for five minutes before you came storming down the stairs like a maniac."

She shifted her gaze back to the TV and tapped her chin. "Then it must have been Grace. She saw me one day at your physical therapist's office."

"She did? When?"

"I didn't think she'd remember me after so long," Mara said, like she was in a trance. "She'd only seen me once before. In the ER the day I lost you. She must have told them."

"She does have a photographic memory."

Mara paced the small room in high gear before grabbing her purse and heading for the door. "I have to go."

Johnny reached for his crutches. "Where are we going?"

She turned and stared at him like she'd forgotten he was there. "Not we. Just me."

"You're not abandoning me here, are you?"

"Don't be stupid. I have an errand to run. There's breakfast on the table."

Johnny looked where she pointed. How had she had time to make a food run and do it without him hearing?

"Stay here, and I mean in this room. I'll be back in a few minutes. Chain the door."

"You're nuts, lady," he said, as he locked the door behind her.

As he ate his breakfast of powdered donuts and cold, hard-boiled eggs, he wondered what life would have been like if that hurricane had never happened when he was a baby. Mara and Criminal Rick would have been his parents. He would have been a normal kid with healthy legs and no headaches or seizures. He would have been able to play sports and go hiking or rock climbing. He'd have a whole different set of friends and a different family. He wouldn't know the Walkers or Emersons, or even Darnell and Ty. The big question he had to answer was whether he was grateful for the hurricane.

He thought next of the other possibility. If Mara and Rick hadn't taken him from the hospital, Craig Stuart would have been his family. He would have grown up in New Mexico without a mom. He'd never been to the southwest and couldn't begin to imagine what that life would have been like, but anything would have been better than being on this mad adventure with Mara.

MARA POUNDED on the door an hour later. Johnny looked through the peephole to see a woman with short, spiked blond hair. She wore heavy eyeliner, thick purple eyeshadow, and a lip-ring. If Johnny hadn't recognized Mara's eyes, he wouldn't have unhooked the chain.

She came in and set groceries bags on the small table. After fishing a pair of pink-rimmed glasses from one of the bags and putting them on, she said, "What do you think? Would Grace recognize me now?"

"No one will," Johnny said. "What will they say at work?"

She unwrapped a breakfast burrito and dumped hot sauce on it. "I can't go back to the hospital. Someone might recognize me from that sketch. I have to find a different way to get money." She pulled a phone from her back pocket. "I have to get my number changed until I can afford a new phone."

Johnny's eyes widened. "Where did you get that? I saw you destroy your phone."

"This is the phone I brought from Portland, the one I used for work. The one I destroyed was my secret phone. I'm hoping changing my number will be enough to throw them off my tail." Johnny watched her shove nurse's uniforms and an ID badge into one of the grocery bags. "I have to dump this, too. Pack up while I'm gone. We need to move again. The guy at the motel desk saw me last night."

Johnny groaned at the idea of having to pick up and move to another place, but he got up to lock the door after her and watched through the peephole until she was out of sight. Whichever family Johnny ended up with in the end, life with Mara would definitely be the most unpredictable.

CHAPTER ELEVEN

REID TAPPED ON MICHAELS' open door. "Any word from forensics yet?"

"Just going over the preliminary reports," Michaels said. "Johnny was at that house, but I'm not sure how knowing that helps. He already told us he was with her." He gestured at a sealed clear bag laying on a table in the corner. "They found some of his clothes, including what I think he was wearing when Mara nabbed him."

"I can run those over to the family if forensics is done with them. I'd like to tell the Walkers about the raid myself," Reid said.

"I called an hour ago and told them Mara got away. We have enough other items of Johnny's in evidence, so those can go to the family. I was going to send Shepherd. Don't you have a strategy session with your team scheduled?"

"There's nothing to strategize about until we have the final forensics reports. My guys are still canvassing the neighborhood, not that I'm expecting to turn up much. Residents in that sort of neighborhood usually keep to themselves and aren't too willing to share with the authorities."

"It was the middle of the night when Mara left with Johnny.

Wouldn't have been many people out that late in the cold, and Mara's smart enough to check. Maybe we'll get a lucky break. God knows we need one in this case."

Reid ran his hand through his hair. "I hate that we got so close and missed them." He paused and looked at Michaels. "What's your gut telling you about our chances?"

Michaels shook his head. "I'm the wrong person to ask. I've been chasing Mara for twelve years, but I thought she would have left Richmond two days ago. Grace said Mara was close. Not sure how she knew, but that might change after the close call last night. I'm trying to stay hopeful, but you and I both know our chances go down with each passing minute, and now Mara knows we're on to her. Unless we do get lucky, we might lose this one. What's your feeling?"

"The same. Mara's no inexperienced amateur. She's had years to plan this. Wish I could predict her next move. They left that house in a hurry. She had to find a place to hide on the run. That might make her desperate enough to make a mistake."

"I agree, but please don't repeat that to the Walkers. Put a positive spin on the raid as you can. I don't want them losing heart this soon. We may have a long way to go."

Reid's gut tightened, and he swallowed down a wave of nausea as he gripped the bag containing Johnny's clothes. It happened every time they found articles belonging to the victims when he was on a case. At least this time, there were no blood stains on the clothes.

MARK HANDED Grace a plate of food and waited for her reaction. She gave him a weak smile and balanced the plate on her knees. The plate held a collection of her favorites from Mark's restaurant; grilled salmon, parmesan gnocchi, and garlic roasted vegetables. She normally would have devoured the meal, but her gut had been in a knot since Johnny's call fourteen hours earlier. Not wanting to hurt Mark's feelings, she dipped her fork in the gnocchi and took a nibble.

"It's a start," Mark said and sat next to her.

Grace swallowed and felt the gnocchi come to a dead stop in her esophagus. She washed it down with a sip of water. "I'm not trying to get rid of you, but shouldn't you be at the restaurant?"

Mark crossed his arms. "I left my sous chef Travis in charge."

Grace was shocked at what she'd heard. The restaurant was Mark's treasured baby. His wife, Valerie, usually had a hard time convincing him to leave the restaurant long enough to take Fisher and Sophi for a trip on a long weekend. "Isn't Travis the new guy? You trust him to run the kitchen?"

"He has solid experience. I'm impressed so far, and I was useless in the kitchen. I couldn't focus on anything but Johnny. They're better off without me."

Grace patted his shoulder. "Thanks for being here. Your dad didn't sleep again last night, so I forced him to take a pill and try to nap. Alec had to take Rosie to the orthopedist for her broken wrist, and Steph went home for fresh clothes. It was the first time I've been alone since, you know." She took a gulp of water. "I thought I'd like the alone time after all the crowds tromping through here, but I panicked as soon as everyone left. I've never been so happy to see you." She took another bite. It went down smoother than the first one.

"Being left out of what's going on here has been torture, but I had to stay at the restaurant until I finished arrangements with Travis. Valerie wants to be here, too, but we decided the last thing you needed was the kids underfoot. We agreed to take turns."

"I miss the kids. Do they know what's happening?"

"We told them right away so they wouldn't hear it from someone else."

Grace flinched and frowned at him.

"I'm sorry, Grace. I didn't mean..."

"Don't apologize. You did the right thing. It's sad they've been thrust into this so young. They must be terrified."

"Fisher wants to punch someone. Sophi cries at the drop of a hat. We've talked about keeping them home from school but decided it would be a distraction for them and gives us a reprieve."

Grace stared at her plate as a new bout of rage tightened beneath her ribs. She'd adjusted to the constant, dull throb that knowing Mara was running free had caused. She'd even learned to forget about her for brief moments, but she couldn't ignore the firestorm raining down chaos on their lives. She handed Mark her plate and got up to pace.

"I feel useless, too," she said. "This waiting and doing nothing is the worst. At least time passed quicker when we were on the search and rescue."

The doorbell rang, and Mark started to get up, but she waved him down. "I'll go." She peered through the peephole and was relieved to see Agent Reid. She let him in and introduced him to Mark. "Any news?"

He shook his head and handed her a plastic bag. "We recovered these in the raid. Are they Johnny's?"

Grace glanced at the bag and recognized the logo of Johnny's favorite band on his hoodie. He'd been wearing it Monday night, the last time she saw him. She tore the bag open and buried her face in the fabric. It still smelled like him. The room reeled, and she reached for Agent Reid, but he was beyond the reach of her arm. Mark caught her just as her legs gave out. The men helped her to the couch.

"I'll take that as confirmation," Agent Reid said.

He sat on the other side of Grace and put his hand on her arm. The tenderness of the gesture pierced her defenses. She slumped against his chest and shook with sobs. Agent Reid stiffened and awkwardly patted her back.

When she regained control, she wiped her face with the

napkin Mark had pressed into her hand and looked into Agent Reid's eyes. "Tell me about the raid. I want every detail."

"Sure you're up for that?" When she nodded, Agent Reid recounted each second of the raid. When he finished, he said, "We were an hour, maybe two, behind them. We're nipping at Mara's heels. She won't escape. I'm going to get her and bring Johnny home. That's my vow to you."

Grace felt the conviction and devotion to duty in his words. It was all the proof she needed that he was the right man for the job.

"I trust you, and my trust isn't something I easily bestow," Grace said.

"I can attest to that," Mark said.

"Given your history, I don't blame you. I promise not to betray that trust."

Grace smiled and squeezed his hand.

"We're waiting for the report on the neighborhood canvas. I'll let you know if anyone saw Mara or Johnny. I'd better get back to the office."

"Thank you, Agent Reid," Grace said and tried to stand.

"Don't get up, and please, call me Wes."

Grace watched as Mark walked Wes to the door. When he came back, she said, "I need to check on your dad."

"I'll stand watch out here," he said.

Grace went to their room and climbed into bed with Ryan. He shifted slightly before wrapping his arm around her.

"Any news?" he whispered.

"No, I just thought I'd join your nap. Go back to sleep."

He pulled her closer and kissed her neck. "I'm glad you're here."

"Me, too."

Seeing Johnny's clothes had been comforting and traumatic. Grace knew she should focus on the fact that Johnny was alive, and Mara appeared to be taking care of him, but all she knew was that he was gone, and she couldn't find him. Knowing she'd betrayed his trust compounded her grief. When Wes brought Johnny home, what would it take to win back his heart?

———

WHEN MARA GOT BACK from the phone store, she threw their bags in the trunk and told Johnny to get in the car. He climbed in beside her, happy to watch the motel recede in the side mirror. It looked even worse in daylight.

"Can you find a better motel this time? That place was a dump," he said.

"Whose fault is that? We had to ditch my house, and I can't go back to work because of your little stunt of calling Grace. I barely had enough money to pay expenses to get us back to Portland as it was. What am I supposed to do about money now?"

Johnny popped a potato chip in his mouth and shrugged. "Get another job."

Mara snapped her fingers. "Just like that? So easy? You don't know anything."

"You're a nurse. Can't you go to another hospital or a doctor's office?"

"The feds might be looking for nurses, and I can't use my Richmond ID anymore. I have to use my one from Portland. I'll have to find something else."

"There's money at my house. My dad keeps an emergency stash. It's like two-thousand bucks. You could sneak in and get it."

"He's not your dad. Don't call him that. Your house is crawling with cops by now. We can't go near that place. I don't even like being in Richmond."

He was glad they couldn't leave Richmond. The thought of her taking him across the country scared him. He hoped to convince her to stay for good. Richmond was the only city he'd ever known.

He caught her watching him out of the corner of her eye. "What?" he asked.

"I'm sorry for being so hard on you. I keep forgetting your life has been turned upside down. Grace sheltered you from the real world. You were rich and pampered. That's not your fault. I'll try to be more patient, but you have to listen to me and do exactly as I say. It'll be better in Portland. You'll like it there."

Johnny nodded and looked out the window. He appreciated what she said, but thought it was funny that she called him rich and pampered. He'd never thought of them as rich. His life was pretty much the same as his friends. He knew people with expensive cars and huge houses. His life hadn't been like that. He knew people who he considered poor, but Mara must have made enough money as a nurse to be more like the Walkers than those people. If she was a nurse, she must have made decent money. He was learning how much he should have appreciated what he had.

Mara smiled. "I'll look for a better place for us to stay." She took her phone from the cup holder and handed it to Johnny. "Do a search for hotels near here."

He typed the search words into Google and waited for the results. He was tempted to text Darnell while Mara was focused on driving, but after what happened when he'd called Grace, he didn't dare. A bunch of hotels came back in the search. He read them off to Mara until she nodded at one that was on the opposite side of town.

"That'll work. It's not too fancy but will have a mini-fridge and microwave in the room."

Johnny's eyes lit up. "And internet?"

"Yes, so you can do homework," Mara said and laughed when he frowned.

Johnny's day was looking up. He finished the bag of chips and downed his soda. If he could manage to avoid pissing Mara off, living in a hotel might not be too bad.

MARA QUESTIONED her judgment as she pulled into the circular drive in front of the hotel. Her money was already running low and the hotel Johnny picked was double what she'd hoped to pay, but she needed to keep him happy. She couldn't risk him trying to contact Grace.

She pulled the keys from the ignition and dropped them in her purse. "Stay here while I check in. We'll go in through a door in back to get to our room, so no one sees you. Pull up your hood."

Johnny gave a slight nod and did as she'd asked. She got out and locked the doors, hoping the window tinting was dark enough that no one would notice him. She put on her Baltimore Orioles cap and forced her feet to carry her through the entrance. As she approached the front desk, she was relieved to see that the clerk was a young, foreign-looking man. Odds were good he paid little attention to local news.

She pasted on her most alluring smile. "I need a double room. Do you have any available?" She glanced at his nametag. Kabir Singh. Perfect.

"How many guests?" Mr. Singh asked in a thick Indian accent while he checked the computer.

"Two adults."

"How long will you be staying?"

Mara hadn't considered the answer to that question. She'd have to pay upfront since she was using cash and she hadn't counted to see how much she had. She did some quick math in her head.

"Four nights. It could turn into more. I'm in town taking care of my sick mother."

Without looking up from the computer, he said, "Admirable. We can put you in a room on the third floor."

"That's fine."

He grabbed a postcard size form from under that counter and slid it across to her. "I'll need you to fill that out with your vehicle information."

He looked at her closely for the first time but didn't register any reaction other than boredom. He picked at his fingernail while Mara filled in the make and model of the car.

"I don't know the plate. It's a rental."

"Just stop by the desk later and give it to us. The year, make, and model are enough for now." She handed the card to him. He looked at it and nodded. "May I have your ID and credit card, please?"

Mara took out her wallet. "Is that necessary? I'm paying the full amount upfront in cash."

He held out his hand. "I still require your ID. I need a credit card on file for incidentals."

"I'd rather not. I've had my credit card number stolen at a hotel. I'd rather not go through that nightmare again. That's why I always use cash when I travel now."

His smile faded. "It's our policy, madam. I cannot rent you room without ID and a credit card, but I assure you, we take the greatest care to protect your information and privacy."

Mara was tempted to walk out, but she didn't want to arouse suspicion, and she'd run into the same issue at every other halfway decent hotel. She huffed and turned her back to him while she dug into the secret compartment of her wallet. She had run out of aliases. Her only option was to use her Oregon ID and hope no one made the connection. She took out the cards under the name she'd used in Portland for the past several years and slapped them on the counter.

The clerk gave her a forced smile as he picked up the cards. "Thank you, madam. I apologize for the inconvenience. The credit card will only be used if you make charges to your room."

He scanned her cards into the system and handed them back

with the key cards. She snatched them from his hand in a huff and headed back to the car.

THE HOTEL WAS in a much better part of town than the motel had been and even had an indoor pool and jacuzzi. Johnny was thrilled that the bed was long enough for his legs and more comfortable than the rickety one at the motel.

He unpacked his few belongings in the drawer Mara set aside for him and went to check out the bathroom. It was clean and had a decent sized stand-alone shower with handrails. That was a relief for Johnny. It was nearly impossible for him to climb in and out of a bathtub alone, and he refused to ask Mara for help showering. He'd had a shower at home that he could roll into with his wheelchair before he could walk with crutches. Ryan had even installed handrails and a seat for him. The hotel shower wasn't as good as the one at home but good enough to manage on his own.

He put his toothbrush and comb on the counter and went back to his bed. After propping himself up on his four pillows, he turned on the TV and started looking for a movie to watch.

Mara handed him the hotel notepad and pen. "Write down the username and password for the pharmacy app. I need to get your meds refilled. You haven't had any doses yet today."

"I'll try," he said, "but my mom might have changed the password."

She glared at him. "You mean Grace. That woman isn't your mother. I am."

Johnny hadn't noticed slipping back into calling Ryan and Grace Mom and Dad, but it felt right. He'd have to watch himself since it made Mara mad.

While he wrote the username and password on the notepad, he said, "It's a habit. I've been calling them that my whole life. It'll take time to get used to calling them by their names."

"Fair enough." Mara read what he'd written and nodded. "If it's not right, can you get into Grace's email to reset the password?"

"Yeah, she uses the same password for everything even though Ryan always tells her it's not safe. For as much as she watched me like a hawk, she wasn't careful about her own stuff."

Mara typed the information he'd given her into the app and waited. A smile crept up her face. "I'm in." She navigated to the refill section. "I hope it's not too soon to do this. Do you remember how long it's been since Grace got your refills?"

Johnny shook his head. He never paid attention to when Grace got his refills. To him, even Thanksgiving seemed like months ago, so it was hard to judge when anything had happened before that. His medicine always just magically appeared in his pill caddy.

"It looks like I can get everything except your asthma meds. How many puffs left in your inhaler?"

Johnny pulled his inhaler from his backpack. "At least enough for a week," he said.

She took a stethoscope out of her backpack and told him to lean forward and take some deep breaths. She listened for almost a minute.

"Your lungs sound clear. You should be fine. Your seizure meds are the important ones. The app says your prescriptions will be ready in an hour. I'm going to wait in the pharmacy parking lot in case they're done sooner, and I can get out of there before anyone gets suspicious." She put on a bright pink wide-rimmed hat. "Think anyone will recognize me?"

Johnny laughed. "No, but they'll remember that ridiculous hat."

"I'm counting on that," she said and gave that eerie smile he didn't like. "Stay here. Don't open the door for any reason. I'll bring dinner back with me. Anything else you need while I'm gone?"

He rattled off a list of junk food.

"Nice try. I'll bring you one treat."

Johnny turned the deadbolt and barred the door like he'd done at the motel. They were on an inside hallway on the third floor, so he doubted anyone would notice them. He found a show he liked and dug through Mara's bags until he found the laptop. The internet password was written on the key-card holder. He logged on and stared at the screen while he debated if he should email one of his friends to let them know he was safe. He decided to wait until Mara told him they were leaving for Portland so he could enjoy living in a hotel a little longer.

MARA'S HEART pounded as she drove to a pharmacy that was furthest from the one where Grace normally filled Johnny's prescriptions. She anticipated the order would be ready when she got there. Her heart sank when she rounded the corner to the drive-through lane saw the sign saying the window was out of order. She hated to go inside but had no choice. She found a parking space near the back of the lot and took a minute to gather her courage up before she ventured through the front entrance.

The clerk at the front counter gave her a cheery greeting, but Mara ignored her. She made a beeline for the pharmacy counter with her hat pulled forward and her eyes lowered. There wasn't a line, so she took three breaths and approached the pharmacy associate at the counter.

"Picking up or dropping off?" the woman asked.

"Picking up for Johnathan Walker," Mara said, without making eye contact and taking care to avoid looking at the security camera.

The woman walked away to check if the meds were ready. Mara did her best not to fidget or look suspicious.

The woman returned four minutes later and said, "The pharmacist is just finishing your order, but we were out of the Brivaracetam. They have it at the pharmacy on West Broad Street. Do you want me to have them fill it?"

Mara resisted the urge to grab her uniform and shake her. Every minute she spent at the counter increased her odds of getting caught, but she had to get Johnny's meds. She pasted on a smile, and said, "That would be lovely, sweetheart," in her best Virginia accent.

"Your other prescriptions will be done in ten minutes. We'll announce when they're ready if you'd like to wait."

"Thank you, I'll just browse while I wait."

She strolled to an aisle near the back of the store where she wouldn't be visible to the cameras. She squatted down and pretended to examine items on the bottom shelf while she reminded herself to breathe. After what seemed like an eternity, Mara heard them announce that the order for Walker was ready. She rushed back to the counter and paid with cash as quickly as she could. She forced herself to walk at a reasonable pace until she was outside, then she ran to the car.

She drove around the block a few times before pulling onto a side street to get her bearings. She looked up the address for the other pharmacy and punched it into the map app on her phone. The pharmacy was only five miles from their hotel. She had no choice but to risk it.

She lucked out to find the drive-through lane open and her order ready at the second pharmacy. She did her best to keep her head lowered and hide her shaking hands as she handed over the cash. She drove straight to the hotel without stopping for dinner. She'd have to hold up for a few hours before daring to venture out of the hotel. Johnny would just have to wait for his treat.

GRACE WAS CALMER after her nap but refused to let go of Johnny's hoodie. She draped the sleeves over her shoulders and tied a knot over her heart. Ryan's face softened as he watched Grace before following her into the living room.

Mark had been dozing on the sofa but swung his feet to the floor when he heard them. "Hey, Dad. You actually look human."

"When did you get here? Why aren't you at the restaurant?" Ryan asked as he gave Mark's shoulder a gentle squeeze.

"Got here hours ago. Needed a break from the restaurant. I'd rather be here with you."

"Glad to have you. The nap helped, but I've got my days and nights reversed. Maybe I'll try another one of Adam's magic pills tonight to get back on track."

"I'm glad to hear that," Grace said. "One of us needs to get sleep."

"I'm jumping out of my skin. I need a way to be useful."

"Know what you mean. Maybe Wes or Agent Shepherd can find something for us to do like he did for Steph," Mark said.

"What's Steph doing?" Ryan asked.

"Wes asked her to go look at photos from the raid. She'd shown him her portfolio yesterday and he was impressed. He wants to show her how forensic photography works. He thought she could get some experience observing on Johnny's case, kind of like an internship."

Ryan eyed him in confusion. "Who's Wes?"

"Agent Reid," Grace said. "I think his interest in Steph has to do with more than forensic photography. At least I hope so. He's a good man, and she deserves some brightness in her life after Greydon and this nightmare."

"Wes will have his work cut out for him. Steph declared at Thanksgiving that she's done with men," Mark said.

Before Grace could answer, her text alert beeped. She unlocked her phone and found a message saying that Johnny's prescriptions were ready for pickup at a pharmacy on the opposite side of the city. She opened the pharmacy app and gasped.

"Ryan, get your shoes. We're going to see Scott."

Ryan ran to their room without questioning her.

"What's going on?" Mark asked.

"Mara just made the mistake we've been waiting for."

His eyes widened when she showed him the message. "And they're still in Richmond."

Grace dialed Scott's number. It rang five times and went to voicemail. She tried Wes next and got the same result. While she was leaving a message, an alert from a different pharmacy popped up on her phone. *We have you, Mara,* she thought and did a fist pump on her way to the car.

AGENT SHEPHERD MET Grace and Ryan at the front desk. "The SAC asked me to give you his apologies for being unavailable when you called," she said as she led them to the elevator. "Even though Johnny's case is our top priority, Scott was needed on another case. Agent Reid and his team were in a strategy session, but they're waiting for you in the conference room. May I see your phone?"

Grace handed it to her, wishing she'd walk faster. They'd lost enough time since she got the pharmacy text, but an encouraging sight awaited them in the conference room. Wes was geared up and just waiting for them to arrive to set his team into action. Agent Shepherd immediately handed Wes Grace's phone. He thanked her and forwarded the pharmacy texts to his cell.

"On my way," he said into his radio as he rushed out of the conference room.

Scott motioned for Grace and Ryan to sit and invited Agent Shepherd to join them.

"I was going to call you to come in and go over the forensic evidence we've gathered. Looks like what you brought is far better." He flipped through sheets of paper stacked on the table in front of him. He removed one and held it out to Grace just as an agent tapped on the door.

"Sorry to interrupt, sir, but we have a lead on the Walker case," she said.

"Come in," Scott said. "Let me introduce you to Mr. and Mrs. Walker. This is Special Agent Cameron. She's the tech advisor on Reid's team. What do you have?"

Agent Cameron glanced at Grace. "I'm truly sorry about your son, ma'am. If anyone can find him, it's Agent Reid." She handed Scott a paper. "This is from the canvas. A resident in the area saw a blue sedan speed off at the time we estimate our suspect would have vacated the house. We have a plate and description. The techs are checking security camera footage from the area to see if we can spot which direction our suspect fled the scene."

Grace jumped up and faced Agent Cameron. "Mara was driving a blue sedan the day I saw her."

"Excellent," Scott said. "If we can place the car at the pharmacy, Mara's done," Scott said. "Keep me posted, Cameron."

"Yes, sir," she said and left.

Grace smiled at Ryan and squeezed his hand.

"Wes was hoping for a lucky break. The car is a solid lead, but I need to warn you not to get too excited yet. This could be unrelated to Mara," Scott said.

"It had to be her." Grace stood and tugged on Ryan's hand to get him out of his chair. "We'll let you get back to work. Please call the minute there's news."

Scott stood and shook their hands. "You have my word. Agent Shepherd will escort you out."

The elevator stopped on the second floor on their way to the lobby. Steph was there waiting to get in when the doors slid open. Grace and Ryan updated her on what had happened.

"This is fantastic and explains why Wes stranded me in the lab without a word. I was glad one of the photographers was in the lab to show me how to get to the elevator," Steph said.

Agent Shepherd stayed in the elevator when they reached the lobby. "I promise to keep you in the loop."

"Thank you," Grace said as the doors closed. "Do you need a ride?" she asked Steph as they walked to the parking lot.

"No, my car's here. I'll meet you at the house. I want to tell you what I learned today. It's fascinating."

Ryan kissed her cheek. "I'm anxious to hear, and we need a good distraction." As Steph walked away, Ryan said, "If Wes continues to give her access, she can be our fly on the wall, and we won't have to wait for the agents to call us."

Grace climbed into the car, and said, "Scott perked up when Agent Cameron told him about the car. I don't think they had much else to go on before we got here. The dominoes might be starting to fall for Mara."

Ryan exited the parking lot and eased into evening traffic. "At least Mara refilled Johnny's meds. That means she's taking care of him."

"But for how long? Caring for Johnny is a challenge in the best circumstances. How long before she gets tired of this game and abandons him like she did when he was a baby?"

"Johnny's not an infant, and he's a smart kid. He'll find his way home. They'll get Mara before it comes to that."

"Maybe she'll be in custody by the time we get home."

WES SPLIT his team between the two pharmacies and went to the one that sent the first text. His team searched the parking lot and drive-through for the blue, four-door sedan with the plate matching the description of the car fleeing Mara's neighborhood. When he was sure the car wasn't there, he left two agents outside and took the rest to search inside the pharmacy. Mara was gone, but Wes hoped they'd get vital information from the pharmacy staff.

He went to the counter and flashed his credentials to the tech. "We have information that prescriptions were filled and sold from this pharmacy for a patient named Johnathan Walker today. Is this correct?"

The tech stared at him for several seconds before saying, "I'm not sure if I'm allowed to share that information."

Wes handed her a form. "Grace Walker, Johnathan's mother, has given authorization for you to share the information."

"Excuse me," she said and walked to the pharmacist. She showed him the form. They whispered to each other before the tech returned with the pharmacist.

Wes again showed his credential. "We're investigating a child abduction. We believe the kidnapper purchased refills for the victim at this pharmacy within the last two hours. We'd like to verify that information."

The pharmacist went to the computer. "What's the child's date of birth?" Wes told him, and the tech stared at him wide-eyed while the pharmacist searched the records. "We filled those prescriptions thirty-five minutes ago. I'll print a copy of the receipt, but the customer paid with cash."

"Thank you, and we'll need the security footage, too."

"I'll contact out security company. Do you have a card so they can contact you?"

Wes nodded and passed his card to the pharmacist. He turned to the tech and said, "Did you process the transaction?"

She glanced at the pharmacist, and he gave a slight nod. "What were the medications?" The pharmacist read them off to her. "Oh, yes. I remember that lady. She was kind of weird. She pretended she wasn't mad that we didn't have one of the medications, but I could tell she was. Another pharmacy filled that one. I can tell you where."

Wes smiled to put her at ease. "We already know, but you've

given very helpful information. Can you describe the woman to me?"

"She was wearing a crazy, pink neon hat. I could see her short blond hair sticking out beneath the rim. She had a lip ring, and a dolphin tattoo on the back of her hand."

"Was she tall, short, heavy or thin?"

"Short to average, I'd say. Kind of thin. I'm sorry, I mostly remember the hat."

By design, Wes thought, but he said, "Are you willing to give a description to our sketch artist?"

"Of course. My shift ends in twenty minutes."

Wes gave her a card with the address to the field office. "Do you recall if she used one of your pens or touched the counter for a fingerprint?"

She shook her head. "If only I'd known who she was. She was right here, and I let her go."

"Don't blame yourself. We appreciate your willingness to help. Citizens like you are vital to our work."

"I hope you catch her and rescue that boy," she said as he and his team were leaving.

Wes radioed the other team. They'd missed Mara by ten minutes.

"She used the drive-through, so all we have is the security feed. The cashier couldn't see Mara's face clearly. She was wearing a wide-brimmed pink hat."

"Same here. Get what you can and head back to the office," Wes said.

He was quiet on the drive back. They'd missed Mara again, but this time they had witnesses and security video. Once they found that car, they'd be only one step away from capturing Mara.

CHAPTER TWELVE

GRACE HUNG up her phone and went to find Ryan an hour after they got home. He was at his workbench in the garage fixing a broken drill.

Grace leaned against his car and crossed her arms. "That was Scott. Mara wasn't at either pharmacy when Wes' team got there, but they collected some good evidence. He wants me to scour through security footage in the morning. I told him I'd come in tonight, but he wants his techs to go through it first. Wes is following up on the car lead."

Ryan put down his tools and looked at her. "How did Scott sound? Did he say anything else?"

"Not much, but he's hopeful."

"Good to know if that's true. My gut says he's not as hopeful as he lets on." Ryan picked up a cloth and wiped the grease off his hands. "Have you eaten? I was just about to go get a plate."

"Can't remember the last time I ate. I'll join you."

Mark was eating at the table, and Steph and Alec were dishing their plates when Ryan and Grace walked into the kitchen. Grace's stomach grumbled at the warm, delicious smells. She took it as a good sign that her appetite was returning. She dished a double portion of chicken casserole a neighbor had brought. The doorbell rang as she lifted her fork to take her first bite.

Steph started to get up, but Grace said, "It's probably Brad or Paul. They both said they might stop by tonight."

She hadn't seen Paul for months, and as she walked to the door, memories of their first meeting flooded over her. He was a lawyer friend of Adam's from their undergrad days. He had a law practice in the city and had come to her rescue more than once during the earlier ordeal with Johnny. She smiled as she remembered how he'd gotten Johnny to take a bottle for the first time after he came out of his coma when she and Alec couldn't. He'd become far more than their lawyer and had remained a dear family friend. She was looking forward to his visit but wished it came under better circumstances.

She opened the door without looking through the peephole and found Craig Stuart on her doorstep. She started to slam the door, but he put out his hand in the way to stop her.

"Move your hand or you'll be sorry," Grace said and pushed harder on the door.

Craig gave a shove, and the door slipped from Grace's hands. Craig pushed it open and held it in place with his foot.

"Please, let me in, Grace. I'm here to apologize and offer my help. I want to do what I can to find Johnny, and I want to up the reward."

Grace eyed him while deciding whether to believe him. He looked sincere, but she'd fallen for his sincerity before only to have him turn on her. She deserved his apology, and the extra reward money might lead to tips about Johnny. She took the risk and stepped aside to let him pass.

She studied him as she followed him into the living room. His light brown hair was still thick and without a touch of gray. He looked slightly more fit and healthy than he had twelve years earlier, and Grace wondered if his third wife had anything to do with that. Grace thought how it wasn't fair that men got better looking with age. He was wearing a polo shirt, khaki pants, and loafers that probably cost more than she spent on clothes in a year. She gestured for Craig to sit in the loveseat, but he remained standing.

"I'm deeply sorry for the things I said on the phone. You aren't to blame for Johnny's kidnapping any more than I was to blame when Mara and Rick took him when he was born. You're a phenomenal mother. Insulting you the way I did in the middle of this terrible crisis was beyond cruel. I am sorry, and I hope you'll forgive me and let me help."

Grace relaxed her fists and blew out the air she was holding. "Sit down, Craig." She worked to regain her composure while she watched him lower himself onto the loveseat. "You could have warned me you were coming."

"True. I flew here on an impulse. I haven't been able to stop thinking about Johnny since I found out he was missing."

"That I understand, and I owe you an apology for what I said on the phone too. I've never believed for one moment that Johnny's kidnapping was your fault. It was a cruel and insensitive accusation."

"That wasn't necessary, but I appreciate it." Before he could say more, Alec burst into the room. Craig sprang up and gave her a sarcastic smile. "Hello, Alec. Great to see you. It's been a long time."

Alec moved two inches from his face and stabbed a finger into his sternum. "How dare you show your face in this house after what you said to Grace? She doesn't need you meddling in this crisis. Please leave, now."

Grace gripped Alec's shoulder and inched her away from Craig. "Down, Alec. He already apologized. We're good. He's here to help."

Without taking her eyes off Craig, she said, "Help? He can help by crawling back to Albuquerque."

Grace kept her hold on Alec. "He's going to add to the

reward." Alec glared at Craig but kept her mouth shut. "It could help Johnny. Nothing else matters but Johnny."

Craig held his hands up in surrender. "She's right, Alec. I told Grace how out of line I was on the phone. I'm sorry for accusing her. Johnny's disappearance stirred up dark memories. It was a knee-jerk reaction."

Alec turned to Grace. "You're buying this?"

The kitchen door opened, and Ryan, Mark, and Steph filed into the living room.

"What's with all the shouting? We've been waiting–" Ryan said but stopped mid-sentence when he saw Craig. He turned to Grace. "You let him in?"

"Yes," Grace said. "Let me explain."

"What's to explain?" He glared at Craig. "You offended my wife at a most vulnerable time. What kind of man are you? I want you off my property."

Alec chuckled. "Get in line."

Grace stepped between Ryan and Craig. "As much as I appreciate you defending me, it's not necessary. I was just telling Alec that Craig has apologized. He's here to offer his help."

"It's true, and I need to tell you how sorry I am, too, Ryan. This is a traumatic situation. We're all on edge."

"Have we all forgotten that Craig lost Samantha and his first-born child on that horrible day fourteen years ago? He suffered for two years before learning Johnny was alive. He's as invested in this as we are."

"I wouldn't go that far," Alec said.

Grace scowled at her. "We've all said and done things we regret this week. Which of us has the right to point fingers?"

Ryan stepped back, and Alec relaxed her shoulders. "You're lucky to have Grace in your corner after what you've done. I'll allow you to stay, but I'll be watching," Alec said.

"I've made many mistakes in my life but giving Johnny to

Grace and Ryan wasn't one of them, Alec. I love Johnny, but I wasn't prepared then to give him what Grace could, and has."

Alec put her arm around Grace's shoulders. "Truest thing you've ever said."

"Do I have your permission to stay, Ryan?"

Ryan dropped onto the couch and rubbed his face. "Why not? We'll take help from anywhere we can get it."

"I'm grateful. I hope we can all remember the real target for our anger," Craig said. "I can't believe Mara had the brass to do this twice. We can't allow her to disappear with Johnny this time. I'll do whatever it takes to stop her and get him home. Melanie and I agreed we can add twenty-five grand to the reward."

Grace sank down next to him and took his hand. "That's as much as the FBI is offering. You can afford that?"

"Yes, and more if we need to."

"So, you do love Johnny," Alec said. "You can definitely stay. I was about to tell Grace and Ryan that Adam and I are planning to donate the same amount."

Grace's eyes glistened as she looked at her friend. "You would do that?"

"We'd sell our house if it would bring Johnny home sooner."

Ryan wiped his eyes with the back of his hand. "I don't know what to say. I'll call Agent Shepherd to get the word out about the reward."

"I'll do it, Dad," Steph said and started dialing her phone before she reached the kitchen.

Craig stood and smoothed his pants. "I'll get out of your hair. I need to check into my hotel and contact Melanie. She was worried about me coming here."

"Smart woman," Alec said.

"You don't have to go. We were about to eat, and we can get you up to speed on the investigation," Grace said. Ryan grimaced, but she ignored him. "You're family. Please, stay."

It was Craig's turn to tear up. "It's more than I deserve, but I accept. I'd like to know more than what they're reporting on the news."

"Good, then let's eat," Grace said and led her family into the kitchen.

REID, Prince, and Elliott waited in the van outside the motel for their target to make an appearance. A Richmond PD officer had gotten a tip from one of his informants about the blue car and passed it to Reid. They'd staked out the motel for two hours, but the car hadn't shown. Reid was beginning to think the tip was a bust.

He was getting ready to call it when the car pulled into the parking lot and drove behind the motel, out of their line of sight. Prince started the van and followed, but the car was empty by the time they got to the back of the motel.

"What now?" Elliott whispered. "She got inside pretty fast. Johnny must not have been with her. Do you think it's the room where the car is parked?"

"She could have parked in front of a different room to throw us off. We can't go busting through every door," Prince said.

"Mara probably has no idea we're this close but get the desk clerk out here just in case. We'll start with the room by the car and go from there. Stay here, Elliott. There's no way to get out the back, so if she makes a run, she'll have to come out the front."

Prince was back in three minutes with the motel clerk. Reid was climbing out of the van when the motel door in front of the car opened. A rough looking guy in his mid-twenties came out carrying a backpack and unlocked the car. Reid called out for him to stop, but the man tossed the backpack in the car and dove into the driver seat. Reid and Elliott were on him before he got the key in the ignition.

Elliott cuffed him while Reid and Prince had the clerk unlock the door. The room was small with a tiny bathroom, so it only took seconds to see no one else was inside.

"Not them," Prince said. "Doesn't look like they've been here either."

Reid went out and slammed the door behind him. "So, who's our mystery man?"

"Richmond PD has a unit in the vicinity. They're on their way," Elliott said. "Turns out they've been looking for Amos here for some time. He hit a liquor store and shot the clerk. The victim is alive but just barely."

"So, Amos, you might be looking at a murder charge to add to armed robbery," Reid said and left Amos lying face down on the sidewalk with Elliott watching him. "We might as well start looking through the car and room to give Richmond PD a head start. We'll head back to the office as soon as they get here. I don't want to waste a second more on this than we have to."

REID FOUND Shepherd going over the pharmacy evidence with Michaels just after their dinner break.

Michaels waved him into his office. "I can tell from your face that I'm not going to like what you have to tell me."

Reid went in and leaned against the desk with his arms folded. "Bad news and good news," he said. "We located the car which the neighbor identified, but it has nothing to do with Mara. Good news is that it was used in an armed robbery and shooting at a liquor store. It led to the capture of Amos Jackson. Richmond PD has been after him for more than a year."

"Another dead end is so not what we need," Shepherd said. "Glad they got Jackson, but this is a blow to our case. Mara could be holding Johnny anywhere in a hundred-mile radius."

"And she's probably ditched any ID tying her to the house she vacated. Who knows how many ID's or disguises she has, and now she has enough of Johnny's medications to last a month," Michaels said.

Reid stroked his beard. "Did she fill all of his prescriptions? If not, she'll have to crawl out of her hole to get them. If we keep eyes on every pharmacy from that chain in the city, we might get her."

"Can you imagine the manpower that would require?" Michaels asked.

Reid dug through the stack of papers until he found Johnny's pharmacy records. "There are two medications Mara won't be able to fill until next week. That's much further off than I'd like, but if we haven't captured her by then, we could use locals to augment my team. Is there a way to red-flag Johnny's account if Mara attempts to get refills?"

"I'll get the techs working on it with the pharmacy, but it's a long shot. Like you said, she has a week's cushion, so we'll keep it as plan D. We need a plan A." Michaels said.

"Working on it, sir. If we're done here, I'll take the unpleasant task of informing the Walkers. And I know, put a good spin on it," Reid said.

"No, call first. If Grace is willing, I want her to go over the security footage tonight. I told her to come in the morning, but I don't want to wait. We can't waste time chasing the wrong person," Michaels said. "Shepherd, I know it's been a long day, but have the footage ready in the tech lab when she gets here."

"Yes, sir," Shepherd said and brushed past Reid on her way out.

Reid followed her and went to call Grace.

———

GRACE SAT NEXT TO STEPH, staring at the computer monitor. She'd been there for thirty minutes and was already having a hard time keeping her eyes focused. She'd been excited to get Reid's call, and Steph had jumped at the chance to go back to the field office with her, but the reality of scanning through the security camera videos was nothing like she'd imagined. As much as she wanted to ID Mara, it was ten-thirty and studying the feed was about as exciting as watching grass grow.

Agent Shepherd had started the video from the mark forty-five minutes before Grace got the text alert. Grace had watched ten or twelve customers approach the pharmacy counter, but none had looked remotely like Mara. Watching the unsuspecting, anonymous people made Grace uneasy. They had no idea they were being filmed, and she felt like a creeper.

The current customer on the screen was an older man who couldn't figure out how the debit card machine worked. The pharmacy tech patiently helped him complete his transaction. The customer before him was a young woman with a little boy who kept picking his nose. Steph had groaned and suggested they bet about whether he'd eat what he pulled out of his nostril. Grace had given her a gentle smack on the arm and told her to focus, but she wondered how many times someone had watched her when she wasn't aware her actions were being recorded. She made a mental note to be more aware of her actions in public in the future.

Shepherd returned with a Diet Coke for each of them thirty minutes later. She pulled up a chair and sat next to Steph. "Anything yet?" she asked.

"Nothing but a new appreciation for people who do this for a living," Grace said. "Have you seen the video of Mara?"

"I have, but we want to see if you ID the person the pharmacy tech thought was her."

Reid came in and stood behind Steph with his arms crossed. Grace caught the slight upward curve of Steph's lips when she glanced at him. She turned back to the screen before Steph saw her watching.

At that moment, a woman with a large-rimmed neon-pink hat

stepped up to the counter. Her face was only visible for an instant before the woman lowered her head, but it was long enough for Grace to get a look at her eyes. She leaned closer to the monitor and studied the woman's movements and body shape.

She pointed at the screen and turned to Reid. "It's Mara. That's her. Does she look at the camera again before she leaves?"

Reid shook his head. "She knows what she's doing. She kept her face hidden with the hat."

"Can you rewind it and freeze it where you can see her face?" Steph asked. Shepherd reached over to the computer and did as Steph asked. She paused the video on the frame where Mara's eyes were visible. "You're sure that's her?"

"Positive," Grace said. "She cut and bleached her hair, but that's her."

Shepherd looked at Reid and dipped her chin. "That's the person the pharmacy tech IDed."

"Have the techs print that frame and try to clean it up so we can disseminate it," Reid said.

"You got it, boss. This is a huge break."

She left in a hurry, and Reid said, "Thanks for coming in so late, Grace. If the techs can get a clean print for the media, someone might recognize her. Even though the tip on the car was a bust, having a shot of her face for the public may bring new leads. The increased reward is making a difference too. The tip line has heated back up. I'm hoping to have Mara in custody by morning."

"Do you ever sleep?" Steph asked.

"I'm heading to the hotel now. I'll keep my phone close by and call the second we have anything promising."

Grace picked up her purse and walked to the elevator a few feet ahead of Wes and Steph. She heard Wes tell Steph that he'd leave a visitor badge for her at the front desk if she wanted to come by in the morning. Steph eagerly agreed, and Grace smiled to herself, still hoping for that one bright spot to emerge from the darkness. She knew Johnny would have been happy about it, too.

MARA'S EYES were glued to the TV while she flipped through the morning news cycle. Johnny watched her while he ate his cereal at the small table in their room. She'd become obsessed with searching for any mention of them in the news, but Johnny was sick of it and wondered if she'd only taken him from the Walkers for the attention.

"Can't we watch a movie or something?" he asked, through a mouthful of cereal. "They're just repeating the same report. We've heard it all."

Mara swung around and glared at him for a second before turning back to the TV. "Fine, we'll watch the news."

He would have asked if he could watch YouTube, but Mara had changed the unlock code on the laptop and restricted his use to homework with her staring over his shoulder. She was afraid he'd try to contact one of his friends. She was smart to do that because that was his exact plan. He missed his friends. He even missed school and would gladly trade a PT session with Tony to another day cooped up with Crazy Mara.

He finished his cereal and out of absolute boredom and desperation, decided to read one of his textbooks. Just as he reached into the backpack to get one, Mara sprang off the chair and stared open-mouthed at the TV. There on the screen was a slightly blurred picture of her in that stupid pink hat. He chuckled, and she turned on him and grabbed him by the neck of his t-shirt. Not again, he thought.

"You think it's funny? That's from the pharmacy. I had to go there because of you. Now I have to figure out a way to change my appearance again or I can't leave this room. It's your fault."

Johnny had gotten used to her tantrums and wasn't afraid of

her. He easily pulled her hand free of his shirt and pushed himself up by pressing on the table.

"Back off. I didn't ask you to bring me here, and it's your fault I need the meds in the first place. All of this is your fault. If you'd left me in that hospital with Craig when I was born, I wouldn't be a damned cripple."

Instead of backing down, she did the last thing he expected and backhanded him across the cheek. The force of the blow knocked him off balance. He fell back, missing the edge of the dresser by less than an inch. His elbow struck the floor hard, and he felt the sting of carpet burn. He sat up and pulled his knees to his chest without daring to look at Mara.

She crouched next to him and tenderly patted his back. "I'm so sorry, Johnny. I just didn't expect you to talk back to your mother that way. I thought Grace had taught you better. You're right that you wouldn't have your disabilities if I'd left you in New Mexico, but it's Rick's fault you got hurt, not mine. I wanted to stay in our house during the hurricane, but he insisted we leave. It's all his fault. I promise never to hit you again, but I expect you to be respectful."

Johnny stared at her, shocked by her sudden mood change and excuses, but he nodded to shut her up. She grinned and helped him into the chair. His elbow hurt when he rested it on the table. When he pushed the sleeve of his hoodie up to examine it, blood dripped onto the table.

"I'm cut. Do we have any bandages?"

Mara pressed a napkin on his cut and told him to put his hand over it and press hard. "I have first aid supplies in my purse, but we'll need more. That's a bad cut. I can't go to the market in the lobby until I do something with my hair."

She dug in her purse and pulled out some antibacterial oint-ment, gauze, and tape. She chatted away at high speed like nothing had happened while she cleaned and bandaged his cut. Johnny became more concerned with each word. He'd never seen someone shift emotional gears on a dime like her, and it disturbed him.

"They have a market in the lobby?" he said to distract her.

She finished with his arm and smiled at her work in satisfaction. "A small one. Not much there."

"Do they have snacks?"

"What's with you and the snacks? I've never seen anyone eat like you. You haven't touched the fruit."

"I had a banana with my cereal." He held up the empty peel to prove it.

Mara looked around the room and sighed. "We need to find somewhere to live that's more permanent and affordable with a real kitchen so I can cook. Not sure how we're going to manage that. I didn't even get my last paycheck from the hospital. It's probably in the mailbox at my house, but that place is most likely crawling with feds."

"Don't you have any friends that could get your mail? And I don't know why you're so worried about getting caught. If you can prove you're my real mom, they can't arrest you."

"Not if. I *am* your mother but proving that will be tricky. What would happen to you in the meantime? And I haven't been here long enough to make friends. No one would want to help anyway. They'd think I'm a kidnapper."

Because you are, Johnny thought but kept his mouth shut. He watched Mara put on her hoodie and pull it tight around her face to cover her hair.

"I need hair dye and extensions, or maybe a wig except they're expensive. My poor hair will never be the same."

She went on mumbling, talking more to herself than him. Johnny took the remote off the table and went to his bed. His elbow was throbbing, and he had a headache. He changed the channel away from the news and turned up the volume hoping to drown out Mara.

"Turn that down," she said. "It's giving me a headache. I'm

going out and may be gone for a few hours looking for a store outside of Richmond where no one will notice me. You have plenty of food here to last until I get back." She put both hotel key-cards in her purse. "Don't answer the door to anyone, just like before, and lock the bolt and bar behind me."

Johnny followed her to the door and locked it after she left but had no intention of staying in the room. He'd been locked up for days and had to get out. He watched the clock for thirty minutes before daring to leave the room. Since he didn't have a key, he made sure to flip the bar to keep the door open like he'd seen his dad do when they went on trips. They didn't have much in the room that anyone would want to steal.

———

JOHNNY NEARLY CHICKENED out while he rode the elevator to the lobby. Mara would kill him if she came back and he wasn't in the room. He hesitated for a few seconds when the doors opened but made himself step out when he saw the rows of snacks on the market shelves.

Instead of going straight to the market, he wanted to explore the hotel first. He found the pool and jacuzzi and wished he had a swimsuit. Tony always said that working his muscles in water was the best thing for him. Mara hadn't even bought him shorts since it was winter, so he was out of luck.

Craving fresh air, he went toward the entrance next. The desk clerk watched him out of the corner of his eye. It gave him goose-bumps, but he kept going since he wasn't doing anything wrong. It was colder than Johnny expected, so he was glad he'd put his hoodie on even though it had blood on the sleeve. He walked around the corner of the hotel and watched the cars speeding by on the street beyond the rear parking lot. He was tempted to flag down a driver and ask them to take him home, but he didn't want to look like a crazy person. He wished again for his phone.

He went back inside after ten minutes and checked out the market. When he saw the high prices, he realized that he hadn't thought about how he'd pay. He couldn't charge it to the room because Mara would know, and he was pretty sure he'd spent all his cash in Charlottesville the weekend before. He pulled out his wallet and checked just to be sure. He saw his debit card resting in its slot and smiled. He'd seen an ATM near the vending machines while he'd been wandering around the hotel. It didn't take long to make his way back to it.

His heart started pounding again while he slipped the card into the slot. The money was his, but his parents had access to the account. He wasn't sure if they'd noticed he'd withdrawn the cash or not. Deciding it was worth the risk, he withdrew eighty dollars. That would be enough to get away from Mara if he decided to escape. He took the cash to the market and bought what he wanted. The clerk stared at him the whole time and even asked his room number. Johnny gave the number for the same room on the second floor and left as fast as he could on his crutches. He was relieved that he beat Mara back to the room.

He bolted the door and settled on the bed with his pile of snacks. He'd eat what he wanted and hide the rest for the next time Mara left him alone. He felt an exhilarating sense of accomplishment while he munched on his candy bar and searched for something to watch on TV. He'd gone on his adventure and taken care of himself without problems or consequences. He just wished Grace was there to see what he could do on his own. Maybe it would get her to stop treating him like a baby. He was disappointed that she'd never know.

CHAPTER THIRTEEN

MARA DROVE the hour and a half to Waynesboro, a small town west of Charlottesville, and used GPS to find the hair supply store. She checked the rear-view mirror before she got out to make sure that her hood was still in place. She left her sunglasses on even though the day was cloudy. The store was lit well enough that she could easily make her way through the aisles.

The store was empty except for the clerk, so she was the only one Mara had to worry about recognizing her. She put a box of auburn hair color in her basket and went to look for extensions to match. They had just enough of the right color to cover her head. Once she had her hair items taken care of, she went to search for tanning lotion and dark makeup. She picked what she needed and carried her basket to the counter.

She relaxed when she saw the sales associate, a girl of about twenty with pink spiked hair and more piercings and tattoos than Mara could count. Mara was confident the girl would care less about a kidnapped teenage boy in Richmond.

Mara put her items on the counter and waited while the girl rang them up. The clerk glanced at Mara a few times but kept going.

After putting the last item in the bag, she said, "Not my business, but is your old man knocking you around?" When Mara raised her eyebrows, the girl pointed at her glasses. "My mom used to wear sunglasses all the time to hide the black eyes my dad gave her until my brother got big enough to toss Dad out on his ass. I think of that whenever I see women wearing sunglasses in a store."

Mara slid off her glasses. "No black eyes. I'm sensitive to fluorescent lights. Sorry about your horrible dad."

She shrugged. "I'm over it. Mom has a good guy now. He doesn't even try to put his hands on me."

Mara was saddened that the girl's measuring stick for goodness was that her mom's boyfriend didn't try to molest her. *Such a messed-up world.*

"Why are you changing your color?" the girl asked, drawing Mara from her thoughts. She pointed at her pink hair. "I like the white. That's how I had mine until the other day."

Mara wished she would stop talking and finish the sale so she could get out of there. She hadn't noticed a security camera but was sure there must be one.

"Just need a change," Mara said and handed her the cash.

"Let me see. I'm in school to be a cosmetologist. My teachers say I have a good eye."

"Another time. I'm in a hurry."

"Come on, let me see."

Mara didn't want to make a scene and figured she wasn't getting out of that store unless she uncovered her hair. She lowered the hood and looked at the girl with no expression. She studied Mara's hair for a few seconds before moving her gaze to her eyes.

"You look familiar."

Mara pulled the hood back over her head. "That's not possible. I'm in town visiting a friend. I've never been in this store."

"But I know you." She narrowed her eyes, and Mara could see

the wheels turning. "You're the lady I saw on the news that took that kid."

She picked up her phone and started to dial. Mara reached across the counter and slapped it out of her hand. As it clattered across the tile, Mara grabbed her bag and started for the door, but the girl came up behind and tackled her to the floor. She flipped Mara onto her back and straddled her, pinning her arms with her knees.

"You're not getting out of here. The FBI is offering seventy-five grand for you. You know what I could do with that kind of bank?"

Mara drew up her knees, planted her feet and arched her back. The girl tipped over, and it was Mara's turn to pin her.

"It's not true what they're saying on the news. I didn't kidnap the boy. I'm his real mother." The girl tried to flip her off as Mara had done to her, but Mara was prepared and didn't budge. "I'll knock you out and be long gone by the time you come to. Here's the deal. I'll give you three-hundred bucks right now if you promise not to tell anyone I was here. It's not seventy-five K, but it's all I have on me. If I get away and they never catch me, you get zero. Deal?"

The girl nodded.

"Say it."

"Deal. I promise not to tell anyone about you but get off me. My manager's in the back room."

Mara rolled off and drew a small switchblade from her purse. She snapped it open before reaching into her purse for her wallet.

The girl climbed to her feet and grinned at Mara. "You think that tiny blade scares me?"

"It should." Mara flung the knife past the girl's ear. It sliced into the wall behind her. Mara dashed past her and had the knife in her hand before the girl moved an inch.

The girl's eyes widened in terror. She held up her hands and said, "Easy, lady. It's all good."

Mara nodded but didn't take her eyes off her while she walked back to her purse. She counted out the cash but didn't hand it to her. "What's your name?" she asked.

The girl hesitated before saying, "Amy."

"Well, Amy, if I find out that you've told anyone I was here, I'll be back for you. Trust me on that."

Mara held the cash out to her. Amy snatched it from Mara's hand and shoved it in her pocket. Mara kept her eyes on her until she was out of the store. She drove three blocks away as quickly as she could without drawing attention and pulled into an abandoned lot. Her hands shook on the steering wheel. She'd managed to fool the girl, but she wasn't as tough as she'd acted. She only knew that knife trick from hanging out in too many bars with Rick.

She was $300 poorer, and her plan was unraveling, but there was no question of backtracking. She'd get Johnny out of Richmond no matter what it took, but she needed to regain control. She had time on the drive back to Richmond to calm down and figure out her next moves. Her only hope was that the bribe was enough to get Amy to keep her mouth shut.

Wes was out of ideas. It was day five since the kidnapping, but his usual tactics were getting them nowhere. Even plastering Mara's photo all over the media hadn't yielded any promising leads, and the pharmacy data had proved useless. Every time he was convinced a piece of evidence would lead to Mara, he came up empty-handed.

He rubbed his face, shook his head to clear it and took a sip of coffee. He had to keep going and find answers. His frustration was nothing compared to what the Walkers were suffering. He recalled the way Steph had looked at him the night before, so hopeful, so trusting. He couldn't betray that trust, and he'd made a promise to Grace that he was determined to keep.

Elliott leaned in through the doorway, interrupting Wes' thoughts. "Hey boss, you need to come with me."

Wes put down his cup and followed Elliott to where a junior agent was taking tip line calls.

"One moment, miss," the agent said and put the caller on hold. "This person says Mara was in her store an hour ago, sir. I thought you'd want to take the call yourself."

Wes took the handset and pressed the hold button. "This is Special Agent Reid. You have information on Mara?"

"Yes, sir," a young woman said.

Wes heard the tremor in her voice, so he softened his tone. "May I ask your name and where are you calling from?"

"I'm Amy Knox in Waynesboro. Mara was in my store. She threw a knife at me when I recognized her." She stopped and took a few breaths. "She missed me, thank God. She paid me three-hundred bucks to keep my mouth shut and threatened to come after me if I told anyone, but she's insane and shouldn't be on the street. She took off an hour ago, but she might still be watching me."

"You were right to call, Miss Knox. Excuse me one moment. Don't hang up." Wes put the call back on hold. "Get Shepherd in here." The junior agent came back with Shepherd a minute later. "Who do we have near Waynesboro?"

"Waynesboro? No one," Shepherd said.

"Elliott, get a team ready. I want you on your way to Waynesboro in ten." Reid took the call with Amy off hold. "Can you leave your location to go to the Police Department? We have agents on the way, but it will take time. We want you to be safe."

"I'll check with my manager. She was in the back room and didn't see Mara."

"If she gives you any trouble, call, and I'll talk to her. Tell her we're sending local police to the store. I'm going to pass the phone back to Agent...?" Wes waved at the agent to give his name. He scribbled on a piece of note paper and handed it to Wes. "To Agent Byers. He'll need the address and contact information."

Wes handed the phone to Agent Byers and motioned for Shepherd to join him in the corner away from the phones.

"Mara's escalating. She pulled a knife on that girl and bribed her to keep quiet. The pressure we're putting on her is making her desperate."

"How far behind Mara are we?" Shepherd asked.

"More than an hour. That girl was too afraid to call sooner. We need to get Waynesboro PD over there now."

"On it," Shepherd said. She started for the hallway but stopped and turned to Wes. "What was Mara doing in Waynesboro?"

"Trying not to get recognized. Guess that backfired. It's a good sign that someone in Waynesboro recognized her. Word's getting out there."

Shepherd nodded and left. Wes listened to the rest of Byers' conversation with Amy. As soon as Byers hung up, he said, "Get the call recording copied and sent to my office. Do they have security cameras?"

"Yes, one but it's not working. Repair guy is coming tomorrow."

Wes rubbed his forehead. "Figures. Call them back and tell them not to disturb any surface Mara touched, and ask them to print a copy of the sales receipt."

"Amy wanted to know if she can keep the money Mara gave her? And if she gets the reward money?"

Wes sighed and shook his head. "Tell her we'll replace the cash with a check. We need the cash to trace it. The reward will depend on if it leads to Mara's capture."

Agent Byers nodded and reached for the phone as Wes left to return to his office. He had no doubt Mara had hightailed it out of Waynesboro. She was most likely safely tucked into her lair in Richmond. Knowing the color of the hair dye she bought would prepare them for which disguise to expect next and having her prints would verify it had been Mara in that store.

The evidence probably wouldn't be any more helpful than what they'd already gathered. The only positive sign was that Mara was staying in the area for some reason. The longer she remained in the city, the higher their odds of catching her.

WES LOOKED up when he heard the faint tap on his door and was glad to see Steph smiling in the doorway. He'd spent the time in his office since getting Amy Knox's call going over every scrap of evidence, looking for the one clue he'd missed, but he'd found nothing. He was eager for a pleasant distraction.

He stood and motioned for her to come in. "I didn't know you were here today."

She settled into the chair opposite his desk and crossed her legs. "I hadn't planned to come, but everyone's so jumpy at home, I had to get out of there. This was the best place I could think of to escape." Her eyes scanned the top of his desk. "Anything good?"

"Nothing more than you already know. You heard about Waynesboro?"

"Yes. Has Elliott contacted you yet?"

He shook his head. "It's too soon, but I honestly don't have much hope that anything will come from it other than a more detailed image of her face. We already have her prints. That's why I didn't inform your parents yet. Do they know?"

"No, I didn't tell them for the same reason." She reached over and picked up a picture of Johnny lying on one of the stacks. She studied it and without looking up, said, "I thought being here would help me feel closer to my brother, but it doesn't. How can

Mara elude us so well in this digital age? There are cameras and electronics recording our every move."

Wes' phone buzzed before he could answer. He pointed at it. "Speaking of electronics." Steph stood to go, but he motioned for her to stay. "You better have good news for me, Elliott."

"Just one thing, the color of the dye and hair extensions Mara purchased," Elliott said. "That's it, other than maybe prints to confirm it was her, but from what Miss Knox says, I have no doubt of that."

"Send what you can and get back here ASAP but set up a detail to keep an eye on Amy Knox first. I doubt Mara would risk going after her, but I don't want to risk further escalation."

"On it, sir," Elliott said.

Wes put the phone down and told Steph what Elliott had said. "Interested in watching us alter the images to give Mara the new hair color and extensions?"

"Are you kidding. I'd love to. It would take my mind off Johnny, and if it helps capture Mara, I'd be thrilled to know I was a part of it."

"It'll take time before you can start. Can you stay until we're ready? I'll order us some dinner to be delivered."

"I was planning to stay as long as the techs would have me, so I'm yours for the evening."

Wes smiled, thrilled by her answer. Her cheeks reddened slightly. *What are you doing, Reid? She's the victim's sister.* Logic told him to pretend he'd just remembered something urgent he had to take care of and ask for a rain-check, but he ignored logic. He promised himself he'd behave and not cross any lines. It was a promise that would be difficult to keep.

GRACE KNELT in front of the Christmas tree just as the first rays of sunrise filtered in through the patio door. She fingered the ornament that had Johnny's birthdate engraved on the front and read Baby's First Christmas. The ornament wasn't really from Johnny's first Christmas. He'd spent that year in a coma. She and Ryan hadn't ordered the ornament until Johnny's third Christmas.

The twenty-fifth was only weeks away. Grace feared her heart would tear in two at the thought of not celebrating his fifteenth Christmas with him or maybe any of the others that followed. She felt the air stir and looked up to find Alec standing over her. She sat beside Grace and crossed her legs.

"I remember when you ordered that. I'd never seen you so ecstatic as when that box was delivered."

Grace's lips curled just a fraction. Without taking her eyes from the tree, she said, "I helped Johnny hang it. He had no idea what was happening and just wanted to eat it. He thought it was a cookie."

Alec took Grace's hand and held it in both of hers. "Our boy would have lived on cookies if we had let him."

"Still would. He's addicted to your biscotti."

Grace felt the tears burn her eyes but refused to let them come. Her eyelids were raw, and she'd had enough with crying. She sucked her cheek between her teeth to stop it. She'd learned that trick when Johnny was a baby.

"He's coming home," Alec whispered. "I refuse to let this end any other way."

Grace leaned her head on Alec's shoulder. "How do we make that happen? Mara seems invincible. If Johnny hadn't found out the truth right before Mara showed up, he might have tried to escape. He'd be snoring in his bed now. Why didn't I listen to you and tell him sooner? Even if he comes home, he's never going to forgive me. How do you recover from the kind of betrayal he must be feeling?"

"Not if he comes home. When. He might be furious with you. He might feel betrayed, but stronger than those feelings is his love for you. He'll remember once he's home." She stood and tugged on Grace's hand. "This tree looks lonely. Let's wrap Johnny's presents and put them under it. Johnny will hear them calling to him. That will get him home."

Grace didn't move. "I can't, Alec. It would be a knife in my chest every time I saw those gifts mocking me."

"No, it would be proof that you believe he'll be here on Christmas morning to open them. Get up and help me find the paper and ribbons. When we're done, you're coming with me to Juliana's for cannoli."

Grace knew there was no fighting the force of nature that was Alec. She slowly climbed to her feet and gazed up at her obstinate friend. "Get the wrapping supplies. I'll get the gifts. Let's get this over with before I lose my nerve."

Alec raced to the basement while Grace dug Johnny's gifts out of their hiding place in the linen closet without allowing herself to reminisce about the time she'd spent shopping for them. If Alec were right, there would be time for that later.

JOHNNY TURNED off the shower and grasped the rail so he could pull his towel off the hook. He started drying off but stopped when he heard Mara slamming drawers on the other side of the wall.

"What's going on out there?" he asked, dreading the answer.

Mara had been agitated since she got back the night before. When Johnny asked what they were having for dinner, she nearly bit his head off and told him to eat cheese and crackers. At first, he worried that she'd found out about his adventure to the lobby, but her behavior didn't seem to have anything to do with him. She'd been calmer when she woke up an hour earlier, but it sounded like something new had set her off.

The closet door slammed, and she yelled, "Get out here."

Johnny dried off and dressed as quickly as he could, which

wasn't fast enough for Mara. She pounded on the door until he unlocked it. She shoved it open, nearly knocking him off his crutches. She held one of the candy bars he'd bought an inch from his nose.

"Where'd you get this?"

Johnny froze. No matter how hard he concentrated, his mouth refused to move.

Mara's jaw clenched. "Answer me," she hissed.

He took a few deep breaths and braced himself against the counter. "I bought it in the lobby. I was hungry. We didn't have anything good."

Mara's fist slammed into his gut so fast he didn't have time to block it. Air rushed out of him and he doubled over, which sent his left crutch skidding across the bathroom tile. He grabbed for the sink counter but missed and struck his head on the toilet on his way to the floor. He looked at Mara as she got all blurry before everything went dark.

IT FELT like someone was pounding a nail into Johnny's head. He forced his eyes open and found Mara staring down at him. The last thing he remembered was getting out of the shower, but he was lying on the floor next to his bed. He didn't remember dressing and glanced down at himself in panic, but he was fully clothed. He closed his eyes against the light over his head and groaned.

"What happened to my head?" he asked. His words came out like a croak. He cleared his throat and asked again, but it wasn't any better. His mouth was as dry as cotton.

"You don't remember what happened?" He tried to shake his head, but it hurt to move. "You had a seizure in the bathroom. I dragged you out here. It wasn't easy, I can tell you. Can you walk? I need to get you to the hospital."

He couldn't lift his head, let alone walk. "I don't think so. Call an ambulance. That's what my mom does."

"Can't do that, and I'm your mom."

Johnny opened his eyes again and squinted at her. He wasn't in any shape to argue about Grace. "Why not?"

"Just can't. I'll think of another way." She swiveled her head as she scanned the room. "I'll be right back," she said and darted into the hallway.

Johnny dragged himself closer to the bed and propped his back against the end of it. His head hurt worse than it ever had in his life. He reached up and ran his fingers over the spot that hurt most. There was a bump the size of an egg. That wasn't too unusual. He'd bumped his head lots of times when he'd had a seizure, but he usually remembered the seizure starting. All he remembered this time was getting out of the shower. It was a blank after that.

The door swung open and a luggage cart rolled in with Mara behind it. "Think you can climb on here?"

"I'm not getting on that. It's for suitcases, not people," he said and crossed his arms.

"You have to go to the hospital. You hit your head on the toilet when you fell. If you have another way to get to the car, I'm listening."

He didn't, and he knew she was right about going to the hospital. His head didn't feel right. He slumped his shoulders. "Fine, but make sure you don't drop me. I don't need any more bumps."

She rolled the cart closer and helped him lift himself on to it. As she pushed him toward the door, he noticed their bags lined up in front of the closet. He was about to ask why, but she went through the door and rounded the corner, so he had to hang on to keep from falling.

Getting him to the car was the easy part, and he wished he'd thought to bring his crutches. It took fifteen minutes to work his way from the cart to the front passenger seat with Mara's help. His headache grew worse with each movement.

Once he was in the car, Mara left him and took the cart back into the hotel. He thought she was returning it to the lobby, but she came back ten minutes later with their belongings piled on it. He watched while she loaded it into the car. She left with the cart again but came back after a minute.

"Why are we leaving the hotel?" he asked when she climbed into the car. "You said we were staying for a few more days."

"You ruined that, didn't you? You went to the market and now they have you on the security camera. We can't stay here."

Mara's words were a foggy jumble that he couldn't understand. He closed his eyes and turned his head to the side so his bump wouldn't press against the seat. He was sad to leave the hotel, but all he cared about was getting relief from his headache. Mara couldn't get him to the hospital fast enough.

CHAPTER FOURTEEN

WRAPPING Johnny's gifts had seemed like a good idea at the time, but when Grace came out of her room after dressing, she couldn't bring herself to look under the tree. Each beautifully wrapped package was a harsh reminder that Johnny wouldn't be there to open them on Christmas morning. She kept her eyes forward and rushed past to the kitchen.

"Keep us posted," Ryan said and hung up his phone as Grace walked into the kitchen.

"Who was that? Wes?" she asked.

Ryan, Steph, and Mark were at the table. They glanced at each other before staring at her.

When Grace reached for Ryan's phone to check the caller ID, Steph said, "It was Jason. Jen might be in labor. They're on their way to the hospital."

Grace rubbed her forehead. "Labor? So early. Give me details."

"Only three and a half weeks early. You know twins typically come ahead of schedule," Ryan said. "Steph and Jen were born two weeks before their due date. It might be a false alarm. They went to urgent care because she didn't feel well. Her blood pressure was slightly elevated. The contractions started while they were there. The doctor told them to go to the hospital."

"It's the stress over Johnny. Worrying about him sent her into labor. Mara did this. The longer this goes on, the greater the chaos in her wake." She stared at the wall calendar Johnny had given her the previous Christmas. "What day is it?"

"Sunday," Mark said.

"Sunday," Grace repeated. "Tomorrow marks a week since Mara tore our world to shreds. We should be with Jen, not here anxious for any scrap of news about Johnny."

Ryan went to Grace and pulled her into his arms. "It's beyond unfair that we can't be with Jen and Jason, but they have one of the best obstetricians in the country. We'll have to trust her. Maybe it's a false alarm, and we'll be there when the babies come, with Johnny."

Grace gazed up at him. "How are you always so calm and rational?"

"Adam's magic pills," Mark said.

Ryan frowned at Mark over the top of Grace's head. "Thanks for the vote of confidence."

Grace squeezed Ryan's hand and turned back to the calendar. She read the notes she'd jotted down for the past week and checked off all the activities she'd missed. The reminders felt like they were for another person from another world. Now, Jen was in labor, and she'd miss that, too. They'd anticipated and planned the birth for all those long months. Grace couldn't have imagined anything could keep her from being a part of the most important event in her stepdaughter's life.

With her back to Ryan, she said, "Have you heard from Wes or Scott?"

His silence was all the answer she needed.

"I was so sure the evidence from Waynesboro would point them at Mara. You were at their headquarters last night, Steph. What were they saying?"

"Not much, but they still had a pile of evidence to sift through. It will take more time. They're working on an image of what Mara might look like with the new hair length and color. She's quite the master of disguise, but the techs showed me some of the innovative new technology they have. It's more than equal to Mara's tricks. They'll be ready when she slips up."

"Good to know," Grace whispered. She sighed and turned an empty Juliana's box on the counter. "Where's Alec? We're supposed to get cannoli."

"She said to ask you for a raincheck because of Jen. She went to get Adam and the kids," Mark said. "Rosie is begging for you to sign her cast. Valerie's wondering if she can bring our two over here. They miss you."

"I'd love to see them. I need a good dose of their energy. There's as much joy around here as a morgue." When Ryan cringed, she said, "Sorry, terrible choice of words."

Mark got up and headed for the living room. "I'll call Val."

Grace saw the mail piled in a basket on the counter next to the empty box. "When was the last time you read through the mail?" she asked Ryan.

"You mean after one of the agents has gone through it with a microscope? Not since Friday. It was mostly just bills and junk. We got a few Christmas cards. I wasn't sure you'd want to see them."

He was right. Reading about their friends and family's perfect lives would be torture while they were living a nightmare. Not that she begrudged them their good fortune. She just needed one less reminder that theirs had been stolen from them.

Grace picked up the basket and carried it to the table. She rifled through it but didn't find anything needing immediate attention. She glanced at the bank statement and said, "Where's my laptop? I should check our accounts to make sure we haven't run out of money."

Ryan cocked his head toward the door. "Dining room."

Grace took the bank statement into the other room with Steph close behind her.

"Tree's pretty," Steph said as she passed it.

Grace grunted and sat at the dining room table with her laptop. She logged into the bank site and checked their accounts. She considered skipping over Johnny's account until she noticed that the balance was almost a hundred dollars less than it was last time she checked. She clicked the link and saw he'd made a cash withdrawal the day before.

"Come look at this," she called to Ryan.

He rushed out of the kitchen, drying his hands on a towel. "What's wrong? Did someone clean out our accounts? It wouldn't surprise me the way our luck's going this week."

Grace turned the laptop to show him. "Steph, call Wes."

It only took minutes for the techs to trace Johnny's ATM withdrawal to a hotel on the west side of the city. Wes' excitement escalated as he mobilized his team. After all the disappointments, moments like that validated his decision to join the Bureau. Capturing Mara and bringing Johnny home would make the sacrifice and struggle worth it.

The driver of Wes' SWAT vehicle parked in the circular drive of the hotel and the two other vehicles pulled in behind them. Agents piled out with Wes on point.

"Prince, take your team and set up a perimeter to the west. Elliott, you go right," Wes said. "Cameron, keep your eyes on the entrance from here. The rest, you're with me."

The desk clerk's eyes widened at the sight of the geared-up CARD team descending on him *en masse*. Wes displayed his credentials and smiled to reassure him.

"Mr. Singh, we believe that the prime suspect in a kidnapping investigation is checked into your hotel." He held up the picture of Mara with short blond hair and the rendering of how she'd look with auburn hair and extensions. "Do you recognize this woman?"

Mr. Singh's gaze flitted over the face of each agent before he nodded. "I remember her. She didn't want to use her credit card. Let me pull up her record."

Wes shifted his feet while Mr. Singh tapped on the keyboard. He was anxious to get to Mara's room before she had a chance to bolt. Mr. Singh printed Mara's check-in record and handed it to Wes.

Wes studied the sheet of paper while Mr. Singh created a key to Mara's room for him. They had some concrete vitals on Mara for the first time. Her full name was Mara May Brennen, or at least that was the name she was using. Wes doubted it was her birth name. It was such an ordinary name for such a notorious person. Her driver's license listed a Portland, Oregon address. Whoever Mara was, she was a long way from home.

"This will open her room. Number 332," Mr. Singh said and gave Wes the room key.

"Thank you." Wes turned to the agents standing in a semi-circle behind him. "Mendez, take your team up the north stairs. Malcolm, you've got the south stairwell."

Wes led the remaining team members into the elevator.

"This is the slowest elevator ever created," Wes said and paced the small space as it crawled to the third floor.

He sprang through the doors the instant they opened. Mendez and Malcolm were waiting for him with their teams when he reached room 332. He rolled his eyes and tapped his knuckles on the door.

"This is the FBI. We have permission to enter. Please open the door." When there was no response, he swore under his breath. "I repeat, this is the FBI. You have five seconds to open the door before we enter."

Silence answered, so Wes counted to five before swiping the keycard against the reader. The light turned green, so he motioned for his team to get ready and turned the handle. They barged in and began their search, but the room was empty. No personal items. No luggage. No Mara or Johnny.

Wes grabbed two of his agents and took the stairs at a fast click to burn off frustration. As he made his way to the lobby, he tried to figure out what tipped Mara off that they were on their way. She must have bolted after Johnny used the ATM. Wes hoped the blood in the bathroom wasn't a reaction to Johnny defying her.

Wes radioed the agents outside the hotel to be on alert for Mara and ordered agents in the room to search every corner. When Wes thought no one was looking, he kicked the bathroom door with his boot. It swung back and slammed into the wall.

Malcolm poked his head out of the bathroom. "Everything all right, buddy?" he asked as he came out and checked where the doorknob had struck. "Accounting won't be happy if they have to repair a hole in the wall."

"Glad it was only you who saw that, old friend. I need to get a grip." Wes propped the room door open and motioned for Malcolm to follow him into the hallway. "How did Mara know? How did she know we were coming?" Wes rubbed his forehead. "Get forensics up here. I want proof Mara and Johnny were here."

"Hey, boss, we've got what looks like blood on the bathroom tile," Mendez called from inside the room.

"I hope it's Mara's," Wes whispered only loud enough for Malcolm's ears. "Look for bloodstains in other parts of the room while you wait for forensics," he told the rest of the agents. "I'm going down to talk to the desk clerk."

He showed the clerk a picture of Johnny when he got to the lobby. "Was this boy with Mara Brennen?"

Mr. Singh studied the photo carefully. "Yes, I think I saw him, but his hair is black and short. The face is the same though. The boy I saw was on crutches. He bought some items from the market."

Wes walked around the corner of the counter to the small market looking for cameras. "Does the security camera cover this area?"

"Yes, sir," Mr. Singh said.

Wes walked back to the registration desk. "We'll need all of your security recordings from the time Mara Brennen checked in."

"Let me call the manager."

While they waited for the manager to come out of the office, Wes said, "Thank you for your cooperation, Mr. Singh. The information you've provided will be vital to our case."

Mr. Singh pressed his palms together and gave a slight bow. "It is my honor to help. I hope the boy will soon be returned to his grieving mother and this villain will get the punishment she deserves."

Wes nodded. "As do I."

MARA JUMPED out of her chair next to Johnny's ER bed when the doctor came into the room.

Without looking up from the stack of papers in his hand, the doctor said, "I have the results of Kyle's tests. The x-rays show no skull fractures, so that's excellent news. Kyle's CBC and chemical levels are all within normal range." He turned to Johnny. "Do you usually have seizures when your levels are normal, Kyle?"

Johnny squinted at the doctor. "Why do you keep calling me Kyle?"

The doctor flipped through the papers. "Isn't that your name?"

Mara stepped between Johnny and the doctor. "He goes by a nickname. Long story. To answer your question, he does have the occasional seizure when his levels are good. The stress of traveling probably caused it. Can I take him home?"

The doctor looked skeptical at Mara's explanation, but he said, "Oh no. I'm admitting him. He didn't have any fractures, but he has a serious concussion. We need to keep him one night at least for observation. They're getting a room ready for him now. The nurse will be in shortly with the forms."

Johnny groaned. "I have to stay? I want to go home."

"I'm sorry, son. I can't release you. You might be able to go home tomorrow." The doctor started to leave but turned before he reached the door. "What do you want us to call you?"

"He goes by Scout," Mara said before Johnny could answer. "It's what his father always called him."

The doctor wrote the name on the top paper. "I'll pass that long."

As soon as the doctor was out of the room, Mara grabbed Johnny's clothes and threw back his blankets. "Get dressed. We're getting out of here."

Johnny raised his eyebrows. "But the doctor said I can't leave. My head is killing me, and the nurse said the doctor would give me something for pain."

"I have pain meds in the car. I'm a nurse. I know how to take care of you. Get dressed before the nurse comes. Do you think you can walk now?"

Johnny stared at her for a second before saying, "I think so."

"If not, I'll get a wheelchair."

She pulled the curtain around the bed and turned her back while Johnny dressed. She wasn't as confident about taking care of him as she'd acted, but there was no question of letting them admit him. All it would take was one person recognizing either one of them for all her plans to be shot.

"I'm ready," Johnny whispered.

Mara lowered the bed rails and handed him his crutches. She helped him slowly raise off the bed. He swayed slightly before steadying himself. She kept a hand on his back until she was sure he wouldn't fall.

"Take a few steps before we leave the room to make sure you can handle it. We'll have to move fast once we get in the hallway."

Johnny walked to the back wall and came back toward Mara without trouble even though he was going slower than she liked.

"Why did you tell the doctor to call me Scout?"

Mara stopped gathering their belongings and stared at him. "That's what Rick always called you. I don't remember why."

"Weird name. I need to pee."

"No time for that. You'll have to hold it."

Mara checked to see if the hallway was clear. There was lots of activity, but no one was near Johnny's room. She motioned for him to go and walked beside him.

They only made it twenty feet when someone behind them said, "Ma'am, where are you going? The doctor is admitting your son." The nurse ran up behind them waving the forms. Mara ignored her and kept walking, but the nurse caught up to them and blocked their path. "Did you not understand that the doctor wants Kyle to stay? He has a concussion that needs to be monitored."

"I understood," Mara said. "I'm a nurse and can look after him. I'm taking care of my sick mother, too. I can't leave her alone. We need to go."

Mara pushed the nurse out of the way and squeezed Johnny's elbow to get him moving.

The nurse didn't follow but called out to them. "You'll need to sign forms saying that you're checking him out against medical advice."

"Keep moving," Mara hissed at Johnny.

They went as fast as Johnny could manage but didn't make it through the door before the doctor came running after them and blocked their exit. He was a large man. Mara wouldn't be able to shove him out of the way as she had done with the nurse.

"Where are you taking your son? He needs a hospital."

Mara crossed her arms and stood as tall as she could manage. "I'm a nurse and can take care of my son. You can't force us to stay. Please get out of our way."

The doctor shifted his gaze to Johnny and searched his face. "Do you want to leave?"

"Yes. She'll take care of me. I want my own bed."

The doctor turned back to Mara. "Can you at least give us a local address so we have it on record? Did you leave a contact number so we can call and check on Scout?"

Mara hesitated before nodding. The doctor handed her Johnny's forms. She scribbled the address for the rental house and her old cell number on the back. She knew he wanted the info to send social services. She'd done it enough times with patients herself to know the drill. He wasn't buying her story. Fortunately, the info she gave him was bogus.

She handed him the paper, and he stepped aside to let them pass. She straightened her shoulders and did her best to hide her shaking hands as she got Johnny moving toward the door. She hardly breathed until she was driving out of the parking lot. She glanced at Johnny, but his eyes were closed, and he didn't seem to care about what had just happened. She'd have answers ready when he had the strength to ask.

FROM THE WAY Johnny's head pounded, he could guess what it felt like to get struck by lightning.

"Open your eyes," a voice that was muffled and distant said. Was he underwater? His shoulder shook which sent another lightning bolt through his brain. "Johnny, wake up. We're here," the voice said. It was louder and clearer.

He opened his eyes for a second before slamming them shut. He was facing directly into the sun. The pain went from a lightning bolt to an electrical storm. Why was this person torturing him? He rotated his head to face her and concentrated hard to focus on her face. His heart sank when he realized it was Mara.

Before she woke him, he'd been dreaming that he was hanging out at Darnell's and had a headache from too many hours staring at video games. He lowered his eyelids hoping to slip back into his dream-world, but Mara unhooked his seatbelt and leaned his seat forward.

"You have to stay awake. I need you to get out of the car. I'll walk you to the door and let you lie down once we're in the house."

Johnny squinted at her. "House?"

She glanced away and said, "Well, sort of."

Johnny craned his neck to look beyond her. They were in a place he didn't recognize. "Is this a trailer park? Where are we?"

"It's our new temporary home. I had to find it online in a hurry. No one will ask questions here."

She put Johnny's crutches in his hand and lifted his elbow to get him moving. He moaned and took three attempts to get on his feet. Mara kept her hands on his waist and steered him toward the house. The trailer-home was the ugliest one Johnny had ever seen.

He stopped before they reached the three rickety wooden steps leading to the door. "You expect me to live here? This thing looks like it will tip over any second."

"I came here and checked it out while they were running tests on you. It's more stable than it looks. The inside isn't too bad and it's clean." She swiveled her head to see if anyone was watching. "Come on, you're almost there."

Johnny was shocked that he made it up the steps without keeling over. He noticed the padlock on the outside of the door as he passed. *Why would anyone have a lock on the outside?* he wondered.

When his eyes adjusted to the darkness inside, he almost

turned and went back to the car. "You and I have very different ideas of what 'not too bad' means." He dropped onto a worn and dusty couch with sunken cushions. He felt the springs poking through the seat of his jeans.

"Quit complaining. This was the best I could do with short notice. If you'd obeyed me and not gone to the hotel lobby, you could still be there in your comfy bed." She handed him two pills and bottled water. "Take these."

Johnny eagerly swallowed the pills, anxious for the sweet relief from his pain. "Where's my room? I do have a bed, don't I?"

Mara pointed to the far end of the trailer. "Over there. After I rented this place, I bought clean bedding and towels while you were knocked out at the hospital. Go lie down while I get our stuff out of the car."

"You left me alone at the hospital? What kind of mother are you?"

"The kind that wants to get you out of this city as soon as she can. A week's rent here is cheaper than one night at that hotel. You left me no choice."

"Sure, blame it on me," he mumbled. "Are you running out of money?"

"It's getting low, but we'll survive. I'd paid for two more nights at the hotel, so that money's down the toilet, not to mention the rest of the month's rent at my house. I've been thinking of sneaking my mail out of the box at the rental house. The feds must know I'm not going back there by now. They might not be watching the place. If I can get my last paycheck, we'll leave for Portland as soon as you're well."

Johnny's heart sank further. He needed a get-away plan from this nut job before she either killed him or carted him off to Portland, but he smiled and said, "Sounds good. Can you help me up?"

Mara rushed to his side like a caring mother. The memory of what had really happened that morning had come back to him during the drive from the hospital. It made Johnny sick to see her act that way after what she'd done to him.

She got him to his room and eased him onto the bed. He scooted to the headboard, and she propped him up on pillows.

"Don't lie flat. Let me know if you get nauseated or dizzy. Those pain meds should start working soon. You'll need to eat and take your other meds, so you don't have another seizure."

"Fine."

Johnny closed his eyes hoping it would coax her to leave and smiled when it worked. When he heard her footsteps retreating down the hallway, he opened his eyes to check out his fourth bedroom in less than a week. The windows had thick plaid curtains that blocked most of the light but left enough for him to see the small room. The bed was a twin, but at least it was long enough for his legs. There was a small, banged-up dresser against one wall and an ancient looking trunk against the other. He shuddered to think of what might be hiding in it. The only other fixture in the room was a tiny closet. He wasn't any more excited to look in there.

The vinyl floor was faded and creaked in places. Johnny worried the floorboards wouldn't support his weight, and he'd end up in the dirt and weeds under the trailer. As much as he didn't want to go to Portland, he didn't want to stay in that disgusting place a minute longer than he had to. If his bedroom was that bad, he could only imagine the horrors that awaited him in the bathroom.

Mara came in with his belongings and piled them on the dresser. "Feeling any better?"

"Not yet. I need food. Pain meds make me sick on an empty stomach. I also need to pee." He ignored the pounding in his head as he swung his feet to the floor and picked up his crutches. "Please tell me I don't have to go in an outhouse."

Mara put her hands on her hips. "Seriously, princess? We have indoor plumbing. Haven't you ever been camping?"

He braced his weight on the crutches and lifted himself off the bed. "Lots of times, but I'm not exactly in a condition to rough it."

While Mara guided him down the hall, she said, "The bathroom is fine. I think the owner must have refurbished recently. We don't have much food. There are some crackers and cheese packs left. I'll get settled and try to find a store nearby. I'm not familiar with this part of Richmond."

"Which part of Richmond?"

Mara's lips tightened into a straight line. Johnny would have to find a way to figure that out on his own.

When they got to the bathroom, Mara reached around him and switched on the light. Johnny had been dreading the condition of the bathroom but was pleasantly surprised by what he saw. The shower was tiny like the closet in his room, but it looked new and shiny like the rest of the fixtures. He wondered why the owner had fixed up the bathroom and left the rest of the place like a dump. Maybe he'd run out of money halfway through renovations.

"Can you manage on your own?"

Johnny pointed a crutch at the hallway. When Mara backed out, he slammed the door in her face. He'd expected to find her waiting outside when he was finished but heard sounds coming from his bedroom instead. He shuffled down the hall and watched from the doorway as Mara unpacked his backpack. She turned and handed him two packets of cheese and crackers with his water bottle.

"You've perked up a bit. How's the head?"

He moved to his bed and laid down. "Better. The pills are kicking in."

"Will you be all right alone while I get groceries?"

"I'm hoping to sleep, but if not, I promise to stay on this bed."

Mara nodded and crossed her arms. "Make sure you do. With that concussion, you need to stay as still and calm as possible. I shouldn't be gone for more than thirty minutes." She stepped to the bed and shined her phone light in each of his eyes. "Your pupils are equal and responsive. That's a good sign, but we have to be careful. Be back soon."

Johnny relaxed when he heard the sound of her car fading. He unwrapped his crackers and munched away while he started planning his exit strategy. He wanted to check out the rest of the trailer, but he'd meant what he said about staying in bed. He could feel the pain meds taking effect, and he'd been wobbly on his way back from the bathroom. He'd have to wait for the next time Mara left him alone to map out his surroundings the way his dad had taught him to do.

GRACE FOLLOWED Agent Shepherd to the table where she'd sat the night before while viewing security footage. "Here we are again," she said.

Ryan took the chair next to her "What are we looking for this time? Grace has identified Mara."

"This won't take long. We'll start the playback at the point Mara approaches the hotel registration desk. The feed is much clearer this time. She doesn't hide her face," Agent Shepherd said. She glanced at the lab tech standing at the end of the table. "And there's something more you need to see."

Shepherd nodded at the tech. He pressed play on the recording. Grace was glad to see that Mara had taken Johnny to a decent hotel. At least she was still taking care of him. Grace watched as a woman in a baseball cap approached the desk. When she smiled at the clerk, Grace had no doubt it was Mara.

"It's her. I'm sure," Grace said.

"She looks like an average mom on vacation. She could be anyone, but seeing her gives me chills," Ryan said.

Shepherd typed something into the tablet propped on the

table behind them. "We wanted additional verification." She motioned for the tech to pause the video and held up a photo for them to see. "This is the computer rendering of how she might look now."

Grace examined the image. It looked exactly as Mara had when Grace saw her for the first time fourteen years earlier. "Now I have shivers," she said.

"Switch to the next segment, please," Shepherd told the tech.

An ATM in a hotel hallway came up but no Mara. Ten seconds later, a teenage boy on crutches appeared on the monitor. Grace was confused. The boy was Johnny's height, but he was wearing a hoodie she didn't recognize, and he had short, black spikey hair. His ears were pierced, and he had a nose ring. Was he posing as Johnny to throw law enforcement off Mara's trail?

"Who are we looking at?" Ryan asked.

"Just wait," Shepherd said.

The camera angle changed when the boy walked to the ATM. When he raised his eyes to read the screen, Grace gasped. It was her Johnny, but not her Johnny.

She watched, mesmerized, while he withdrew cash. When he turned and walked away, the camera angle changed again, and Johnny appeared at a small hotel market. He chose various items that Grace recognized as his favorite snacks. He carried them to the small shop window and paid the desk clerk before shoving them in his pockets.

Grace jumped out of her chair and backed away from the table. The tech paused the video, and he and Shepherd stared at her. Ryan came to her side and put his arm around her waist.

"Start it over," Grace ordered.

The tech glanced at Shepherd, and she nodded, so he replayed the clip.

As Grace watched, her breaths came faster and faster until she struggled to draw air and her legs gave out. Between gasps, she said, "What has that bitch done to my son?"

Ryan offered his hand to help her up, but she brushed it aside and climbed to her feet. She leaned close to the monitor and stroked her fingers over the screen. "When was this?" she whispered.

"Yesterday around noon. We estimate it was when Mara was in Waynesboro. As far as the hotel staff could tell, Johnny and Mara were there until this morning. Agent Reid's team just missed them by hours," Shepherd said.

Grace dropped into her chair when the video ended. "Waynesboro was yesterday? Seems like days ago." She pointed at the monitor. "Again, please."

Ryan moved close to the monitor as Grace had done. "If not for the crutches, I wouldn't recognize him if I passed him on the street. It's disturbing."

They watched the video through again. "One more time," Grace said when it finished.

"We can't stay here all night replaying this," Ryan said to Grace before turning to Shepherd. "Can we have a copy to take home?"

"I'll check on that, but it probably won't be ready until tomorrow noon at the earliest. Most of the techs are gone for the night." She gestured for Ryan to sit and took a chair facing them. "I have more to tell you. They found traces of blood in their hotel room. It was Johnny's."

Her words were a punch in Grace's gut. "What?" she gasped. "How much blood?"

"Very little. We decided to tell you because we're checking hospitals in the area, hoping Mara took him to one. The best-case scenario is that he had a seizure. Mara hasn't shown signs of violence toward Johnny that we've been able to ascertain. I haven't received word yet, but Agent Reid will report to the ASAC as soon as there is any information."

"Hospitals," Grace said. She stood to look for her phone until she remembered that she'd had to leave it downstairs. "Is there a phone I can use? I need to call Alec."

Ryan raised his eyebrows. "Right now? Why?"

"There's something about Mara. I need to confirm it with Alec."

Shepherd led her to a desk in the bullpen. "There you go. Dial nine for an outside line. Be aware the call will be recorded."

Grace called Alec's number and drummed her fingers on the desk while she waited for her to pick up.

"You nearly gave me a heart attack, Grace. I was asleep. What's happening? Is there news from Jason or Wes?"

"No news. I have an important question. Think hard before answering. When Mara called us on Johnny's second birthday to tell us she was the one who kidnapped him, did she tell us she was a nurse?"

The line went quiet for about five seconds. "Yes, I think she did. She said she had such an easy time kidnapping Johnny because she was a nurse and knew her way around hospitals."

"That's what I remembered. Thanks, Alec." Grace hung up and turned to Shepherd. "Mara's a nurse. We know she'd been in Richmond for at least two months probably more. How has she been living? She'd need money for rent and food, and Johnny's medications. She could have been working at a hospital. Nurses are fingerprinted at Virginia hospitals. If Mara were hired at one, they'd have her on file. While you're looking for Johnny, search for Mara, too."

Ryan hugged her. "Thank goodness for that incredible memory of yours."

"We'll get the techs started on that before I leave," Shepherd said.

"I have contacts in the medical community all over Richmond. I'll start contacting them in the morning." Grace took Ryan's hands. "Let's get out of here. Alec's interview is early tomorrow, and I want to make a list of contacts." She turned back to Shepherd. "Call any time with news. I won't be sleeping tonight."

Shepherd nodded and headed for the door but stopped when Grace turned to the monitor. She kissed her fingers and pressed them to the screen.

"Goodnight, my little man. We're going to find you. Just hang on a little longer."

CHAPTER FIFTEEN

GRACE'S PHONE vibrated and startled her out of a dead sleep. Her face was smashed on the dining room table in a puddle of drool. She'd expected to be awake all night but surrendered to her fatigue around two. She picked up her phone and saw it was Jason. She glanced at the time. It was five minutes to six.

As soon as Grace answered, Jason said, "I have to be quick. Jen's water broke an hour ago. They've been prepping her for a C-Section. They tested the babies' lungs. Both are developed enough for delivery. They may have to stay for a week or so, but the pediatrician is confident they'll be fine."

Tears of happiness, frustration and concern filled Grace's eyes. "That's great news, Jason. Ryan and I wish we could be there more than you'll ever know. We love you both. We'll be praying and waiting for pictures. Please give Jen a hug and kiss from us."

"We understand why you can't be here, Grace. We love you, too. Don't worry. Jen and the babies are doing fine. We weren't expecting them to make an entrance today, but we're thrilled. I'll be in touch the second the babies arrive." Grace heard Jason talking to someone before he came back on. "Jen's ready. I have to go. Talk to you soon."

"Thanks for calling Jason and congratulations."

The line went quiet. Grace wiped her face with a crumpled napkin left from dinner the night before and sighed as she stared at the screen. The anger and bitterness toward Mara that she'd struggled to suppress erupted. Once again, Mara was siphoning joy from her life.

"I hate you, Mara," she said to the silent room. "I hate you, and I'm coming for you."

Her phone buzzed again, and she growled at it until she saw it was Wes. "Good morning. Do I want to know the reason for this call or not?"

"Yes and no. Sorry to call so early. Did I wake you?"

She told him about Jason's call and said, "I'm furious that I can't be there for Jen and Jason. I'm trying to stay in control, but it's not working. I've been beaten, neglected and abandoned in my past, but I've never hated anyone like I do Mara. Is it wrong that I do?"

"I'd be worried if you didn't. Don't try to ignore or suppress it. Take your feelings out and look them in the eye. There will be time for forgiveness later. For now, face how you're feeling honestly. Pretending those feelings don't exist is unhealthy."

"How psychological of you. You sound like Adam, but thanks for the pep talk. I needed that. Now, about why you called?"

"We found the hospital where Mara took Johnny. It's just north of the city."

Grace sat up straighter and her heartbeat quickened. "Is he there? Can we see him?"

"No, I'm sorry to say he's gone. Mara told the doctor that Johnny had a seizure and hit his head on the toilet. The doc was skeptical when he saw how Johnny reacted to her explanation, but Mara said they were from Oregon so that doc didn't suspect he was Johnny. His name was listed as Kyle Brennen on his ID."

"What's his condition? He must have been well enough to leave, right?"

"He has a concussion, but otherwise, he's fine. The doctor wanted to admit him, but Mara checked him out AMA. The good news is that he was able to walk out when they left. The doc said Johnny should be fine in a few days with rest, and he hasn't shown up in any other medical facility so far. We'll keep checking."

Grace was shocked but relieved that Johnny was able to walk after the seizure. That usually wasn't the case, so his condition must not have been critical. The fact that Mara was a nurse gave Grace some comfort. Johnny should have been in a hospital, but hopefully, Mara knew what she was doing.

"Kyle was the name Mara gave him when she kidnapped him as a baby," Grace said. "If Johnny didn't contradict her to the doctors or nurses, he must be terrified of her."

"Don't jump to conclusions, Grace. The doctor said Johnny was disoriented when they got there. He might have just been confused."

"Hope you're right. Who was the doctor?" She was encouraged when Wes gave her the name. He was a neurologist Grace knew and respected, and she'd sat on a seminar panel with him once. "He's a good man. I'll go see him after Alec's interview. Any more news for me?"

"Between evidence we gathered from the hotel, the hospital, and Mara's house and bank accounts in Portland, she won't be able to sneeze without us knowing. We found out that she was working as a nurse in Portland, so that was an excellent call on your part. We're contacting hospitals here to see if she's employed at any of them. It's no longer a matter of if we catch her but when. The noose is tightening, Grace."

"You can't imagine how happy I am to hear that. With the reward, the FBI on her heels and the national coverage of Alec's interview today, she won't have anywhere to run. I just hope Johnny can hold on until we find her."

"He sounds like a smart, tough kid, and he has amazing parents. My money's on him."

"Thanks again, Wes, but I need to get going. Alec's interview is this morning, and she has to be at the studio in time for the seven-thirty local break on the national news broadcasts."

"Wish her luck for me. I hope it leads to the break we need."

Grace said she would and, after extracting a promise from Wes to keep her updated, she woke Ryan and Alec to fill them in on Jen and Wes' news. She and Ryan went to their room afterward while Alec went downstairs to get dressed.

"What do you have planned today?" she asked him.

He glanced at her and hesitated before saying, "Would you be too mad at me if I go into work? Between Alec's interview and contacting your professional connections to see if they know anything about Mara, you have important things to do, but there's nothing I can do here. I need a distraction from obsessing about Johnny. I need to feel useful."

Grace wrapped her arms around him and kissed his cheek. "I understand and won't be mad at all. Just promise to keep your phone handy."

"I will if you promise to call me with the slightest bit of news, or even just to tell me you love me."

"That's a promise. Wes said the noose is tightening on Mara. Do you believe that?"

"I do. With the media coverage and Wes on her heels, it won't be long before they rat her out, and I keep hoping Johnny will find a way to escape. Even if he doesn't come here, just getting away from her will be a victory."

She pulled him tighter and rested her head on his chest. "Be careful today. I'll check in as often as I can. I hope you know I love you and couldn't survive this without you."

Ryan kissed the top of her head. "I do. I feel the same. Call as soon as the interview ends. I love you."

Grace nodded and watched him go, hoping she'd have good news the next time they spoke.

GRACE WAS quiet as Alec drove them to the local network studio for her interview. Returning to the studio dredged up unwelcome feelings of interviews she'd done during Johnny's ordeal as a baby. Nothing but Alec's request that she come along for moral support could have enticed her to set foot in that building. She was just glad she'd be behind the camera instead of in front of it.

"I'm nervous," Alec said, startling Grace out of her thoughts. "I'm usually excited about these interviews."

"This isn't a typical interview," Grace said quietly. "There's much more riding on it than book sales."

Alec squeezed her hand. "Book sales mean nothing to me now. I'm doing it for the national exposure to bring results in finding Johnny. I hope you believe that. I'm glad Wes called this morning. It's a relief knowing Johnny is alive and still in Richmond."

"I believe you, and I hope it stays that way long enough for Wes to catch Mara. She could get spooked and take off to Portland or wherever."

"Something is keeping her here. That gives us the advantage."

Grace nodded and looked out the window wondering how long it would be before they discovered where Mara was hiding.

GRACE SAT BY HERSELF, facing the set where they would film Alec's segment, while she waited for taping to start. When she and Alec arrived at the studio, the producer offered her hopes that the broadcast would lead to the speedy capture of Mara and the recovery of Johnny. After Grace thanked her, the producer explained that the first broadcast would play live on the local affiliates and would be followed by typed replays each half hour. She was confident that the national broadcast and cable networks would pick it up and replay it during their morning shows.

Grace's heart raced as Alec and the anchor doing the inter-view took their seats facing each other. As the makeup artist touched up Alec's face, Grace could see her friend's hands shak-ing. She flashed Alec a smile and mouthed that she would do just fine. Grace shouldn't have worried. The instant the camera's rolled, Alec became her poised and confident self.

The interviewer was a young man named Ethan James. He'd interviewed Alec before, so she felt comfortable with him. He was trying to get name recognition in a cut-throat business so he could be aggressive, but fair. He introduced Alec and welcomed her.

Ethan: "Tell us about your book which releases tomorrow. This is a drastic departure from your children's books isn't it?"

Alec: "Before we get to that, I want to thank you for agreeing to have me here on such short notice."

Ethan: "We're privileged to have you."

Alec: "Thank you. To answer your question, *Baby John Doe* is a very different project for me, and one I've worked on for years. Having personal involvement with the subject matter makes it all that much more important to me, especially now."

Ethan: "Can you please tell us about it?"

Alec: "Of course."

Alec gave the summary of "Baby John Doe" that the copy-writer had given her. It felt strange for Grace to hear Alec discussing her life right in front of her as if she was just some character from a novel.

Ethan: "Many of us remember this story playing out in the news, although I was still in high school at the time. Why have you waited so long to publish the book?"

Alec: "Partly because I didn't become a writer for several years after these events, and also to have time to do the research and gather all the facts. Some of the criminal trials went on for years."

Ethan: "Are those the only reasons?"

Alec froze, and Grace could see her figuring out how to answer.

Alec: "Yes, those are the only reasons, other than the fact that I was recovering from a rock-climbing accident."

Ethan: "Yes, most of us are familiar with your accident, but for those who aren't, can you tell us what happened?

Alec: "Of course, Ethan. My husband and I were on a rock-climbing trip in Alaska for our tenth anniversary. My equipment malfunctioned and I fell nearly thirty feet." She paused for dramatic effect. "I fractured my spine along with other serious injuries. I was fortunate to have survived, let alone be able to walk. That might not have happened without Grace's support and encouragement. Learning to walk again was painful and challenging, and I gave up. It was Johnny who convinced me I could do it, and Grace who gave me the courage to see it through. Johnny was also the one who encouraged me to become a writer."

Ethan: "We're grateful he did. It's a heart-warming story. So, this is what prompted you to write the book?"

Alec: "In part, but I had many reasons. One of the biggest is to help women see that they don't have to have superpowers to overcome their challenges. It's my deep conviction that ordinary women, which I consider myself to be, have the capacity to overcome seemingly insurmountable trials. Grace's story is proof of that conviction."

Ethan: "Admirable. I have another question that might be more difficult to answer. Isn't it a bit of a coincidence that your book hits the shelves tomorrow, a week after Johnny's abduction?"

Alec: "I'm not sure what you mean, but yes, it is a terrible coincidence. I would have preferred the book to come out under much more favorable circumstances."

Ethan: "What I mean, Mrs. Emerson, is that many find it curious that your book goes on sale exactly when the subjects of the story are all over the news."

Alec: "What are you implying. Ethan?"

Ethan: "I'm not implying anything. I'm stating it outright. Did you manufacture this news story to coincide with the release of your book? I've been in this business long enough to know that coincidences are rare. This feels more like an expertly manufactured publicity stunt."

Alec's poise and composure disappeared as she sat forward and stared at Ethan with her mouth hanging open.

Ethan: "I take your reaction as confirmation."

Alec: "My reaction is shock that you'd have the audacity to suggest such a thing. Are you assuming that I paid off the FBI and local law enforcement to put on a show for the country? You're accusing me of a federal crime."

Ethan: "I'm saying law enforcement has nothing to do with this because they know it's a publicity stunt."

Grace jumped out of her chair and was about to run on to the set when someone grabbed her arms from behind and stopped her. She turned to find the producer grinning at her. Grace tried to break free, but she held her tighter. Alec slowly stood and balled her fists.

Alec: "How dare you accuse me of such a thing. Johnny and Grace are family. I would never exploit their tragedy. Not for money, fame or any reason. You think I'm some heartless PR mastermind?"

Alec turned to the camera and pointed at Ethan, who sat grinning like the cat who caught the rat.

Alec: "Ignore this self-absorbed weasel. Johnathan Walker's abduction is real. He's been kidnapped by the woman named Mara who also kidnapped him on the day he was born. I'm not here to sell books. I'm here to plead with all of you to please help us find Johnny and bring Mara to justice. The number and web address for the tip-line is scrolling across the screen. Please, help us."

Alec tore off her microphone and stomped off the set. She pushed the producer aside and took Grace's hand. They heard the crew applauding as they left the studio.

When they reached the parking lot, Grace tugged on Alec's hand to get her to stop and swung her around to face her.

"That's it? You're just going to leave? You need to go back in there and stand up to that little prick," Grace said.

Alec put her hands on her hips and locked her eyes on Grace. "That would be playing into his hands. He was baiting me and trying to manufacture a scandal. The point of this interview was to get the public to help find Johnny, not pump up the latest news cycle or Ethan's career. I said what I came to say."

"But what if people believe him? This could destroy all our efforts."

"Reasonable people will believe the truth. Going back in there would only backfire," Alec said, before marching to the car.

Grace watched her go and knew she should follow, but she was tempted to go defend her friend and salvage the situation. They needed any help they could get to rescue her boy, but the interview had been a catastrophe. When Alec waved her to the car, Grace decided to trust her and hope the aftermath wouldn't be as big of a disaster as she feared.

"OH, MY GOD," Wes whispered when the news segment ended. He and his team had watched Alec's interview in the conference room with the Assistant Special Agent in Charge, Jamal Wilson. "That was a train wreck. Could anyone possibly believe Johnny's abduction is a hoax?"

"People are so cynical these days that they'll believe any conspiracy theory that comes along," Wilson said. "Facts are worthless. Elliott, get the techs on this to see if it's viral yet."

"Yes, sir," Elliott said and rushed out of the conference room.

"I'll notify Michaels myself and get him down here. I told him we'd cover things so he could come in later today. He was here until two-thirty this morning."

"He's taking this personally since he was on the case when Mara got away with kidnapping Johnny the first time. I'm letting him and the Walkers down. We have piles of evidence, but I still can't get my hands on Mara. Now this," Wes said and pointed at the screen.

"Don't blame yourself, boss," Prince said. "People with half a brain will see the interview for the grab at sensationalism it is."

"Keep following up with the hospitals and medical offices. We'll keep a close eye on the tip-lines. If they drop off, we may have to manipulate that media to our advantage even though I hate to justify this with a response," Wilson said.

"I agree, sir," Wes said. "We have enough to keep us busy until we wait for the fallout."

Wilson left to contact Michaels, and Wes sent the rest of his team back to their assignments before replaying the interview. Seeing that smug upstart Ethan made Wes sick. The only satisfaction he derived was from Alec calling him a self-absorbed weasel. *That guy had better hope he never comes face to face with me*, Wes thought. *I'll do more than call him names.*

Johnny felt worse when he woke up the next morning. The knot on his head had doubled in size and throbbed like someone was using it for a drum. He sat on the edge of the bed and gave himself time to get his balance before daring to go to the bathroom. Even though his head was killing him, he wasn't as dizzy, so he took that as a good sign.

He went to the living room after using the bathroom, hoping Mara was gone, but she was sitting at the small table in the corner of the kitchen. She got up and helped him to his chair.

"What are you doing out of bed? I was just getting ready to check on you and bring breakfast. How are you feeling?"

"Like my head's going to explode. Do you have any more of those pain pills?" Johnny asked, while Mara checked his pupils and bump.

"Enough for today and tomorrow, but we'll have to manage with ibuprofen and acetaminophen after that, but your pain should have lessened by then." She slid two muffins and a bowl of fruit across the table. "I'll get you some juice and milk. You didn't eat much, and you need to drink as much water as you can."

Johnny watched her pouring the orange juice that he didn't want. He'd never liked OJ, but Mara wouldn't know that and hadn't bothered to ask.

He looked around the room. "Is there a TV or internet here?"

"Yes, to both, but no cable. The antenna works well enough. The internet is a little slow but usable. It works well enough for you to do homework when you feel better."

Johnny grunted and took a bite of the muffin which he almost spit out after tasting it. "What is that?"

Mara set the juice and milk in front of him. "A gluten-free bran muffin. It was all they had left at the gas station store last night. I found out where a grocery store is near here. Once you're situated, I'll go shopping. You need to eat that so you can take your pills."

The muffin tasted like sawdust, but Johnny choked it down and gulped the OJ to follow. At least he liked milk and fruit.

Mara went to her room and came back, pushing a small TV on a cart. She plugged the TV in where Johnny could see it and adjusted the antenna until there was a clear picture. She flipped through the channels until she found a national news show. Johnny shook his head and went back to eating his fruit.

The anchors covered international and national stories before going to a commercial. When the show came back on, they announced that they had breaking news, and Johnny wondered what the president had done this time. He whipped around to face the TV when he heard the headline.

"Is the abduction of Johnathan Walker fact or fiction? The following is an interview from a local affiliate with author Alec Emerson recorded earlier today."

Johnny was dumbfounded as he watched the replay. As upset as he'd been with Alec for hiding the truth about his past, he couldn't imagine anyone thinking her capable of making up the story of a kidnapping to sell books. Seeing how the interviewer treated her made him furious. Even worse, hearing the anchors discussing his disappearance like it was a joke devastated him.

Mother or not, Johnny was ready to get away from Mara and was hoping the FBI would find them before he had to escape on his own. If they thought the whole thing was a hoax, they might stop looking for him. Tears welled up in his eyes at the thought.

He flinched when Mara started laughing. Johnny wanted to punch her.

"Did you hear that? They're saying the whole thing was a hoax. They'll stop looking for us. It's incredible." When Johnny didn't answer, she turned to face him. "Are you crying? Why? Alec and the Walkers are getting what they deserve. You should be glad."

She'd caught Johnny off guard. He lowered his head and stared at the melon floating in his bowl while he tried to get control of himself.

"I just feel sorry for her. She's not a bad person, and she's telling the truth. You *did* kidnap me," he said, just loud enough for Mara to hear.

She sprang out of her chair and lunged at him with her arm raised but stopped herself from striking. She studied him for a moment and said, "Yeah, she's a decent person, but I didn't kidnap you. You came willingly. You need to toughen up and stop acting like a helpless victim. I'm your real family, and I'm going to take you home where you belong. Forget these people. They're nothing to you."

Johnny kept his eyes lowered. "Sure, Mara, you're right. It's just my headache. I'm sorry."

Mara patted his shoulder. "I forgive you but think before you open your mouth next time."

She returned to watching the news like nothing had happened. Johnny went back to his room without Mara bothering to notice. He crumpled onto the bed and cried into his pillow to muffle the sound of his sobs. He was getting desperate to escape, no matter what he had to risk to do it.

GRACE AND ALEC ranted to each other about the interview during the drive home, but it had done little to alleviate their anger or frustration. Wondering if Alec could have done anything differently was pointless. Ethan had gone into that interview with an agenda and blindsided Alec. Ryan was outraged when Grace called to tell him what had happened and he offered to come home, but Grace told him that as much as she'd love to be with him, it wouldn't make any difference.

"Stay where you are and do some good there. I'll call in an hour."

"I love you. The truth will come out and we'll weather this. It's just a setback," Ryan said.

"Love you, too," Grace said and ended the call.

"Are you still going to talk to your contacts after what's happened?" Alec asked.

"Yes. Ryan's right. The truth will come out soon enough. I'm moving forward despite the interview. What choice do I have? Come with me?"

"You need to keep your distance from me right now. I'm going home to lie low until this blows over." Grace was about to protest, but Alec's phone rang over the car's Bluetooth. "That's my agent. This will be good." Alec pressed the button on her steering wheel to answer. "Hey, Marissa. What took you so long?"

As Grace climbed out of the car, she heard Marissa say, "What in the hell was that?"

CHAPTER SIXTEEN

WES DREADED DELIVERING his latest update to the SAC that afternoon. Alec's interview had gone viral, and it seemed like half the country believed that Johnny's abduction had been an elaborate hoax. They still had their supporters, but the tips-lines had gone silent, and the evidence from the hospital and Portland had gotten them nowhere. Wes was at a loss for where to turn next.

Michaels was on the phone when Wes got to his office, but he waved him in and ended the call as quickly as he could.

"That was the director," Michaels said. "He called after having a lovely chat with the Attorney General. They agreed the interview makes them look complicit in a publicity stunt. They want to know what we're doing to fix the situation. Half the American public believes we were patsies to a massive fraudulent PR scheme. So, thoughts on damage control?"

Wes shook his head. "In light of other recent scandals the Bureau is facing right now, the only option I see is to hold a press conference. My recommendation is that it be you and Grace. Since the director is a political appointee and you're a career agent, the public might have more faith in you. Having Grace along might regenerate trust and influence emotions. I'm at a loss beyond that."

Michaels studied Wes while he mulled over his suggestion. "Agreed. I'll get public affairs to arrange it as soon as humanly possible. I'll leave it to you to convince Grace. She has an aversion to getting in front of the camera."

"Given the dire circumstances, it won't take much convincing."

Michaels rubbed his forehead. "Do you have any good news to share? God knows I could use some."

"Just bad and worse." Wes looked down at his phone when it buzzed.

He looked at Michaels, who said, "Take the call. Maybe it's that good news we're dying for."

Wes nodded and answered. "This is Special Agent Reid."

The color drained from his face as he listened to the caller.

"Oh, God no, not that. Anything but that. Text the location. I'm on my way," he said and hung up.

"So, not good news," Michaels said.

"The worst possible. You may want to hold off on contacting public affairs. That was the police chief. They've found a body."

WES ARRIVED WITH PRINCE, Elliott, and Cameron at the location the sheriff had given him thirty minutes later. It was a littered, weed-covered lot on the south side of the city. The scene was crawling with Richmond PD and sheriff's deputies. One of the deputies that Wes had met at the Walkers' on the day he arrived in Richmond approached him and extended his hand.

"What do we have?" Wes asked, dreading the answer.

He pointed at two African American men of about nineteen or twenty, standing by their bikes at the edge of the crime scene. Another deputy was questioning them. "Those two were on the way to work when they spotted the body and called 911. They're pretty shaken up. Neither has even seen a dead body."

"The first one's always the worst. Hope it will be their last. How long ago did they find him?" Elliott asked.

"Approximately an hour and forty-five minutes ago. The Medical Examiner beat you here by a few minutes."

"Prince, get forensics down here and guard the crime scene," Wes said. "Do you think it's our boy?" he asked the deputy.

He led Wes to the body without answering. What Wes saw made his breakfast churn in his stomach. He'd seen more dead bodies than he could count, and it never got easier. It was so much worse when it was a child. The body was fresh, and the boy looked to be about Johnny's age and height. There were no crutches at the scene that Wes could see. The corpse's fingertips had been removed and the face was disfigured, so it was impossible to tell if it was Johnny. Even if it wasn't, Wes was sick with grief for the dead boy's parents, whoever they were.

Wes took a breath and knelt to make a closer inspection.

After Wes completed his inspection, the deputy introduced him to the ME, who extended his hand. "Dr. William Forest."

Wes glanced at him as he shook his hand. He was a sturdy, middle-aged man with close-cropped, graying hair. Wes decided he liked him on sight. "Special Agent Reid. Is there anything you can tell me?"

"No bullet or stab wounds that I can see. It appears the body was dumped here post-mortem. Did you see the face? I'd say someone beat this poor soul to death with a baseball bat, but you didn't hear that from me. We're preparing the body for removal now. I've been instructed to make this case a top priority, so I'll begin my examination as soon as we have the body in the lab. May I have your card so I can contact you the instant I have test results?"

Wes took out a card and handed it to Dr. Forest. "I appreciate that. We're facing a firestorm today. The sooner we can put this situation to rest, the better."

Wes asked the deputy who'd interviewed the two witnesses to forward his report to the field office before rounding up his agents. They peppered him with questions on the way back to the office, but he had no answers. The best they could do was wait for the ME's report and hope the corpse was unrelated to their case.

GRACE SAT in her car in the hospital guest parking lot facing the main entrance. She'd been to five other hospitals desperate to find anyone with news of Mara or Johnny. Her friends had been sympathetic, but none had anything useful to tell her. Most of her acquaintances in the medical field had been supportive, but a few eyed her with skepticism. Grace wished she had gone on her quest to the hospitals before Alec's disastrous interview, but she wasn't going to let a little suspicion deter her.

She summoned her courage and forced herself out of the car. The walk to the entrance seemed to fly further away the closer she got, but eventually, she made it through the doors. She bypassed the lobby and went directly to the internal-medicine floor to look for her friend, Amelia, who she'd worked with at Brad Carter's office years earlier. Amelia had left the medical office to take a job at the hospital in the hope of becoming a charge nurse. She and Grace had kept in touch at first and met for the occasional lunch, but Grace hadn't seen her for more than two years. She wasn't sure what kind of reception to expect.

Grace had donned her nurse's uniform and clipped on her ID badge before leaving the house. She didn't have privileges at this hospital, but she hoped to not be too conspicuous. She walked to the nurses' station like she belonged there and asked for Amelia. One of the nurse assistants pointed her to the breakroom and went back to the computer without so much as raising an eyebrow. Grace let out her breath as she made her way down the hallway.

Amelia jumped up and hugged Grace as soon as she walked into the lounge.

"I'm so sorry about what's happened, Grace. I've been thinking about you every minute since I heard about Johnny on the news." She took Grace's hand and led her to a small couch in the corner. "How are you managing? Is there any news?"

All Grace could think was that Amelia had been too busy on her shift to have time to watch the news or check her phone. She was the first person Grace had met with that hadn't seen Alec's interview.

"It's been beyond horrific," Grace said, "but we keep moving forward hoping Johnny will be found any minute. It's all we can do."

Amelia took her hand. "Why are you here? What can I do?"

Grace pulled her hand free and pulled the pictures she had of Mara from her purse. She gave Amelia time to study them before asking if she'd seen Mara working there. Amelia ran out of the room without a word and came back thirty-seconds later with another nurse.

"This is Candice, the charge nurse. Candice, you're probably aware who Grace is," Amelia said.

Grace stood and shook her hand.

"Amelia told me why you're here and showed me the pictures. I think this woman worked here for about two months. She showed up the other day when she wasn't on duty and was acting strangely. I think she was trying to steal drugs. She took off when I confronted her and hasn't shown up for her shifts since."

Grace moved closer to Candice. "Did you report this to the FBI? Didn't you see her photos on the news?"

"Honey, I never have time to watch the news. I've practically been living here. We were short-staffed as it was before Mara bailed. You can't imagine."

"She can, actually," Amelia said. "Grace was the Internal Medicine charge nurse at Richmond City."

Candice nodded. "You understand then?"

"Did Mara ever mention a son? Can you tell me anything else about her?"

"She was an odd one but a hard worker who knew her stuff. She kept to herself most of the time," Candice said. "I never had anything more than job-related conversations with her. Did you, Amelia?"

Amelia shook her head. "I only worked with her a few times. We never spoke much."

"Would you be willing to talk to the FBI and share her records with them? There might be something there that can help us find her," Grace said.

"I'd be honored to do whatever I can to help them capture her and rescue your son."

Tears welled up in Grace's eyes. "You can't imagine how much that means to me after the day, no, the week, I've had." She handed Candice a copy of Wes' business card. "This is the direct line to the commander of the task force looking for Johnny. He'll be thrilled to hear from you." Grace hugged her and Amelia. "I'll let you both get back to work. Amelia, I promise to call if I hear anything. We need to keep in better touch when this nightmare ends."

Amelia kissed her cheek. "I agree. Best of luck. I'll be praying for all of you."

Grace smiled and just managed to make it inside the elevator before breaking down. She pushed the hold button and rested her forehead against the wall while she cried. She had no way of knowing if Candice's information would lead to Johnny, but it had touched her to be reminded that people were good and truly wanted to help them. They would need all the goodwill they could gather to bring her little man home.

WES' team gathered around with the SAC and ASAC in the bullpen while Wes gave his report from the crime scene where the body was discovered.

"My gut tells me it's not Johnny. The evidence doesn't fit. The ME is making the autopsy and ID process top priorities. The victim's face was disfigured, and the fingerprints were removed, but his teeth were intact. Hopefully, his records or DNA are in the system. I'm expecting ID confirmation in the next few hours. It's my opinion this is drug related and has nothing to do with Johnny, but don't quote me."

There was a gasp at the back of the group, and Wes turned to find Steph staring at him with eyes the size of saucers.

When every head turned to face Steph, Wilson said, "Who's that?"

Steph spun around and ran for the stairs before anyone could answer.

"I've got this," Wes said and took off after her. He caught her before she reached the first floor and grabbed her arm to stop her. She struggled to break free, but Wes held tight. "What were you doing in the bullpen? You were supposed to be in the lab."

Steph grabbed Wes' shirt with both hands. "Is Johnny dead? Did you find his body?"

Wes covered her hands with his. "We found a body, but I'm almost positive it's not your brother."

"Almost?" Steph said, and her voice caught. "Just almost positive?"

"I wish I could tell you for certain it's not him, but I can't until we have the report from the ME. I meant it when I said my gut tells me it's not Johnny, and my gut is pretty reliable."

Steph collapsed against him and sobbed on his chest. Wes stroked her hair to calm her. "I'm sorry you heard that, Steph. It wasn't meant for you. These investigations move fast. Evidence and directions change on a dime. It's not Johnny. Trust me."

Steph pulled free and looked up at him. "I want to, Wes, but I'm so scared. I'm putting on a brave act, pretending to be strong for my dad and Grace, but I'm terrified. On top of that, I couldn't be with my sister when my niece and nephew were born. Jason told me it may have been the stress that sent her into labor early, but he made me promise not to tell my parents that. Now, this. What if you're wrong?"

"I'm not, but I'll be here for you no matter what happens. We're getting close to catching Mara and rescuing Johnny. It won't be long now. Go home and rest. Please, don't say anything about this to your family. I'm sorry to ask you to keep another secret, but I don't want them to suspect in case this comes to nothing."

Steph's hands dropped to her side. She stared at Wes before continuing down the stairs without a word. When the stairwell door closed behind her, he sank onto a stair and ran his hands through his hair.

He'd tried to appear as strong and sure of himself to Steph as she with her parents, but he was as scared as she was. He'd told her the truth that he didn't believe the dead boy was Johnny, but there was a minuscule chance it was him. If it was, Wes didn't know how he'd go on knowing he'd failed Steph and her family.

"Please, don't let it be Johnny," he cried to the ceiling before dragging his feet up the stairs to get back to work.

Grace had turned off her phone while she was in the hospital but powered it back on as soon as she was in the parking lot. She had two calls from Jason, one from Ryan and ten texts from the two of them. She smiled and waited until she got in the car to read her messages.

The texts from Jason were mostly pictures of their new little grandbabies. They'd named them Whitney Grace and Zachary James. They were precious, and Grace's tears dripped onto the screen while she swiped through the photos.

Jason's last text said, *Jennifer and babies doing great! We miss you all and can't wait for you to meet Zach and Whitney!*

Neither can we, Grace wrote back. *Hope it's soon. Congratulations again! We'll call you soon.*

She checked Ryan's texts next. They were copies of the pictures Jason had sent.

Aren't they amazing? Talked to Jason. He said they're doing great. I told him to prepare for no sleep for the next eighteen years. I love you. Where are you?

Grace was about to call him when her phone rang. The caller ID said it was Steph.

"Have you seen the pictures of the babies? Aren't they gorgeous?" Grace said before Steph got a word out.

Steph's breath shuttered, and Grace smiled, assuming she was overcome with emotion over the birth of her twin sister's children.

"Grace," she gasped, "I have news."

Grace's gut tightened and bile rose in her throat. "What's happened? Tell me, no matter how terrible."

"They discovered a body. It might be Johnny. Wes swears it's not, but I'm terrified."

The world started to spin, and Grace dropped her phone on the seat. She opened the car door and planted her feet on the pavement before lowering her head between her knees.

"Grace, are you there?" she heard Steph's muffled voice saying.

She stretched her arm behind her and felt for her phone. "I'm here," she said without raising her head. "What did Wes tell you? Where's the body?"

"It's at the ME's lab. They're waiting for ID." The line went quiet for several seconds. "The boy's fingerprints were cut off, and the face was disfigured. They're hoping to identify him with dental records and DNA."

"I know the ME. I'm going to his office."

"Is it safe for you to drive?"

Grace got out of the car and took a few steps. "I'm fine. Just shocked. Stephanie, please don't tell your dad or anyone else about this until I contact you. Promise me."

"I promise. Just don't take too long. This is torture."

"Go home and wait for my call. I'm not far from the ME's office." She took a few breaths and climbed into the car. "If Wes says it's not Johnny, it's not. I trust him. It's not Johnny. It can't be."

She hung up and started the car. Her hands shook on the steering wheel, but nothing could stop her from finding out the truth about that body in the morgue.

THE DISTANCE from the hospital to the ME's office was short, but the drive felt like it took an eternity. Grace refused to let herself think about where she was headed and forced herself to focus on her new grandchildren getting their first view of the world.

She parked and marched to the door without giving herself a chance to lose her nerve. What she faced inside that building could be the realization of her worst nightmare, but she had to know. She walked through the entrance like she belonged there and hoped the fact that she was wearing her nurse's uniform and badge would prevent suspicion.

No one so much as gave her a second glance as she made her way to the forensic pathology lab. She found her way with no trouble. There was a shelf with sterile clothing outside the door. She took the time to put on a gown, mask and gloves before reaching for the door. Her hand hovered over the handle as she struggled to force herself to turn it. She could see the ME and his assistants through the window as they surrounded a body on the table. She found her courage to enter after the third try and burst into the room.

The ME's head snapped up, and he swung around to face her. His eyes widened when he recognized her. "Grace Walker? What are you doing? You're not authorized to be here."

A beanpole of a young man standing next to the ME stepped between Grace and the table. Grace ducked past him and pushed her way closer to the body.

"I'm sorry, William, but I have to know if it's him. That could be my son lying there."

William left the table and motioned for his team to give them space. William stopped two feet from Grace and blocked her view of the body.

"I'm sorry for what's happening to you, Grace, but the FBI shouldn't have informed you about this. It's an official part of the investigation. There's more than just my butt on the line."

Grace hadn't seen William for three years, but she'd known him for more than twenty. He saw dead bodies every day, but this was different. He knew her history with Johnny. She searched the eyes behind his protective glasses hoping to find empathy and compassion.

"They didn't tell me," she said softly. "I found out by accident. I know you have protocols, and I respect that, but this is my Johnny we're talking about. If that's not enough to convince you, I can save you and every law enforcement agency in the state hours or even days of time and effort if you let me give a visual ID. Please, William."

His jaw clenched, and his lips tightened, but Grace saw him wavering. Aside from their personal connection, she could tell he was calculating the time and effort that would be spared if she identified the body on his slab.

William stepped to the side and waved his hand for her to pass. She gave a slight bow and started for the table but only made it a few steps before her feet refused to budge like they'd become glued to the floor. William pressed his hand into the small of her back to get her moving. She lowered her eyes and took the last steps to reach the body. She could feel the eyes of William's team on her.

"Take your time," William said. "I'm glad the days of having next of kin come in to identify bodies are behind us. I know this must be torture. Just remember your medical training, take a breath and examine the body."

Grace nodded and raised her chin. What she saw wasn't what she'd expected. The victim's face was so bruised and distorted that it was hard to tell he was human, but that didn't matter to Grace. It only took seconds for her to determine that it was not her Johnny. Her relief was so overwhelming that her legs started to give way. The young woman standing next Grace caught her under the arms and lowered her to the floor.

"No, Grace. Is it him? Is that Johnny? I was so sure it wasn't," William said.

Grace pulled her knees up and wrapped her arms around them. She tried to answer but words wouldn't come. Someone put a bottled water into her hand. She twisted the cap off and took a gulp.

"It's not Johnny," she croaked and took another drink. "Even with the injuries to this poor boy, I can tell it's not Johnny. Body shape is all wrong."

William removed his glasses and gloves and ran his hand over his face. "Thank God," he whispered. "Help Grace to a chair." The beanpole intern lifted Grace to her feet and guided her to a plastic chair on the far side of the room. William turned to his team. "Let's take a ten-minute break."

His staff stripped off their sterile clothing and tossed them into a biohazard receptacle before filing out of the room. A few nodded and smiled at Grace as they left. When they were alone, Grace stood and hugged William, ignoring the tears streaming down her cheeks. She still didn't trust her legs when she backed away, so she dropped back into the chair. William handed Grace her water and sat on a rolling stool facing her.

Grace wiped her face on her gown and sipped her water. "I'm so elated. Johnny's still missing, but there's hope. It would have killed me if that had been my boy."

"It wouldn't have, but you would have been facing a nightmare time. The months, or maybe years after we lost Marissa were unbearable, and we knew her death was coming. You think you're prepared, but you never are. We survived it, though. Diana even laughs and smiles again and is able to focus on the other kids. Chelsy is pregnant with our first grandchild."

Grace squeezed William's hand and smiled. "Ryan's daughter, Jennifer, gave birth to twins this morning." She took her phone out of her pocket and showed him a picture.

"Beautiful." He handed the phone back and crossed his arms. "You have been through the wringer today. Does Jennifer live in Richmond?"

"No, DC. Who knows when we're going to get to meet the babies? Did you see Alec's interview?"

He looked away which told Grace all she needed to know. "Damned media."

The feeling had returned to Grace's legs, so she stood and removed her sterile clothing. After throwing it away, she glanced at the body. "Feels wrong to sit here chatting in front of that poor soul. I'm beyond ecstatic that Johnny's alive, but he's someone's son. I feel guilty for feeling this happy with him in the room. Some mother is going to get terrible news soon."

William stood and followed Grace to the door. "I get so focused on my investigations sometimes that I forget these victims aren't just evidence. I needed this reminder. I suspect that he was involved in a drug deal gone bad, but he was a person."

"I need to call Stephanie and Agent Reid."

"Leave Reid to me." William rubbed his chin. "How am I

going to explain IDing the victim so quickly? He had no dental records on file, and the initial DNA analysis won't be back for hours."

"Have you done x-rays?" When William nodded, she said, "Did he have signs of healing from an old fracture on his right forearm?"

William went to a laptop sitting on the counter. He searched through some images and shook his head.

"Tell the FBI you compared Johnny's medical records to the victim, and they didn't match," Grace said. "You would have done that, right?"

"That works." He walked back to Grace and took her hands. "Congratulations for this and the new grandbabies. The four of us should have dinner once Johnny is home, and this nightmare is over and done."

Grace kissed his cheek. "I don't know how to thank you. You didn't have to do this. I owe you more than you'll ever know."

"It was worth it. Now, get out of here. I need to re-scrub before my team gets back."

Grace gave a small wave as she went into the hallway and fought the urge to run back to her car. She called Steph the instant she was in the parking lot. When she gave her the news, Steph broke down and sobbed into the phone.

Grace let her cry it out. When Steph quieted, she said, "Don't ever tell anyone about this. It's our secret. Your dad would kill me if he knew I stormed in here, especially without him."

"I agree, but has it occurred to you we could still have to face the same situation? I'm trying not to admit it to myself, but it could happen. Maybe we should be preparing ourselves for the worst now that we know what to expect."

"No, Steph. I refuse to think that way. I wish you'd never overheard Wes talking about the body. Whatever Mara's twisted plan is, killing Johnny isn't part of it. She loves him in her own sick way. You need to remember that and focus on finding Johnny, nothing more. Promise me."

"Fine, but I have no idea what to do next. I think it would be best to avoid the field office for now."

"Probably. Have you talked to Jen?" Grace asked to change the subject. "It would be good for both of you if you called and raved over her little darlings. Aren't they gorgeous? I can't wait to meet them."

Steph gushed about her new niece and nephew as Grace drove for home. She was glad to have distracted Steph from the harrowing ordeal they'd experienced and hoped her stepdaughter wouldn't suffer any lasting trauma. Grace hoped the same for herself but knew it would take time to erase the image of that brutally murdered boy from her mind.

CHAPTER SEVENTEEN

THERE WAS a car Grace didn't recognize in the driveway when she got home. She was too exhausted to give it much thought. A stream of unfamiliar people had paraded through her house since Johnny's abduction, and they still had two Richmond police officers standing guard. They wouldn't have allowed the car's owner to enter the house unless they were cleared to be there.

Her gut tightened for a moment at the thought that it could be someone from the press until she remembered that Scott Michaels had arranged for them to be barred from closer than a hundred yards for security reasons.

Grace parked in the garage, went inside and dumped her purse on the kitchen table as she passed. All she wanted was a long hot shower and to change into sweats and a t-shirt after the day she'd had. She opened the door to the living room and had to stifle a groan when she saw Craig reading Alec's book on the couch. She'd forgotten about him in all the chaos and hadn't talked to him since Saturday. She secretly hoped he was on his way back to Albuquerque.

He put the book down and sat forward. "I hope you don't

mind that Mark let me in before he left to deal with some crisis at his restaurant. I was going insane waiting for news at the hotel."

Grace gave him a weak smile. "I wish I had news to give you. What do you think of that?" she asked and pointed at the book.

Craig relaxed back into the cushions. "Alec's an amazing writer. I was just reading the part about your childhood. I'm so sorry. I never knew. What was it like reading about yourself from Alec's perspective?"

"I haven't read it. Alec gave it to me just before the kidnapping. She'd kept it a secret, and I was furious with her for not giving me more warning." She stared at the book for a few moments. "Seems like such a trivial thing to have been upset about."

"You should read it. You might be surprised."

Grace dropped onto the loveseat and hoisted her feet onto the ottoman. "You sound like Ryan. Has he been home since you got here?"

Craig shook his head. "It's just been me. I saw the interview this morning. It was painful to watch. That Ethan is a moral degenerate. I'd like to strangle him."

"You and half of Richmond. The FBI is working on damage control. I'm not sure what that means or if it will do any good. Have you eaten? I haven't had a bite since breakfast." She checked her watch and the lingering elation of knowing Johnny was still alive drained out of her.

Craig leaned forward and drew his brows together. "What's wrong?"

"Johnny stormed out of the house and into Mara's web a week ago this very minute."

Craig got up and moved next to her. "It's just time on the clock, Grace. It doesn't signify anything. The FBI could bring Johnny through that door five minutes from now. You can't let it get to you."

Grace peered into his eyes. Her interactions with Craig had

been limited in the past, but they'd usually been intense. She realized that she knew very little of him as a person or what his life must be like. She wondered if she'd misjudged him.

"You're right. The minute has passed, and nothing's changed. Let's go make a dent in the mound of food in the kitchen."

Her phone buzzed as Craig extended his hand to help her off the couch. "It's Scott Michaels." She tapped the screen to answer and didn't hesitate to put it on speaker so Craig could hear. She'd declared him to be family and there was no longer a point in hiding anything from him. "Hello, Scott. Why are you calling instead of Wes?"

"Because this involves you and me. We've arranged a press conference to put this nonsense about a hoax to rest. The director himself has requested that you join me in front of the cameras and make a statement. Are you willing to do that? I know it's a great deal to ask, but it could make a world of difference in our efforts to recover Johnny."

She frowned, but Craig nodded to encourage her. "I don't know what to say."

"Public affairs will help with that. We need you to come now."

"Now? I thought you meant in the morning."

"We're jumping on this before it spins any further out of control. We would have arranged it earlier, but we had another situation to handle first."

Grace knew what the situation was but kept that to herself. "I'll have to trust that you know what you're doing. See you shortly." She hung up and stared at Craig before burying her face in her hands. "It's too much. I don't have the strength to go on live TV in front of the entire country."

"Scott didn't say it was the entire country, but what does it matter? Johnny needs you to do this. Don't lose sight of that." He reached out his hand to her. "I've eaten. Let's fix you a to-go bag, and I'll drive. You can eat on the way."

Grace took his hand and let him lead her to the kitchen,

confirming for her that there was no question she'd misjudged him, and she was glad to have him at her side.

RYAN WAS WAITING for Grace at the field office entrance. He raised an eyebrow when Craig walked in behind her. "What's he doing here?"

"Long story, but I wouldn't have made it here without him," Grace said and took Ryan's hand.

"I called Steph and the Emersons. They're on their way. Mark's still at the restaurant, but he'll do his best to make it," Ryan said.

"That's not necessary. He should stay at work. Did you say Alec's coming? Is that wise?"

"Like I could stop her, but she already knew about the press conference. Her publicist told her. We'll hide her in a corner."

"Hide Alec in a corner? Good luck with that."

A public affairs specialist met the three of them in the lobby. After introducing herself as Megan Nelson, she said, "Please, follow me," and led them to a tiny annex attached to the press conference room. "Mr. and Mrs. Walker, I'll need you to stay here. Mr. Stuart, you may take one of the chairs reserved for family in the press room."

Craig gave her a nod and took Grace's hands. "I'm proud of you. Remember, this is for Johnny."

As if I could forget, Grace thought as she watched him go.

Ms. Nelson handed Grace a sheet with talking points just as Scott came in with Wes and a tall, striking man Grace had never met. Wes introduced him as Assistant Special Agent in Charge, Jamal Wilson.

He shook Grace's and Ryan's hands. "I'm truly sorry about Johnny's abduction. Please know his case continues to be our top priority. The director himself has taken an interest and has allocated whatever resources we need to bring your son home."

"We're deeply grateful," Ryan said and turned to Scott. "How bad is the fallout from Alec's interview? I've abstained from the news or social media today to preserve my sanity."

Scott rubbed his face. "It's been a hell of a day, but it could have been worse. You have no idea."

Grace caught the glances between the three men. They had no way of knowing how much she understood the significance of Scott's comment.

"This press conference will slam the lid on the hoax rumors, and we can get back to focusing on finding your son. Ready for this, Grace?" She nodded and tried to project more confidence than she felt. "Great, then let's get this show started."

Ms. Nelson gave them instructions and told Grace what to expect. Grace struggled to hear her over the pounding in her chest.

"You may speak from your heart or read the statement I prepared which will scroll on the teleprompter. Do whichever feels more comfortable for you."

Ms. Nelson opened a door leading to the small press room and motioned for them to follow. A podium covered with microphones faced the room packed with reporters from every news outlet Grace had heard of and some she hadn't. She froze in the doorway.

Ryan tenderly placed his arm around her waist. "It'll be fine. You've done a dozen of these."

"But never one like this, and it's been years. What if I freeze up there?"

Ryan kissed her cheek. "Just imagine you're talking to Johnny."

Grace took a deep breath and squared her shoulders as she followed the ASAC into the room. She was pleased to see Steph already waiting for them. She squeezed her hand, and they shared a knowing look.

Scott stepped to the podium, and the buzz in the room quieted. As he began to speak, Grace glanced at the front row to find Alec sitting with Adam and her agent. Alec mouthed an *I love you* and blew a kiss. Grace's fears melted away, and she had to bite the inside of her cheek to keep from smiling.

She switched her focus to Scott as he began to speak.

"I'm Special Agent in Charge Scott Michaels. Behind me are Assistant Special Agent in Charge Jamal Wilson and Grace Walker with her family. I will make this brief as we have urgent work involving life and death situations to attend to. We're only taking time from that work to counter false and dangerous accusations made during an interview with author Alexandra Emerson this morning. Ethan James insinuated in that interview that the abduction of Johnathan Walker by Mara Brennen was a publicity stunt planned and executed by Mrs. Emerson to sell more copies of her latest book which releases to the public tomorrow. My colleagues and I are here to emphatically refute that accusation and assure the nation that Johnathan Walker was in fact forcibly removed from his home by Ms. Brennen one week ago today."

Scott paused and waited for the buzz to again quiet. Several reporters raised their hands, but he ignored them.

"We again plead with the citizens of this country to aid us in locating Ms. Brennen and Johnathan, who goes by the name Johnny. As of this moment, we believe they are still in the greater Richmond area, but we have no concrete proof of this at the moment. We're asking citizens across the country to be on the lookout. In conjunction with private contributions, the Federal Bureau of Investigation is offering a reward of $200,000 for information that leads to Ms. Brennen's capture or Johnathan Walker's location. Information with the phone number and website address for the tip-lines is scrolling across your screen. I'll now turn the podium to Mrs. Grace Walker, Johnny's mother, to make a statement."

Grace stepped to the podium without hesitation. She looked at the words on the teleprompter, but they didn't represent what was in her heart. She gazed into the faces of the reporters and spoke from her heart.

"As many of you know, Mara kidnapped Johnny from the hospital nursery on the day he was born more than fourteen years ago. Six months later, she, along with her husband, abandoned Johnny at Richmond City Hospital in his time of greatest need. This proves the kind of person she is. Through the intervening years, while the FBI has hunted for Mara, Johnny's father and I have lived with the constant threat of Mara resurfacing and trying to steal our son from us. That fear became a reality one week ago today."

The room was silent while Grace paused to catch her breath and gather her thoughts. Every eye was locked on her face.

She raised her chin and said, "Alec Emerson has been my closest friend for many years and stood by me during Johnny's ordeal early in his life. She stands by our family now and thinks of Johnny as her nephew. She was with me the night Mara called twelve years ago to confess to kidnapping Johnny. She wrote her book, *Baby John Doe* and gave me a copy just days before Johnny's abduction. She was completely unaware that Mara had resurfaced, as we all were. I'm incensed that she's been accused of manufacturing this crisis to sell books. That is a complete and offensive lie. Alec is suffering from this tragedy as much as our family is."

Alec looked to Grace with tears streaming down her cheeks. Grace again bit her cheek, but this time to quell her own tears.

"I have a message for Mara. Johnny *is not* your son. He doesn't belong to you now and never has. I'm his mother, and Ryan is his father. Give up your insane scheme to steal him away from us. Set him free to come home where he belongs."

Grace scanned the crowd seated and saw several reporters

wipe their eyes. If her words had touched them, maybe she had reached Mara.

She looked directly at the camera. "Johnny, we miss you and need you to come home. Don't believe the lies Mara tells you. She's a dangerous criminal who only cares about herself. Do what you can to contact us or escape. We'll be waiting to welcome you with open arms. Auntie Alec and I wrapped your Christmas presents. They're waiting for you under the tree. We love you more than you can imagine. Please, come home."

Grace turned without another word and rejoined Ryan and Steph. Several reporters raised their hands. Scott went back to the podium and began taking their questions, but Grace heard little of what they said as she silently prayed that Johnny and Mara had heard her plea.

WES FOLLOWED Steph out of the press room and tapped her on the shoulder.

"May I speak with you? It won't take long," he asked quietly.

Grace and Ryan heard him and stopped. "We'll wait in the car," Grace said and tugged on Ryan's arm.

Steph turned to face Wes. "Did you tell anyone about the body?" he asked.

Steph looked down and pushed a ball of lint around on the carpet with the toe of her shoe. "I told Grace."

Wes squatted in front of her, and she lifted her eyes to his. "I'm not angry. Did she go to the ME's lab?" Steph glanced away, and that told Wes all he needed to know. "I thought telling Grace about discovering that body was a terrible idea, but I was wrong. Dr. Forest filed his results in record time without mentioning her name. We probably wouldn't have been able to hold the press conference until tomorrow if Grace hadn't verified that the body wasn't Johnny's."

"Will we get in trouble? Have we committed a crime by interfering in an active investigation?" Her words tumbled out in a rush.

Wes stood, and Steph's eyes followed him. "No, it was an accident that you found out, and I won't tell anyone. I'm sure the ME won't. Your family isn't the only one relieved that boy wasn't Johnny. We all were. We're doubling our efforts to find him. We have *carte blanche* from the top to use whatever resources we need. I will find your brother. I'm not supposed to say that, but it's true."

"Thank you, Wes." She wiped her eyes and smiled at him. "This has been an insane day. Did you hear about my sister's babies?"

"I did. Congratulations. I'm thrilled your family has a happy event to focus on in the middle of this ordeal. I'll make sure to end this so you can meet your niece and nephew as soon as possible. Are you coming back to the tech lab tomorrow?"

Steph shook her head. "After what happened today, I need to keep my distance for a bit. I'm too emotionally invested in this investigation. I'm sure we'll still see each other, and you better promise to keep us notified of any new leads."

"You have my word."

"I'd better go. My parents are waiting. Bring my brother home, Wes. I'm counting on you."

Wes watched her go and felt the weight of his obligation more than he had since arriving in Richmond. Failure wasn't an option. If he had to work 24/7, he was going to lock up Mara and return that boy to his family.

MARA THREW the TV remote at the screen after the replay of the press conference on the ten o'clock news.

"Hey, that TV's my only connection with the outside world from this prison," Johnny said.

Mara swung around and glared at him. "Don't you see what this means? For $200K, everyone in Richmond is going to be hunting me. Hell, I'd turn myself in for that kind of cash if it wouldn't mean prison time."

Johnny shrugged and pretended not to care, but secretly, he was thrilled. Seeing his mom and dad, and Steph had gotten to him. The fact that he'd gotten so mad over them hiding his past from him no longer made sense to him. The Walkers were amazing parents who loved him, and Mara didn't. Even more, he loved them and wanted to go home.

The press conference meant they were searching for him again. It gave him hope of getting away from Mara. She'd been right about the reward. For that much money, people would be falling over themselves to find him.

Mara picked up the remote and handed it to Johnny. "Do what you want. I'm going to bed."

"Can I get on the laptop?" he asked eagerly.

"Just to play games. No internet. And don't stay up too late. You've complained about your head all day. You need to sleep."

She went to her room without another word. Johnny dropped the remote on the couch and got up to figure out how to carry the laptop to his room without using the backpack. He tried tucking it under his arm, but it kept slipping. He gave up after two more tries and unzipped Mara's backpack. Four baggies filled with white pills tumbled to the floor.

He quickly shoved three of the baggies into the backpack and lifted the fourth close to his face to get a better look. The tablets were just like the ones Mara had been giving him for pain since his seizure. There must have been hundreds of tablets, but Mara told him she only had a few left. They had to be opiates, and he was afraid to imagine where Mara had gotten them.

His gut tightened as he put the last baggie back with the others and zipped up the backpack. If Mara was desperate for money, she probably stole those pills to sell. Johnny hated to think that she'd had them since kidnapping him. His health teacher had talked about the street-value of opiates and how addicting and dangerous they were. Mara could make a boatload of cash from selling them, but what kind of people would buy them?

He gave up on the laptop and went to his room. He needed to be as far from that backpack as he could get. If Mara had lied about the pills, was anything else she'd told him true? If Mara was dealing drugs, it meant Johnny could be in danger from more than her crazy temper. He dropped onto his bed and lay in the dark trying to figure out a way to escape. Getting away from Mara had become about more than homesickness. His survival might depend on it, and he could be running out of time.

GRACE CHECKED the hour on her phone for the tenth time, making sure not to let the glow disturb Ryan. He'd only been asleep for an hour. Her phone said three-twelve, only seven minutes later than the last time she'd checked. It felt more like hours. The 'magic pill' she'd taken to sleep had done nothing but give her dry mouth. She stifled a groan and got up for some water.

She'd been keeping the house lit up like a Christmas tree during the night since Johnny's abduction. Ironically, the only lights she turned off each night were on the Christmas tree. Even though Ryan had tried to convince her that it was safe to keep them on, she didn't want to tempt fate with the way their luck was running. She couldn't have Johnny come home to find she'd burned down their house.

She carried her glass of water to the living room and switched on the surge-protector behind the tree. She sat cross-legged in front of the quilted skirt that Ryan had inherited from his grandmother and sipped her water. Admiring the glowing tree in the darkness had always brought her comfort. She needed it more than ever that year.

The image of the body in the ME's lab flashed into her mind. It hadn't been Johnny. As long as he was alive, there was hope. She hoped someone in the world would mourn that poor beaten and broken boy. Had he died knowing he was loved? Had he died alone? No one should have to die alone.

Refusing to allow her mind to descend into dark places, she took another sip of water and called up memories of past Christmases. How fortunate they'd been to be surrounded by love and laughter. No matter what it took, she'd make sure Johnny would enjoy those experiences for the rest of her life.

She longed to turn on her Christmas playlist but didn't want to wake Ryan. She gazed around the room at the other decorations, but her eyes stopped on Alec's book that Craig had left on the couch. Everyone kept pushing her to read it. She'd resisted to prove a point. *How selfish of me,* she thought and got up to carry the book in front of the tree to read by the light of her phone. What did she have to lose?

CHAPTER EIGHTEEN

WES' gaze wandered over the group circling the conference room table. Everyone looked fresh and eager to get started for the day, except SAC Michaels. He looked about as bad as Wes felt. He pitied Michaels. He was roughly twenty years older than Wes and married. His wife hadn't seen much of him in the past week. Wes had no one at home waiting for him. It made for some lonely nights, but his single life was simpler when he was on a case. His loyalties were never divided.

He and Michaels had stayed at the office all night going over the evidence for the fourth time. They had more than enough proof that Mara was the kidnapper, but none of that was doing them a bit of good. Tips had skyrocketed since the press conference, but they were all dead ends. Everyone in the country seemed hellbent on collecting the reward money.

Wes downed another gulp of coffee wishing he'd had time to shower before the strategy session to clear his head. Showering, shaving and putting on clean clothes would make him feel like a new man. He was in desperate need of that.

"Mara seems to have fallen off the grid," Michaels said. "Tips are pouring in, but they just confirm Mara's identity. I need to know where she's hiding. I hope she's trapped in the city without necessary funds to leave and that she's too afraid to show her face. The interview and press conference did their job keeping this case in front of the public."

Scott gave Wes a nod. He stood and started to pace while he picked up where Michaels left off. "In spite of that scare with the body that was discovered yesterday, I feel confident that Mara won't injure Johnny." He stopped and turned to the RPD chief. "Do we have any word on who the boy was?"

"His name was Noah Jensen. He was sixteen years old. According to our informant, a local dealer was trying to recruit him, but he resisted. Apparently, the dealer doesn't take no for an answer. We collected enough evidence against our primary suspect to take him out when we catch him."

"Good to know, Chief," Wes said. "As far as Mara is concerned, even if she's on the run, she can't move easily or inconspicuously with Johnny in tow. We've got eyes on the airports, bus, and train stations. His medical issues also make traveling with him under the radar a challenge. According to the pharmacy, he's running low on two medications, so we've red-flagged that as well. Does anyone have anything to add?"

Wes held his breath hoping someone would mention any scrap of a clue he'd overlooked, but blank stares were the only response he got. He didn't fault them. He was the one failing Johnny and the Walkers.

"My team will revisit the rental house, the hotel, and the hospital to see if there's anything we've missed. Let's stay in touch and make today the day. Eyes wide open," he said.

The group dispersed, and Cameron handed Wes the report with the latest tips. It would have to wait until after his shower. He glanced at the digital calendar on the wall as he left the conference room. It was Tuesday. Day eight. He was determined there wouldn't be a day nine.

SUNLIGHT BLASTED in through moth holes in Johnny's curtains. *I'll have to cover those if my escape plan fails*, he thought as he rolled over to face the wall. He ran his fingers over his bump. It was the same size, but he was glad it hadn't gotten bigger. Between his pounding headache and the anxiety over discovering drugs in Mara's backpack, he'd been awake most of the night. He didn't dare ask for pain medicine since he had no idea where it had come from. He'd have to make do with Advil and Tylenol.

He laid quiet and tried to go back to sleep, but it was pointless. He gave up and went to see what Mara was doing banging around in the kitchen. She was in a terrible mood after the press conference, so he had no idea what he'd be facing. He used the bathroom and went to confront his kidnapper.

"It's about time," Mara said, without turning away from the fridge when he came into the kitchen. "I thought you were going to sleep all day."

Johnny checked at the clock on the microwave. "It's only quarter after nine."

She carried the carton of OJ to the table and set it in front of him. "You're usually up before this." She put her hand under his chin and tipped his head back. "You look like hell." She picked up her penlight and shined it in his eyes. "I don't like your pupils. They're sluggish. You should be showing signs of improvement today. How's your headache?"

He lowered his head and locked his fingers behind his neck. "The same. Killing me. By the way, I can't stand orange juice."

Mara put her hands on her hips. "Why didn't you tell me? I can buy other kinds of juice."

Johnny raised his eyes. "I didn't want to make you mad."

"Why would that make me mad?"

"Never mind."

Mara watched him for several seconds. "I think you should

stay in bed all day. Go lie down and I'll bring you breakfast before I leave for the store."

Johnny went to his room without arguing. Mara's concern over his eyes worried him. He knew what sluggish pupils meant. He should be in a hospital.

She brought him two cinnamon rolls and hard boiled eggs, along with a glass of milk and a sports drink. She watched him eat for a minute before asking what kind of juice he liked.

He swallowed a bite of the cinnamon roll. It tasted much better than the gluten-free garbage she'd given him the day before, and he perked up a little. "Grape or apple."

"Easy enough." She reached into her pocket and took out two pills. "Take these so you can sleep."

He took them from her but didn't put them in his mouth. "Where did you get these? I don't have a prescription for pain meds."

"Leftover from an ankle surgery I had. You didn't care when I gave them to you yesterday. Why the questions?"

"Just wondered." He set the tablets on the edge of his plate. "I'll take them after I eat, so I don't get a stomachache."

"Fine. There's a bottle of ibuprofen on the kitchen counter. Take four in two hours."

"Two hours? Won't you be here?"

"I don't know how far away I'll have to go shopping. I'll look for an out of the way country store. It may take a while. Stay in bed and rest. No computer. It'll make your headache worse. I'll bring the TV in here. It's fine if you listen to it."

"Thanks," he said and finished his roll.

"Your color is better. Maybe you just needed to eat."

"That's probably it."

He lowered his eyes to his plate while he ate, hoping she'd go. She stared at him a few seconds before leaving to get the TV. She was back with it a minute later and had her electric hair clippers.

"What are you doing with those?" he asked, through a mouthful of egg.

"I'm going to shave your head."

Johnny sat forward. "No, you're not. Get away from me with those things. My hair's short enough."

"The video from your escapade at the hotel has been all over the media. We have to drastically alter your appearance. No one expects a bald head. You'll look like a cancer patient and people won't question you. It will be easier for me to keep an eye on that bump, too."

Johnny didn't have the strength to fight her, and he was too afraid of her to try. "Can I grow it out once we get to Portland?"

"Of course. Finish your breakfast." She set up the TV and picked up his dirty clothes while he ate. "They have a laundry room in this complex, but it's expensive. We'll have to wear our clothes more than once, so try not to get too dirty."

"I never leave my room. How am I supposed to get dirty?"

"Good point. Hurry up. I need to get going." She went out and came back with a kitchen chair and a large trash bag. She put the chair on the bag. "Sit here."

Johnny huffed but did what she ordered. His hair was already so short that it took no time to shave it. He cringed when she went over his bump with the clippers. She apologized and was more careful on the next pass. Johnny was relieved when the buzz of the clippers stopped. Mara was quiet after she examined his head.

"How does it look?" he asked.

"Fine," she said softly.

Johnny turned and raised his eyebrows. "Bring me the mirror."

She went to the bathroom without reminding him to say please. She handed him the mirror for him to inspect his new look. He barked out a laugh when he saw himself. He looked like a freak, especially with his black eyebrows.

"Like you said, it won't take long to grow back, and it'll be blond again. I'll lighten your eyebrows when I get home from the store."

She cleaned up the mess and handed him the remote. She stared at him with a strange look on her face. "I'll get back as soon as I can."

Johnny gave an exaggerated wave as she went out and fell back on his pillows. *A few hours of freedom*, he thought as she drove away, leaving him in peace.

JOHNNY FLUSHED the pain meds down the toilet and took some ibuprofen and acetaminophen when he woke up from an hour nap. He went back to bed and waited for the medicine to take effect, so he'd have the strength to execute the escape plan he'd come up with during the night.

He flipped through the TV channels while he waited but didn't care about any of the shows that came in with an antenna. He wondered if that was what it was like in the old days before cable and internet. *How boring*, he thought and tried to find anything about his kidnapping on the news. All he saw was the tip-line number scrolling on the screen. He was already old news.

When the medicine kicked in, and his headache faded to a dull roar, he went to the front door to see if Mara had forgotten to lock it from the outside. He turned the knob and pulled hard, almost falling off his crutches. The door didn't budge. He tried two more times with the same result, and his heart sank. It would have been so much easier if he could have walked out the door and been long gone by the time Mara came back.

He gave up on the door and turned to the windows next. Two had rusty old bars, and another was nailed shut, but a fourth at the back of the trailer opened with no trouble and didn't even have a screen. It was higher up the wall than the others, but Johnny was sure he could manage it.

He went to his room and emptied his backpack before carrying it to the kitchen. He put the laptop and last two water bottles inside before adding a cinnamon roll and some packets of cheese crackers to be safe.

His dad had always told him to carry a knife and a flint or lighter when he went on an adventure. He was sure he wasn't going to find a flint or lighter in that trailer, but he dug through the drawers and found a book of matches. He next took a dull carving knife from the silverware drawer. He would have preferred his pocketknife, but this would have to do.

The last thing he needed was to find some money. He searched the trailer for fifteen minutes but didn't find so much as a penny. Mara had taken the cash he withdrew from the ATM at the hotel. He searched the backpack once more to be sure. He found two one-dollar bills and a dime stashed in an inside pocket, probably left from when he went to Charlottesville. He wouldn't be able to buy much with that, but it was something.

He put the backpack on and went to the window. He considered throwing the backpack out first but decided against it in case he couldn't climb out to retrieve it. Instead, he hung it on a bent piece of metal jutting from the trailer that he could reach from the ground. All that was left was to get his body through the window.

He leaned his torso against the sill and lifted himself by pushing his arms on the hand rests of his crutches. He was grateful for the upper body exercises Tony always made him do at PT. It was a tight fit in the window, and his shoulders kept getting stuck, but he was making progress. Once his body was high enough, he grabbed the top of the window frame and twisted sideways. Using every bit of muscle he possessed, he lifted the leg closest to the window through the opening. It wasn't as hard as he'd expected. Tony would have been proud. He took a minute to catch his breath before lifting his other leg through the opening with his free hand.

Getting that far had drained him, but he'd nearly reached his objective. He picked up his crutches and hung them on the same piece of metal as the backpack before looking down to see how far he'd have to fall. The sloping weedy lawn was farther down than he'd hoped. His only choice was to pitch himself forward and tuck into a ball before he hit the ground and pray that he didn't break anything. After that, he'd have to use the siding on the trailer to raise himself up to grab his crutches.

Being so close to freedom gave him a burst of adrenalin and the energy he needed for the final step. He didn't know how long Mara had been gone, but it had been long enough that he knew he needed to hurry. He scooted as far forward as possible without falling, then took a few deep breaths and crossed his arms over his chest. Just as he leaned out to launch himself through the window, he heard Mara's car in the driveway.

In his panic, he toppled backward, and his head slammed into the floor right on the bump. A light flashed through his vision, and he lay on the floor in a daze. With the adrenalin still in his system, his head cleared quickly enough for him to drag himself to the couch. Sweat dripped into his eyes as he pulled himself across the floor in a military crawl. He heaved himself onto the couch and grabbed a textbook off the floor just as Mara came through the door.

She carried grocery bags to the table before turning to face him. "What are you doing out here? I told you to stay in bed."

Without taking his eyes from the book, he said, "I got bored. It's dark, and it stinks in my room."

She stared at him before shaking her head. "Whatever. I have to get the rest of the groceries."

Johnny's gaze flew to the back of the trailer the instant she went outside. The window was wide open, letting in the cold. If Mara didn't notice that, she would definitely notice Johnny didn't have his crutches, but there was no way he could crawl to the window and walk back to the couch before she came in. If Mara realized he'd tried to escape, she'd give him more than a headache. His head and heart pounded so hard he was afraid he'd pass out.

She made two more trips to the car before closing the front door and putting away the groceries. Johnny tried not to look at the window while she chatted away about her adventure to buy food. At least she seemed to be in a good mood.

She came to the couch and checked his pupils after she finished in the kitchen. The pain was blinding when she shined her penlight in his eyes. She stepped back and bit her lip when she finished. The concern was clear in her eyes.

"I don't like this. You should have stayed in bed."

And you shouldn't have punched me in the gut, Johnny thought but wished he had stayed in bed. Aside from his pain and panic, he could feel something was seriously wrong.

"I'll go back to my room in a few minutes. Can you fix me something to eat? The cinnamon rolls didn't fill me up."

She went to the kitchen and came back with a sub sandwich. "Figured you'd be hungry. You always are, but I guess that's a good sign." She handed Johnny a paper plate and his sandwich. While he unwrapped it, she went back to the kitchen for his drink. "I need a nap. I didn't sleep much last night. Do you need anything else before I go to my room?"

He said no, and she squeezed Johnny's shoulder as she walked by the couch. She passed the window without a glance. His escape plan had failed, but he'd been damned lucky not to get caught. He ate his sandwich and waited thirty minutes before dragging himself to the window. He grabbed his stuff and quietly shut the window before taking his backpack to his room to wait for the next time Mara left him alone.

MARA WOKE with a start to the sound of shouting and a blaring car alarm. Her heart sank when she realized where she was. *Still in this damned stinking trailer,* she thought. She had planned to whisk Johnny back to Portland three days after nabbing him. Instead, they were stuck in Richmond after more than a week with no money. Her face was plastered all over the news and the FBI was hunting her like a dog.

She'd been foolish to believe she could take Johnny without anyone knowing where he'd gone. She'd considered ditching him more than once since everything blew up in her face. It would be simple to drop him at a hospital or street corner, disappear in the wind and start over in a new place. She'd done it before. She could do it again, but she'd have to cross into Canada like Rick had done. There wasn't anywhere left in the U.S. for her to hide.

In the end, she had no choice but to see it through no matter the outcome. She'd agonized over the loss of Johnny in the years after Rick forced her to leave him and couldn't go through that a second time. She'd devoted years and invested thousands of dollars in putting her plan into action. She wouldn't abandon Johnny.

It would take a boatload of cash to set up a new life in Canada, and she only had one way to get it. She thought of the bags of drugs hiding in her backpack. The kind of people who'd buy her goods wouldn't care about Johnny or what they'd heard on the news. They'd just be desperate for their next hit. Mara just needed to figure out how to connect with buyers without getting caught.

She sat up and rubbed her face. The room was dark, and it felt late but must only be around two. Her stomach growled. She hadn't eaten since early morning, but before she fixed lunch, she needed to check Johnny. She hadn't liked the look of his pupils when she came home from the store. Two days had passed since he bumped his head on the toilet, but he was getting worse, not better. As a nurse, she knew odds were that he had a subdural hematoma or maybe a slow bleed, and his intracranial pressure was increasing. If she was right, he'd need the kind of medical care she wasn't equipped to provide.

She went to Johnny's room and found him in a deep sleep. His breathing was regular, and his forehead was cool and dry. She lifted his arm and pressed her fingers into his wrist. His pulse was strong and steady. The only red flag was that bump on his head. It felt bigger than it had been that morning.

Johnny didn't stir while she examined him, so she left him to rest. She rolled the TV into the living room and turned on a craft show. The novelty of being famous had worn off, so she was glad there wouldn't be any news on that time of day. She relaxed and learned how to make greeting cards while she ate her lunch.

She heard Johnny coming from the bathroom just as she finished eating. She put her plate down and stood as he approached. His left eye was swollen shut, and his cheek drooped. When he came into the light from the window, she saw that his face was ashen.

"Help me, Mara," he said. "Something's wrong."

The last words came out in a slur as his legs gave out. He crumpled to the floor and began to seize. Mara shoved a pillow under his head and waited for the seizure to end, but it went on much longer than it should have. He didn't open his eyes or respond when his body became still.

She picked up her phone to call 911 but debated whether it was worth the risk of exposing their location. She shoved her phone in her pocket without dialing and grabbed Johnny under his arms to drag him to the car. She didn't worry about any of the trailer park residents reporting them. By the looks of most of them, the last thing they wanted was cops crawling around the area.

It took Mara ten minutes to get Johnny lying flat and seat-belted into the backseat. She ran through her options as she squealed out of the driveway. The closest hospital was Richmond City where she'd abandoned Johnny as a baby, and it had the best trauma center in the city. They stood the greatest chance of being recognized there, but she hoped the FBI had their eyes pointed elsewhere and wouldn't think she'd dare take Johnny to such a conspicuous place.

Richmond City Hospital was in a different system than the one she'd taken Johnny to a few days earlier so they wouldn't have access to his records. Her only chance of not getting caught was if the FBI hadn't red-flagged the files, but she had to risk it to save Johnny's life.

She pulled the car in front of the ER and ran inside shouting for help. Two orderlies rolled a gurney to the car and loaded Johnny onto it. Mara left the car and ran to keep up with them as they raced Johnny to the trauma center. Her heart pounded as much from fear of being recognized as from concern for Johnny.

A nurse blocked her way at the doors of the trauma room and directed her to a row of chairs in the hallway.

"Let the doctors do their work," the nurse said. "Tell me what happened."

Mara hesitated as she tried to concoct a new story to tell, but she was too distraught to think and decided to stay close to the truth in Johnny's best interest. She lowered the pink ballcap she'd grabbed from the car over her forehead as she answered.

"My son has a seizure disorder from a car accident as a baby. He had a seizure the other day and hit his head. The doctors thought it was minor and released him, but he's been getting worse. He passed out just as I was getting ready to bring him here. It's never happened like this. I'm scared."

The nurse put her hand on Mara's arm. "This is the best trauma center in the region. We'll take good care of your son. Come with me to registration, and we'll do his paperwork."

Mara thought it was best not to mention that she was a nurse. "I forgot my purse at home in my rush to get here. I think I can remember most of the information. We're visiting from out of town."

"Don't worry. Just give us what you can. We'll get the rest later."

Mara brushed away a nonexistent tear and followed her to registration.

MARA PACED the surgical waiting room like a caged tiger five hours later. She'd never been on that side of the operating room doors and had worried how another person's surgery was going. She felt the security cameras watching her and knew her odds of getting caught increased with each passing minute.

Johnny had been in surgery for three hours. The surgeon said Johnny had a massive subdural hematoma and his intracranial pressure was critically elevated. They'd also found a densely packed bundle of vessels in his left frontal lobe that was probably a result of his earlier injury. The surgery was delicate and could take eight to ten hours, which meant they had five to seven hours left to go.

Mara remained in the waiting room as long as she could before needing to escape. She gave her phone number to the volunteer at the surgical desk and said she had an urgent matter to tend to. She forced herself to walk to the parking lot instead of bolting to the car. She didn't know where she'd go, she just knew she had to get away from the hospital.

She headed to the trailer first to retrieve her purse. She hadn't lied to the nurse about forgetting to bring it to the hospital. She unlocked the trailer and dropped onto the couch to take advantage of the quiet and get her head straight.

The urge to abandon Johnny and run resurfaced but she resisted, knowing she'd regret it for the rest of her life. She was destined to be Johnny's mother. She had to stay the course to prove she was worthy of that destiny. She'd worked too hard to give up this close to her goal. She just needed to keep her wits sharp.

Asking herself what a real mother would do in her situation, she went to his room to put some of his personal items in his backpack to take to the hospital. After searching for a few minutes, she found it shoved under the bed and wondered if he'd been hiding it from her. She knew the answer as soon as she unzipped it. Her laptop, a kitchen knife, some food, water, and toiletries were stuffed inside. She sank to the floor with the pack on her lap. Johnny had been planning to run away from her.

The realization infuriated her. After all she'd done for him? Knowing all the plans she had for him, how could he dare leave her? A tear rolled down her face and dripped off the end of her nose. Wasn't he coming to love her? Didn't he care about the sacrifices she'd made? How could he not?

She pondered these questions for some time before an idea popped into her brain. Johnny was homesick. That had to be all it was. He was a teenage boy who was homesick for the only life he'd ever known. It didn't matter how much he hated the Walkers; he missed his friends and his life. It was so simple. Mara told herself that she'd have to give him time to adjust to her and his new life. The week they'd spent together hadn't exactly been normal. She'd have to learn patience and give him time to come to love her if he survived.

She took out the items he wouldn't need at the hospital and left them in the middle of the floor. She left the toiletries and laptop where they were and packed his video game, and the comic books she'd bought that morning. It might be days before he'd be in any condition to need them, but she wanted them there for him when he was ready. It would be good for him to see what a thoughtful mother she was.

She left the trailer with her purse and the backpack and got some fast food on her way back to the hospital. Remembering her purpose had helped her focus, and she was prepared to do whatever it took to save her son.

CHAPTER NINETEEN

GRACE FINISHED Alec's book on the sixteenth day since Johnny's abduction. She tenderly laid the book on her lap and closed her eyes in the stillness, absorbing the lovingly crafted words her friend had put to paper. It was a profound and masterful work of art. Grace felt humbled and unworthy of the tribute Alec had paid her. The recounting of some details from Grace's early life was not exactly as they'd happened, but the rest mirrored Grace's memories.

The book had flown off bookstore shelves and online retailers in the week since its release. Alec's publisher was scrambling to print enough copies to keep up with demand. Grace was happy for Alec. She had a promising future writing nonfiction, just as she did in children's books. None of that mattered to Alec, though. Like the rest of the family, all she cared about was finding Johnny.

Grace had been so sure the $200,000 award would spark a frenzy around the country of people searching for him, but Mara's trail had gone cold in the past week. The promise of an award hadn't been enough to produce evidence that led to her capture.

It was pure torture each morning when Grace opened her

eyes and realized Johnny was still missing. Her dreams were filled with bizarre and disjointed images of him that left her breathless and anxious. There were mornings she wished she hadn't woken up, not that she'd do anything to cause that to happen. The strain and despair of their ordeal were enough to do her in.

She'd read the same despair in Wes' eyes. He did his best to assure her that Mara had taken Johnny underground to wait for the uproar to quiet down and the public to forget the two of them. He didn't believe those words even as he spoke them.

Grace had concluded that either Mara had killed Johnny and dumped his body before going underground, or she'd abandoned him, and he'd died of exposure or starvation and thirst. Images of Johnny lying dead in a ditch invaded her thoughts. She appreciated Alec's book giving her a tangible reminder of him as her little man and not as a decomposing corpse.

She lowered her gaze to the book and studied the picture of Johnny as she tenderly ran her thumb over the cover. Alec came into the living room from the kitchen eating cannoli and stopped when she saw Grace.

"How many of those have you had today? It's only ten in the morning," Grace said, attempting to lighten her mood.

"Lost count around five. Who cares?" Alec glanced at the book on Grace's lap. "Did you finish? What did you think?"

Grace wiped her tears and gazed up at her friend. "Extraordinary."

"I had extraordinary material. Made my job easy." She sat next to Grace and held her hand. "What's the plan to look for our boy today?"

"No more plans. I'm empty. You can go home, Alec. Adam and the kids need you, and there's nothing to do here. I've sent Mark and Steph back to their normal lives. They're making plans to go to DC on Saturday to see Jen and the babies. Even Ryan is back at work."

"Trying to get rid of me so you can sit here alone and wallow in your misery?"

"I'm going to do that whether you're here or not." Grace got up and went to the Christmas tree. She straightened an ornament and adjusted a string of lights before stepping back to admire her work. "Christmas is two weeks from today." She wanted to say more, but the words caught in her throat.

Alec came up behind her and wrapped her arms around Grace's waist. "I'm not abandoning you. I told you at the start of this nightmare that I'm not leaving until Johnny comes through that door. Adam and the kids are fine without me. They prefer the nanny. She spoils them. Adam is dealing with this by throwing himself into work as usual. I'll bring the kids over tomorrow, and we'll make our gingerbread houses."

The thought of their annual gingerbread house tradition was too much for Grace. She slid out of Alec's arms and curled into a ball in front of the tree, fearing the force of her sobs would tear her in two. Alec rubbed her back and muttered words of comfort, but no words existed to soothe her pain.

JOHNNY STARED at the shapes in the ceiling tiles while he waited for the nurse to answer his call button. He'd been staying awake enough during the day that the doctor ordered the nurse to remove his catheter. Johnny had been relieved and disappointed. The catheter had been uncomfortable and embarrassing, but it had also meant he didn't have to worry about having an accident while he waited for his nurse to help him to the bathroom. He wasn't allowed to get up on his own. Most of the time they responded quickly, but sometimes they didn't show up until he was about to burst.

He didn't really need to go to the bathroom this time. He'd used that as an excuse to get the nurse to his room so he could tell him who he was. Mara had finally gone home to eat and shower, so Johnny needed to take advantage of the chance while Mara was gone. She hadn't left his side once while he was awake in the week since his surgery.

The doctor had kept Johnny sedated for the first three days after his surgery. When he woke up on the fourth day, he didn't know why he was in a hospital. He was more lucid by the next day but still so drowsy from the drugs they were pumping into him that it was impossible to force himself to stay awake.

As he grew more alert in the days that followed, he bided his time until he could nark on Mara and get free of her. She'd made that impossible by putting on her Mother-of-the-Year act and refusing to leave his bedside. Johnny had finally managed to convince her that it was hard for him to rest with her staring at him all the time. He also played the angle that she needed to take better care of herself, so she'd be strong enough to take care of him when he got out of the hospital. He was shocked when she bought it.

Johnny was about to push his button again when the nurse came in and gave him a fist bump.

"You have to go again, bro?" the nurse asked. "It's only been an hour."

"Sorry, Luke. You know how it is," Johnny said. He pushed himself up higher in the bed and swung his feet to the floor.

"Guess this means you don't want the bedpan." He handed Johnny his crutches and started unhooking him from the monitors. "Doc says no more wheelchair if you think you can manage."

"I can," Johnny said.

Luke held the IV bag as he followed Johnny toward the bathroom. They'd almost reached the door when Mara walked in and asked what they were doing. Johnny wanted to scream.

"Why isn't he in the wheelchair?"

"Don't worry. The doctor said crutches are fine," Johnny said. He hoped to catch Luke's eye and signal that he wanted him to get Mara to leave, but Luke was busy watching Johnny's feet.

"Can you get me one of those smoothies I like from the cafeteria? I ate all my lunch," he asked Mara.

She held up a large paper cup with a straw. "No need. It's much better than the hospital ones."

"I'll take it if you don't want it," Luke said and winked at Mara.

"Nice try," Johnny said and went into the bathroom with Luke trailing him.

He was tempted to whisper to Luke about Mara while the bathroom door was shut, but he was too afraid she'd overhear. He didn't know what she'd do if he crossed her and he was more helpless than ever. She'd probably behave herself in front of Luke or the other nurses, but the thought of what she might do to him when they were alone terrified him.

He relieved himself and Luke helped him back to bed.

"I'll come back in an hour to see if you're up to sitting in the recliner for half an hour. The doctor says as soon as you can sit without getting a headache, we'll move you out of ICU to the step-down unit. They have much nicer nurses down there, and they won't have to bug you as much."

"Bet they're cuter, too," Johnny said and did his best to smile.

Moving him out of ICU meant he was recovering, and he wouldn't be in the hospital much longer. He had to find a way to get free of Mara before that happened. There was no way he was leaving with that monster.

"ALEC TOLD me what happened this morning," Ryan said when he got home that night. "God, I'm worried about you, Grace."

Grace was on the bed watching some mindless sitcom. She couldn't even remember the name. After her breakdown, Alec had helped her to bed. Grace had cried herself to sleep and woke two hours later with a roaring headache. Alec forced her to eat a few bites of lunch and take a pain pill. Grace had relented, not having the strength to fight her.

She had to admit she was feeling better and had an appetite for the first time in days. Alec always knew what was best for her. She'd been pestering Grace to have a good cry, but as always, Grace resisted. She'd been taught as a child that crying equaled weakness. It was still a challenge at times to get past that backward conditioning.

Grace patted the bed for Ryan to sit with her. "Stop worrying. All I needed was a good cry. You have to face it that I can't put on a brave face and pretend our son hasn't been in the clutches of a maniac for more than two weeks."

"I'm not asking you to pretend. In fact, I'm glad you cried it out and that you're defending yourself. It's the silence that scares me. Have you decided to go to your girls' dinner tomorrow? Contrary to what you say, it would be good for you to get out for a few hours."

Grace had hoped Ryan forgot about her annual dinner out with a few of the friends she'd worked with over the years. The only excuses any of them allowed for missing the occasion were serious and/or contagious illness or a death in the family. None of them could have imagined one of them missing due to a kidnapped child.

Grace had tried to beg out, but her friends insisted she join them. She'd texted them two days earlier that she'd go if none of them brought up Johnny. They answered that they wouldn't agree to that, and it would do her good to talk. She was certain they were motivated more by curiosity than concern.

She couldn't conceive of going to dinner and chatting with her friends about their children's grades and sporting exploits or gossiping about so and so's divorce while Johnny, if he was still alive, was out there suffering. Alec and Ryan thought it was the perfect distraction, but even garnering the strength to dress up and do her hair and makeup was overwhelming. Her breakdown that morning was proof that she wasn't up to girls' night out.

"I'm not going. It takes all I've got left to get out of this bed every day. Can't that be enough for now?"

"Put off your decision until morning, but I say you can be miserable in a restaurant as well as here."

She sat up and swung her feet off the bed. "I don't want to talk about it anymore. I'm starving. Let's go find something to eat."

Ryan followed her to the kitchen without a word, but she knew he wasn't done with her. She wasn't the only stubborn one in the family.

ALEC WATCHED from the bed as Grace put on her makeup the following evening. "What made you change your mind about going?" she asked.

Grace grimaced at her reflection. "I'm only doing it to get you and Ryan off my back. Ryan brought it up first thing this morning, and you've been pestering me all day."

"All day? I asked you once. Maybe twice."

"Felt like all day. I look like hell. No amount of makeup is going to cover the bags and circles under my eyes."

"Cut yourself some slack. You look like a mother whose son was kidnapped. No one expects you to be a cover girl. What would you do if one of us was in your shoes?"

Grace stared at Alec through the mirror. She put down her blush and rested her hands on the counter. "I'd do anything, and everything, just like all of you have done for me. I'm sorry if I seem ungrateful. I'm not. There's no way to express how thankful I am."

Alec fell back onto the bed and sighed. "I'm not looking for gratitude. I'm trying to get you to see that we're doing this because we love you and Johnny, just as you love us. Let your friends show their love. Are you almost ready? I told Katrina we'd pick her up at the hospital."

She grimaced at her reflection and scooped her makeup into the drawer. "This is as good as it's going to get. Let's get this over with."

———————

GRACE WATCHED the scenery speed past as Alec drove them to meet Katrina. How many times had she crossed that bridge over The James River from her house to Richmond City Hospital over the years? She did the math in her head. Close to six thousand trips. She squeezed Alec's hand as the memories welled up. Alec raised her eyebrows but Grace just smiled.

Grace shifted her gaze to the city skyline. She hadn't been downtown since searching hospitals for Mara the previous week. In fact, she'd hardly left the house since the press conference. Ryan had been right to pressure her to go to dinner. The change of scenery was refreshing, and she looked forward to eating at the Italian restaurant they'd chosen. It had only been open for two months but was a big hit in Richmond. Even Mark had given it his stamp of approval.

Alec pulled into the parking garage and drove around for five minutes before finding a spot at the far end.

"I miss access to staff parking," she said. "We have to park in the sticks like civilians. Almost makes me want to go back into nursing."

"And give up all that fame and money? You're just spoiled from pulling up to the curb in your limo," Grace said as she climbed out of the car.

"I wish. I could be a nurse and author, too." Alec fell into step with Grace as they walked to the hospital entrance and said, "Speaking of my career, I'm glad the book is doing so well, but it's so frustrating that it hasn't helped Johnny. I hope that bitch Mara is taking care of him."

"Wes and Scott insist she is, but they just say that to placate me. The strain is showing in Wes' face. I wish he wouldn't blame himself. I'm not sure what else he could have done."

Alec stepped in front of Grace, blocking her way. "Stop talking like Johnny is dead. I know that's what's rolling around in that brain of yours. Mara has no reason to kill him. That doesn't even make sense. She's in hiding, plain and simple."

"Maybe it got to be too much for her, taking care of Johnny on the run. She probably realized how much work it is and abandoned him in the middle of some secluded field."

Alec rolled her eyes. "Even if that were true, why wouldn't she just drop him on a street corner and get the hell out of Richmond? She would be long gone before Johnny made contact with us."

Grace held Alec's gaze while she pondered her logic. It made sense, but her gut wouldn't accept it. "You know I want you to be right with all my heart. I'm just preparing myself for the worst."

Alec turned and started walking. "Why don't you put all that energy into thinking of a way to find him instead? That's what I'm doing. Maybe one of our friends will have a fresh perspective."

Grace followed Alec in silence. She wanted to be optimistic and hopeful like Alec, but she was too afraid of the devastation that would come if it turned out to be the one that was right and Johnny was dead.

She caught up with Alec and said, "I'll try. I will, but please do me a favor and steer the conversation away from Johnny as much as you can. I know it will come up, but I don't want him to be the sole topic tonight. I agreed to come to dinner as a way of distraction, remember?"

Alec nodded. "Deal. I'll do my best."

Grace gave her the best smile she could muster and followed her into the lobby. Katrina worked in the cardiac wing, so it took four hallways and two elevators to get to her. Grace marveled at how much the hospital had changed since she'd left nearly thirteen years earlier. A wealthy patient had donated the lion share of the funds for the new cardiac wing and had raised more for a massive refurbishing of the rest of the facility. The hospital was modern with state-of-the-art medical equipment and systems. Grace wished it had been that way when she'd worked there.

Katrina was coming out of the locker room when they reached the nurses' station. Grace was happy to see her and gave her a quick hug. She was about ten years younger than Grace but looked ten years younger than that, and it didn't show that she'd just worked a twelve-hour shift. Her light-brown hair was highlighted and had a stylish, layered cut that complimented her face and sparkling green eyes. Grace had always told Katrina how jealous she was of her thick, wavy hair.

Alec and Katrina hadn't seen each other in the past year, so they had catching up to do. Grace walked behind them quietly lost in her own thoughts. She glanced up as they passed the cafeteria on the main floor. A woman in a pink baseball cap came out of the cafeteria and headed down the hallway in the opposite direction. She was at least twenty feet from Grace when she turned, but it was close enough for Grace to get a look at her profile.

It was Mara!

"Alec, it's Mara," she called and ran in the direction she'd gone.

"What are you doing, Grace?" Alec said and chased after her with Katrina not far behind.

Grace wove her way through the halls and checked inside a few rooms, but Mara had disappeared. She ran as far as she could until she came to a door that only medical staff was authorized to enter. She came to a halt and pounded her fists on the door. Katrina came up behind her and put a hand on her shoulder.

"Grace, stop that. I'll open the door." Katrina slid her badge through the reader, and the doors swung open. Grace burst into the surgical wing. "Wait," Katrina called after her. "Mara wouldn't have access to this area, but I'll ask if anyone has seen her. Retrace your steps in the hallway. Alec, call the girls and tell them we'll be late."

Grace debated with herself before going out the way she came. She and Alec searched every hallway on every floor, but there was no sign of Mara. Katrina texted to say she hadn't had any luck either and asked them to meet her in the lobby.

Grace went directly to Katrina and said, "Can you contact anyone in HR and see if Mara works here?"

"HR is closed. No one will be back until Monday, and I don't know anyone that works in that department, but I alerted security. They're searching for her."

Alec faced Grace and said, "You're sure it was her? You only saw her for a split second."

"Yes, I'm sure just like I was when I saw her at Johnny's PT appointment. I was right then, and I'm right now. I recognized her profile and the way she walks. It was her. I'm going to call Wes to meet me at the field office. Maybe they can get a security feed for this hospital, and he can get the personnel records. Mara was here. I'm positive it was her." She took out her phone and called Wes before Alec could protest. "Go to dinner. I'll get an Uber."

Alec started to protest as Wes answered. Grace held up a hand to quiet Alec and told Wes about their hunt for Mara. Wes was as skeptical as Alec.

"That's the last place Mara would be," he said.

"That makes sense, but what about Johnny's abduction has made sense? It was Mara. Work on getting the security footage and live feed from the hospital. Meet me at the office. I'm not far."

Wes chuckled. "Yes, ma'am. I guess we have nothing to lose by trying. I'm still at the office."

Grace called an Uber and ran out of the lobby entrance. Alec and Katrina caught up with her, and Alec offered to go to the FBI with her.

"Go enjoy dinner. You can't ID Mara. You've never seen her, so there's no point in coming with me," Grace said as she scanned the road leading to the parking lot for her ride.

"I feel guilty going to girl's night when you're dealing with this."

Grace turned to face her. "Don't. I'll be more upset if you miss it. You needed a night out as much as I did. If we find Mara because of my seeing her tonight, it will have been worth it. Here's my ride. Hug everyone for me. I'll keep you posted."

Grace got into the car and gave Alec a reassuring smile as the driver wove his way out of the parking lot.

———

WES AND STEPH met Grace in the field office lobby. Steph peppered Grace with questions as they walked to the elevator.

Grace interrupted her and said, "I'll tell you the whole story if you answer a question for me first. What are you doing here?"

Grace caught the glance that passed between Steph and Wes.

"We were having dinner. To discuss the case," Wes said, without meeting Grace's eye.

Grace was pleased to hear that they were spending time together. Steph had taken a step back from involvement in the case after the incident with the ME. Grace thought that meant she'd taken a step back from Wes, too. She wasn't sure what kind of future the two of them could have given their unique careers, but she was glad Steph had someone to spend time with who could empathize with her situation.

Wes took them to the bank of monitors that Grace was coming to know and detest, but that night she hoped they'd reveal the answers they sought. She settled in for the long haul, and Wes and Steph looked over her shoulder while she watched the prerecorded security footage from the timeframe where she saw Mara.

There wasn't a camera in the hallway near the cafeteria, but they had recordings from cameras in that area. Grace's heart pounded with excitement. Seeing Mara meant that not only was she still in the city, but they might also have a way to track her!

Once they'd studied the footage with no luck, a tech switched to the live feed that hospital security had allowed them to patch into. The feed rotated between zones of the facility. Grace's heart rate slowed to normal after thirty minutes passed with no sign of Mara. Wes came and went during that time, but Steph stayed at her side. Even though she'd talked Alec out of coming with her, Grace was glad not to be alone.

She jumped when Steph broke the silence and said, "Does Dad know you're here?"

Grace put her elbows on the table and rested her chin in her hands. "No. I didn't want him trying to convince me that I'd imagined seeing Mara, and I didn't want to get his hopes up either. I'll call him as soon as we confirm she was at the hospital."

Steph nodded and turned her eyes back to the screens. Another hour passed while Wes came and went but still no sign of Mara.

When Wes' phone buzzed for the tenth time, he checked it and said, "We have access to the HR records. A team is combing through them now. I'm going to join them. I'll be more help there than here."

Steph stood and stretched. "I could use a break. You must be starving, Grace. What can I get you?"

Grace hadn't noticed how hungry she was until Steph mentioned it. "Just a chicken sandwich and salad. And something small and sweet would be nice."

"I know just the thing," Steph said, as she left with Wes.

Grace followed Steph's example and stood to stretch, but she kept her eyes on the screen. It was after ten, so there were no visitors at the hospital, and the hallways were quiet. Grace wondered if staring at those screens all night hoping to see Mara was an exercise in futility. Mara could have been long gone by then.

Grace tried to figure out what Mara had been doing at the hospital. She hadn't been wearing a uniform, but that could have meant she was getting dinner before starting her shift. That was Grace's hope because it meant she might catch sight of her while she worked. The other possibility was that Mara had just come off her shift and had changed before getting dinner and heading back to her hideout.

Wes had insisted that Mara wasn't foolish enough to try to get a job in the most likely place they'd look for her, but they hadn't been looking for her there for that very reason. Maybe getting a job at Richmond City had been one of Mara's evil-genius tactics.

Grace swung her arms and paced a few quick laps to get her heart pumping before dropping into her chair. She hoped the added blood flow to her brain would be enough to solve the Mara puzzle. If Wes was so insistent that Mara wouldn't apply for a job, why else would she have been there? She was puzzling over her questions when the camera panned over a sign in the ICU that posted visiting hours.

Grace sprang out of her chair and leaned closer to the monitors. Mara hadn't been at the hospital to work. She'd been there because Johnny was a patient. If Johnny was there, Mara wouldn't leave him alone overnight. The ICU had a lounge for immediate family to sleep, eat and shower, so they wouldn't have to leave their loved ones.

It only took two more minutes of watching the security feed to prove her hunch right. As the image of the ICU came on the center monitor, Mara stepped out of a patient room and went to the nurses' station to talk to a doctor leaning against the counter. She wasn't wearing the baseball cap, but her hair was pulled into the same ponytail. Grace tapped the button on the keyboard to freeze the feed just as Mara raised her face to the camera.

Grace grabbed her purse and raced down the stairwell. She retrieved her phone at the reception desk and opened the app for an Uber. Since it was Friday night, she wouldn't have to wait long for one to arrive and carry her to her Johnny.

WES RUBBED his face and yawned before flipping to the next record in the HR file from the hospital. It was his third time through the records. It had been a revelation to him how many people are employed in a big facility like Richmond City, and he didn't even have all the files. The team looking for Mara had split them up to save time, but much to Wes' frustration, none of them had found anyone who remotely resembled Mara.

"Agent Reid," someone said, startling him just as he was about to take a sip of coffee. Half of it spilled down the front of his shirt. "Ms. Walker is asking for you. She says it's urgent."

Wes jumped up and rushed to meet Steph in the hallway. "What is it? Did Grace see Mara?"

"Better than that. Come on." Wes had a hard time keeping up with her as she ran back to the room where Grace had been watching the security feed. "I've been trying to call you for five minutes," Steph said over her shoulder.

"I turned my phone off so I could concentrate. Explain what's happening."

They reached the AV room, and instead of answering, Steph pointed at the monitors. Mara was frozen on the screen looking directly into the camera.

Steph handed him a sheet of paper. While he read it, she said, "Johnny's in the ICU. Grace has gone after Mara. You better get your team over there ASAP. Who knows what she'll do?"

Wes didn't wait to hear more. He got on his radio and barked orders for his team to gear up and meet him at the SWAT vehicles.

CHAPTER TWENTY

GRACE JUMPED out of the car the instant the driver stopped at the hospital entrance. As she raced through the halls after taking the elevator to the third floor, she racked her brain for anyone she knew that worked in the ICU but came up empty. Her only hope was that someone from her past would recognize her and buzz her into the unit. If not, she would fight her way in. She refused to let a little thing like a locked door keep her from her son.

The problem was solved for her when a middle-aged couple came out just as Grace arrived at the ICU doors. The man held tightly to the woman who was sobbing into a bloodied flannel shirt. Grace's heart went out to them as she grabbed for the door before it closed. Her actions didn't even register with them as they passed, consumed with their grief.

Grace stepped into the ICU and forced herself to stop and regain her composure before forging ahead. The ICU staff would recognize all authorized visitors. They'd toss her out in an instant if she barged in gunning for Mara. Grace had to act like she belonged there. She waited for her breathing to slow before continuing down the hallway.

The unit had been refurbished since she was last there, but

the layout was the same. The circular nurses' station was in the center with the rooms laid out in a larger circle surrounding it. There was a clear view of the patients from any angle of the nurse's station, and few people were as familiar with that department as Grace was. From the video she'd seen of Mara, she knew exactly where to find her.

Grace turned in that direction, but the hallway was vacant. In the twenty minutes that had passed, Mara would have had time to get to the parking lot and speed off in any direction, but Grace's gut told her the enemy was close.

Grace made a circuit of the floor without finding Mara. She had paused to step into an empty room if anyone gave her a second glance. She was about to make a second loop when Mara stepped out of room four and started for the exit. Grace crossed the ICU in record time and bowled into Mara with as much force as she could muster. The momentum slammed them into a wall. When Grace caught her breath, she spun Mara around and held her shoulders against the wall. Mara struggled to break free, but the adrenaline pumping through Grace gave her strength she didn't know she possessed.

"Where's my son?" Grace asked through clenched teeth.

Mara's lips curled into a sadistic grin. "You don't know? Then that's too bad. I'll never tell you."

Mara braced her left foot against the base of the wall and pushed. The movement shoved Grace off balance and she fell backward. Mara tried to run past but Grace caught her foot and toppled her onto her back. The fall knocked the wind out of Mara, so Grace used the advantage to straddle her and pin her arms at her sides.

"Trust me, you're going to tell me where to find Johnny."

A cart stacked with medical supplies stood inches from where she held Mara. Grace grabbed a sterile suture kit off it and tore it open. A pair of scissors clattered to the floor. Grace picked them up and held the point half an inch from Mara's throat.

Grace felt a hand on her shoulder but shrugged it off without moving the scissors. She watched as a pair of feet moved to the top of Mara's head and stopped. "Grace, is that you?"

Grace recognized the voice. She tore her eyes from Mara and looked up to make sure. "Marci? What are you doing here? You're supposed to be in Baltimore."

"I started here as the charge nurse three days ago."

"Touching reunion," Mara said, "but could you get this maniac off me, Marci?"

Marci knelt next to Grace. "I'm not sure who you think this is, but she the mother of one of our patients. You need to hand me the scissors and let her go."

"No! This is Mara Brennen. She's kidnapped Johnny twice, the first time on the day he was born. Amanda and I saw her in the ER when she abandoned Johnny. I'll never forget her eyes. And she's done it again. She took my boy. She knows where he is. I'm going to make her tell me." Grace faced Mara. "Tell me where he is now!"

Mara sneered. "You'll never prove it," she whispered just loud enough for Grace to hear. "Amanda's long gone. I checked when I got to Richmond, so it's your word against mine. I'm not afraid of you, Grace. You don't have the guts to stop me. One thrust and I could toss you like a ragdoll. Johnny's my son, and you can't have him. He'll always belong to me."

Marci called for security as Grace touched the point of the scissors to Mara's throat and imagined them piercing the skin. The violence of the thought frightened her but proved she was capable of more than Mara imagined. She squeezed her other hand into a fist and lifted it to strike.

"Mom?" The word dispelled Grace's rage and pierced her heart. "Is that you, Mom?"

Grace kept the scissors at Mara's throat as she turned her head toward the sound. Johnny's voice was weak but close. "Johnny? Where are you?"

Mara chuckled beneath her. "That's right. Your precious boy is on the other side of that wall. If you go to him, I'll disappear again, and you'll never find me. So, what's it going to be, him or me?"

Grace glared at Mara not knowing what to do. Her little man was only feet away, but if she went to him, Mara would escape, and they'd never have another chance to capture her. But how could Grace ignore Johnny? The days and weeks separating them had been agony, yet there he was, right within her reach. She only had to take a few steps to hold him in her arms.

She threw the scissors to the floor and climbed to her feet. Mara would get away, but Grace didn't care. All that mattered was Johnny. All that had ever mattered was Johnny.

MARA SCRAMBLED to her feet and started for the exit, but Marci blocked her path.

"You're not getting out of here. Security is on their way." Marci glared at her with her hands on her hips.

Mara sized Marci up. Grace was a tiny slip of a thing, but Marci was a different story. She was at least five-ten and looked like she was no stranger to a gym. Mara had hoped to get out of the hospital without having to play her last card, but there was no way she could take Marci down in a hurry, and security arrives any second.

"You'll let me go," Mara said and lifted the pant leg hiding the gun strapped to her calf. She pulled it from the holster and pointed it at Marci. "If you don't want to add more patients to this ward, you'd better get out of my way." Marci raised her arms and backed up to let Mara pass. "Good choice."

Mara tore Marci's badge from her uniform and used it to activate the scrub dispenser. She held the gun in one hand and grabbed a pair of scrubs with the other before running toward the

ICU exit. She threw the scrubs over her clothes as she went and put on a sterile cap and surgical mask for good measure. She took time to stop and flip off the stunned ICU staff before heading out the door.

GRACE RAN to Johnny's room but froze when she saw him lying on the bed with his head shaved and bandaged. She knelt at his bedside and whispered, "Is it all right that I'm here?"

She held her breath as she waited for his answer. Johnny lifted his hand to her and said, "Mom, it is you. I knew you'd find me."

It was all she needed to hear. She pulled him into her arms and held him as tightly as she dared. Her tears spilled onto his pillow as Johnny shook with sobs.

When he quieted, Grace looked into his eyes and said, "I can't believe you were here all this time. Why are you in ICU? Did Mara do this to you?"

"In a way." He told her the story of his ordeal and said, "It only took two days to figure out what a creepy nutcase Mara is, but by then it was too late to escape. I tried but I couldn't do it. If I hadn't hit my head when I fell off the window sill, she would have hauled me off to Portland or somewhere where you never would have found me."

"That didn't happen. Mara's gone. You're safe. Let's just be grateful for that." She tenderly brushed her fingertips over his bandages. "I had her, but I had to let her go. She was in my grasp but getting to you was more important than capturing Mara. It was more important than anything. You have my promise I'll never let that monster within miles of you again. Your dad and I will do whatever it takes to keep you safe."

Wes divided his unit into three groups. He left four agents to guard the main lobby and prevent anyone from leaving. He'd tried to get hospital security to order a lockdown, but all they were willing to do was post guards at the remaining exits including those used by staff. Wes split his other two groups between the elevators and stairs. His team took the elevator.

He was silent and tried to steady his thoughts as they ascended to the ICU floor. He didn't know how he'd bear it if Mara slipped through their net for the third time. Or was it the fourth? He'd lost track. His gut told him this was his last chance.

He was worried about Grace, too. After the way Mara had attacked the store clerk, Wes hated to think how far she might go if Grace threatened or cornered her. Dread rose in his gut at what they'd face in the ICU.

He sprang through the doors the instant they opened and led his team to the ICU entrance. A woman in scrubs wearing a surgical mask and sterile cap came out as they reached the door.

"FBI. Please hold that open," Wes called as he pulled his credentials from of his pocket.

The woman pushed it open as far as it would go and stepped aside for them to pass. Wes gave her a quick glance as he brushed by. She had her eyes lowered, but he saw enough of her face to recognize her. She flicked her eyes at him for less than a second, but it was long enough to confirm his suspicion.

She reached into her waistband as she turned to run in the opposite direction. Wes grabbed the back of her scrubs and yanked her back through the ICU entrance. Mara thrust her weight forward and broke his grasp, but Wes tackled her, and they slid across the slick tile floor.

Mara fought to break free while Wes pulled the gun from her waistband and held it up for Agent Cameron. He flipped her onto her back and straddled her as Grace had done. He ripped off the surgical mask and cap to get a better look. Mara struggled beneath his weight, but Wes just held her tighter.

"Get off me, you brute," she cried. "I'm a nurse here."

"Glad to," Wes said as he climbed off and rolled her on her side to cuff her. "Mara Brennen, you're under arrest for kidnapping, carrying a concealed firearm into a hospital, and resisting arrest. I'm guessing they'll be adding illegal possession of that firearm and who knows what else. Now, before I send you away to be locked up for the rest of your life, tell me where Johnny is."

"Bite me," Mara said.

Wish I could, Wes thought as he handed her off to Cameron. "Get her out of my sight."

Wes had agents Prince and Elliott start questioning witnesses while he went to find Grace and figure out what Mara had been doing in the ICU. He hoped it would lead them to Johnny. Capturing Mara was only the first step in ending this nightmare. His promise to Grace didn't end until her son was safely home.

He saw one of the nurses watching him scan the unit for Grace. He marched up to her and took out his phone to show her a picture of Grace. "I'm Special Agent Reid, ma'am. I'm searching for this woman. Have you seen her? Can you tell me where she is?"

A smile crept up the nurse's face and she motioned for Wes to follow her. "I'm Marci. I've known Grace for years." She stopped outside room four and said, "In there."

Wes raised his eyebrows at her. He was afraid Mara had shot Grace and couldn't imagine why Marci was smiling. He went in and stopped in shock at what he found. Grace was seated next to the bed holding Johnny's hand.

She jumped out of the chair and grabbed Wes' hands. "Mara was here. You have to go after her. You just missed her."

It was Wes' turn to smile. "Mara's in custody. Don't worry, Grace, it's over."

"You caught her?" When he nodded, Grace threw her arms around him and squeezed so tight that Wes was surprised at how strong she was. "I knew you would," she said.

Wes gently freed himself and looked her in the eye. "You're the hero, not me. But what were you thinking of going after her on your own? She had a gun, you know."

Grace's eyes widened. "I had to get to her and make her tell me where she was holding Johnny. Nothing else mattered. Turns out, Johnny was right here."

Wes stepped close to the bed and held out his hand. "You must be Johnny. I'm Wes. You can't imagine how happy I am to meet you."

THE PAST TWELVE hours had been incredible and kept getting better by the minute. Johnny had smiled so much his face hurt.

After his mom found him the night before, she called his dad with the news, and he got to the hospital in record time. He'd been so overwhelmed at seeing Johnny that he couldn't speak for two minutes. They both bawled like babies and made fun of each other for it.

They were only able to talk for five minutes before the doctor came in to tell his parents they would have to sleep in the family lounge down the hall. They begged him to bend the rules under the circumstances, but he stood firm. Johnny needed his rest.

Even though Johnny hated seeing his parents go, he was comforted to know they'd be close if he needed them. He felt even better that the hospital had posted a security guard outside his door. He knew he didn't need to be afraid of Mara anymore since Agent Wes had locked her up, but having the guard there made him feel safer.

His parents and the doctor had come in as soon as Luke finished taking Johnny's vitals in the morning. The doc announced that they were moving him to the step-down unit so he could have more visitors, and his parents could stay the night in his room if he wanted them to. His mom said she was staying whether he wanted her to or not. Johnny laughed but was happy to know that some things never changed.

Moving to his new room had tired Johnny out, but he was still thrilled when Steph, Uncle Adam, and Auntie Alec showed up as soon as he finished lunch. Steph and Auntie Alec each hugged him so many times that he finally had to beg them to stop. When they'd been there for just over an hour, his mom stood and announced that it was time for everyone to leave.

"We just got here," Alec said. "I was planning to stay for the rest of the day. Adam and I even came in separate cars."

"Johnny has another visitor coming and they need time alone. You can stay as long as you want once he's home," Grace said.

"Who's coming?" Johnny asked.

"You'll see," was all his mom would say.

His sister, aunt, and uncle all hugged him again before reluctantly agreeing to leave. After they left, his dad said, "I have an errand to run, so I'm going to head out for a bit, too. I'll be back soon with a surprise." He kissed Johnny's head and waved as he left.

"What's going on, Mom? You're not keeping secrets from me again, are you?"

"Never," Grace said. "Someone is coming that you need to meet."

As she said the words, a man with short brown hair peeked his head in and tapped on the open door. "Can I come in?" he asked.

Johnny's mom went to the man and led him to Johnny's bedside. "Johnny, this is Craig Stuart, your biological father."

Johnny stared at the man with his mouth gaping. Craig was the last person he'd expected to come walking through his door. He didn't know how to act or what to say.

Craig stepped closer and said, "I've dreamed of this day for so long. It's wonderful to see you again, Johnny."

Craig held out his hand, but Johnny said, "It's all right if you want to hug me. Everyone else is."

Craig's eyes welled up as he leaned down to wrap his arms around his son. Johnny gingerly lifted his arms to return the hug. He thought it would be awkward with this stranger, but it felt familiar to him.

"Thank you," Craig whispered and wiped his face as he sat in the chair that Grace offered him.

"You should know that I read about you on the internet. Not personal stuff, just news stories about you." He glanced at his mom, not sure if he should ask the question that had haunted him since he read Alec's book. When she nodded, he said, "How come you didn't want me when you found out that I was alive? Why did you give me back to my mom?"

Craig looked Johnny in the eye. "I don't want you to ever think that I didn't love or want you. It makes me sad to know that you've thought that for even a minute. It was never about me wanting you. It was...complicated."

"Tell me. I want to know everything."

It was Craig's turn to glance at Grace. When she nodded again, he said, "I need to start at the beginning. Your mother's name was Samantha, and she was the most amazing person I've ever known. I still miss her and think of her every day."

Craig's lip trembled, so he stopped and took a breath before going on. Johnny's eyes were riveted on his father. He'd waited his whole life to know the story of where he came from and who his parents were. He was relieved to know they loved each other.

"Your mom was the one who pushed us to have a baby, and it took a long time for you to come along. Sometimes we worried it would never happen. We were both thrilled when it did."

He stopped again, and Johnny was tempted to beg him to get on with it, but he kept quiet. He understood why talking about it was hard for Craig.

"Something went wrong when your mom went into labor. Grace can explain it to you later, but they had to do an emergency delivery. The doctors did a Cesarean and whisked you off to the nursery before I even got to hold you. Your mom hemorrhaged. The doctors couldn't stop it. Mara and her husband stole you from the nursery while I held your mother's hand as she slipped away from us. She died without ever seeing your face. It was the worst day of my life. I lost your mom and you."

Johnny didn't try to hide his tears as he silently watched Craig. He heard his mom sniffle from her chair in the corner.

"That's so horrible. How did you go on living after something like that? You lost your whole family in one day."

"This gets to the explanation of why I didn't keep you when I found out you were alive. My best friend had a sister named Kristen. We'd never been close, but she was there for me after I lost you and Sam. I wouldn't have survived that time without her. We fell in love, or at least I did, and we got married. We found out she was expecting at the same time I found out you were alive. We brought you home, but Kristen is a selfish person and didn't want to share her love between you and our son."

"That's harsh," Johnny said. "I kind of don't blame her, though. I know I'm not easy to take care of."

"It was more than that. I think Kristen would have rejected you if you were perfectly healthy. You were miserable and home-sick when we took you away from Grace, too. She was the only mother you'd ever known, and you cried for her day and night. Kristen threatened to leave if I kept you. I had a terrible choice to make, but I made the one that was best for you, and I don't regret it. No one could have raised you or loved you better than Grace and Ryan."

Johnny smiled at his mom. "I agree. Thanks for explaining. I know it wasn't easy."

"I'm glad I got to tell you. When you disappeared, I was afraid I'd never get the chance."

"Does Kristen still feel the same way? Does she mind that you're here?"

"Kristen did us all a favor and ran off after your brother was born. My new wife is Melanie, and she's dying to meet you."

"So, I have a brother?" Johnny asked.

"Two brothers, Sam and Charlie, and a sister named Laurel. I've told them everything about you. We're all hoping you'll allow us to be a part of your life, Johnny. I should have done this years ago, but I hope it's not too late."

"It would be incredible. I have a whole other family. That's freaking amazing."

"Come to stay with us this summer if your parents agree to let you out of their sight."

"Of course," Grace said. "But first we have to get him well and home. Then we'll make plans for summer."

Craig stood and squeezed Johnny's hand. "Melanie is on her way from Albuquerque. We'll visit in a few days when you're stronger. I love you, Johnny. Thanks for understanding."

"Love you, too." He paused before he said Dad. "What should I call you? Dad doesn't feel right. Ryan's my dad."

"We'll have to work on that but pick whatever feels right to you."

"I'll let you know," Johnny said and smiled when his second father waved on the way out.

GRACE PICKED up the copy of Alec's book that Alec had brought in for her and carried it to Johnny. She showed him the cover before holding it out to him. He hesitated before reaching for it but took it and laid it on the blanket without looking at it.

Grace pulled her chair close to the bed and sat facing Johnny. "You and I need to have a talk. I know seeing that book must stir up some terrible memories, but you need to read it. I resisted when Alec gave it to me, just before you disappeared, but your dad eventually convinced me to read it. I'm glad I did. Remembering the obstacles we overcame when you were a baby kept my hope alive."

Johnny glanced at the book before turning his eyes back to Grace. "I'm afraid to read things I don't want to know. For so long, I wanted to know where I came from more than anything, but that story Craig told is brutal. Maybe I'm better off clueless."

"No, Johnny, you aren't. I made a terrible mistake in not telling you the truth about your past years ago. I know it will take time for us to get past what I did, but I don't want there to be any more secrets between us. You need to know the truth of who you are, and who I am. The first part of that book is the story of my early life that I've kept hidden too. Your father tried for years to get me to tell you, but I was afraid to for some reason. I can't remember why now, after all that's happened."

"I'm so sorry for running out, Mom. If I hadn't gone ballistic instead of facing my problems, this wouldn't have happened. I can't believe I was stupid enough to get in Mara's car. I was just so freaked out and confused."

"Don't apologize to me. You did *nothing* wrong. This was all on me. And Mara. Mostly Mara, but you had a right to the truth, and I lied to you. It's unforgivable. Losing your love and trust was almost as painful as losing you physically. I've wondered so many times how you'd react to me when we found you. If we found you. I'm deeply grateful that you didn't push me away when I walked into your room last night. I understand that it will take time to regain your trust, but I hope you're willing to try."

"Stop it, Mom. I'm over it. I get why you didn't tell me. You don't have to regain my trust. You have it. Five minutes with Mara was enough to prove what an amazing mom you are. I think moms like you are rare."

Grace tried to thank him, but the words caught in her throat. She didn't deserve his love or trust, but he gave them freely. It was more than she dared hope.

"I promise never to keep anything from you. We'll talk when

you've finished reading the book and go forward from there. No looking behind us. I hope you know that you are my life. I'd do anything for you, even fight a deranged kidnapper."

"Nurse Marci said you were like a superhero. I'm proud of you, and I love you, Mom. I'll always love you, and I can't wait for you to take me home where I belong."

END

ACKNOWLEDGMENTS

First and foremost, I must thank Joseph Nassise, my mentor/editor/*Sensei* and NYT bestselling author in his own right, for his invaluable guidance and encouragement. I can say with all honesty that this project would have died a slow, agonizing death without his help. Instead, he helped me create a story I can be proud of.

I'd also like to thank my award-winning cover designer Timothy Barber for his patient and pleasant nature, and most of all, his incredible talent. He created a cover that was just as I envisioned it.

Next, I need to thank my wonderful sisters for their constant support and enthusiasm. They have been with me every step of the way from concept to final proofread. You are the best sisters a person could hope for, and I owe so much to you.

Thank you to my friends, who helped me carry on to The End. I feed off your energy, and it strengthens me in times of doubt.

Thank you to my readers. None of this would have a point without you. I appreciate your kind and enthusiastic support.

Thanks to my sons who are my reason for being and who make me laugh on a daily basis.

Lastly, I must thank my husband of thirty-five years who tolerates my hours-long ramblings about how much I love to write. He never gives up on me and constantly reminds me that I've got this. I love you and couldn't do it without you.

ABOUT THE AUTHOR

Eleanor remembers the thrill of learning to read at the age of five. Her passion for writing would emerge a few years later. She cherishes books that influence her writing and her life. She hopes to create the same experience for readers. She loves creating stories that celebrate everyday superheroes. Eleanor's debut novel, Arms of Grace, was a finalist in consideration for production by Wind Dancer Films and won a silver medal in the Readers' Favorites Awards. Arms of Grace is also a recipient of the B.R.A.G. medallion.

Eleanor has traveled the world and lived in five countries. She resides in the Williamsburg, Virginia area with her husband, is the proud mother of four grown sons, and Nana to one amazing grand-darling.